LINE OF SUCCESSION

DAVID BRUNS

J.R. OLSON

SEVERN RIVER
PUBLISHING

Copyright © 2025 by David Bruns and J.R. Olson.

All rights reserved.

No part of this book may be reproduced in any form or by any electronic or mechanical means, including information storage and retrieval systems, without written permission from the author, except for the use of brief quotations in a book review.

Severn River Publishing
www.SevernRiverBooks.com

This is a work of fiction. Names, characters, businesses, places, events and incidents are either the products of the author's imagination or used in a fictitious manner. Any resemblance to actual persons, living or dead, or actual events is purely coincidental.

ISBN: 978-1-64875-657-3 (Paperback)

ALSO BY BRUNS AND OLSON

The Command and Control Series

Command and Control

Counter Strike

Order of Battle

Threat Axis

Covert Action

Proxy War

Line of Succession

The Third Option Series

Weapons Free

Also by the Authors

Weapons of Mass Deception

Jihadi Apprentice

Rules of Engagement

The Pandora Deception

Never miss a new release! Sign up to receive exclusive updates from authors Bruns and Olson.

severnriverbooks.com

*To our mothers
Regina Bruns & Pam Olson*

1

Saransk, Republic of Mordovia, Russia

Nikolay Sokolov felt his eyelids growing heavy. The heat of the concert hall was making him drowsy.

The venue, packed with proud parents, every local dignitary within a hundred kilometers, and a substantial contingent of national politicians, was one of those events where everyone wanted to be seen. This grand opening of a cultural hub in one of the smaller provinces was the third such event he'd attended in as many months. It looked as if his national strategy to reengage with citizens in their local communities was working brilliantly.

But only if he managed to stay awake.

Nikolay sat up straighter in his seat, filled his lungs with stale air, and refocused his attention on the stage. All it would take is one citizen with a mobile phone to snap a picture of the President of the Russian Federation dozing at the grand opening of the Saransk United People's Center for the Arts to screw up what was thus far a public relations coup.

On the stage, a gaggle of children dressed in brightly colored tunics and loose Cossack-style trousers finished their dance. The audience erupted in applause. The beaming children lined up along the edge of the stage, joined hands, and bowed together.

The audience stood and roared approval, so Nikolay got to his feet as well. Next to him, Zave rose in a fluid motion, like the dancer that she was. Her hair cascaded down her back in auburn waves and she smiled broadly as she clapped.

Nikolay leaned close—she smelled wonderful—and whispered in her ear, "What are we clapping for exactly?"

Instead of answering him, she slid her hand down his back and stepped close to him. He could feel the sinewy tautness of her body molding to his. Zave rested her head on his shoulder. Nikolay could almost feel the photographs being taken, sense the headlines being written on websites all over the country.

Our bachelor President has a special friend...Are there wedding bells for Nikolay?

He smiled and put his arm around her waist, drawing her closer. He'd known Yelizaveta Kovaleva only six months, but she was a perfect match. A former ballerina at the famed Bolshoi, Zave had retired in her early thirties, at the peak of her career. She taught privately to international clients now, which meant she was gone for weeks at a time. Lately, Nikolay found that each time she left, he missed her even more.

His grin widened. He'd successfully negotiated the Kazakh partition deal with the Chinese to secure his southern border and made amends in Ukraine to solidify his western flank. Domestically, his plan to embrace the dozens of ethnic minority enclaves all over the Federation reduced internal divisions and built trust in the federal government. *His* federal government. In the coming months and years, that public trust would allow him to make the reforms necessary to pull Russia into the modern world.

He surveyed the jubilant crowd. Mordovia, once a harsh penal colony, was now the home of a brand-new center for the arts celebrating the very people that Moscow once considered enemies of the State.

His smile widened as he slid his hand over the curve of Zave's hip. The hard-right minority factions in the Duma were agitating again—they were always yammering about something—but they were on their back foot and they knew it. In the upcoming elections, they would get their twenty percent of the seats in the Duma and things would return to normal again.

Unless he did something to change that dynamic, he thought. A wedding announcement close to the fall elections might be an excellent way to draw the attention of the public away from the pettiness of politics.

The orchestra started playing again and the hall filled with the din of hundreds of people taking their seats. Zave kept his hand in hers as she sat down. Spine erect, shoulders back, the scooped neckline of her dress settled over the curve of her breasts. She drew his hand into her lap and he felt her leg muscles taut against his palm. In profile, the corner of her lip turned up. She was teasing him. He dug his fingers into the inside of her thigh. She cocked an eyebrow in response.

The music started again with a crash and male dancers trailing red sashes leaped across the stage. Nikolay dragged his gaze away from the woman to the action below. He vaguely recognized the music as a famous Russian composer who loved to use heavy percussion in his pieces.

A popping staccato in the background caught his attention, but Nikolay wrote it off to a problem in the sound system. A few seconds later, it happened again and he saw people in the audience turning their heads looking for the source of the popping sound.

His security lead appeared at his shoulder, leaned in. "Mr. President, we need to—"

The back doors of the theater crashed open. Four men dressed in black poured into the theater and the popping sound took on a harsher tone as they opened fire.

There was a split second of frozen silence, then chaos broke loose. The audience erupted like a living thing, dispersing in every direction. On the stage, the music continued. Half the dancers stopped, half kept going. They crashed into one another as they sought to make sense of what was happening in front of them.

Nikolay's security lead manhandled his President out of his seat and half dragged him toward the back of the box. Nikolay reached back for Zave's hand, but she was too far away. He tried to pull away from the arms propelling him forward, but the man was strong.

Just as they reached the door, a second guard appeared. "They're in the hallway," he shouted. "The exit is—"

A three-round burst of rifle fire sounded in the dark passage behind the security guard. The man spun, caught himself on the doorjamb, and twisted. His handgun was out and he fired blindly down the hallway. A second burst of gunfire caught him in the neck and suddenly there was blood everywhere as the man collapsed.

Nikolay felt a spray of wet warmth across his face.

His security lead kicked his comrade's body into the hall and slammed the door to the box closed. He seized a chair, jammed it under the knob. He stepped back, took a knee, and drew his sidearm. "Get behind me, sir."

Nikolay looked over the edge of the box. It was a ten-meter drop into the audience. He'd break a leg for sure—or his neck. A wave of panic hit him and he leaned farther out.

Zave grabbed his arm, drawing him back behind the cover of the railing. "Stay down!" she whispered urgently.

He noted in the moment that although her voice showed concern for him, there was no trace of fear. His gaze ping-ponged around the box. Two rows of free-standing chairs, with light cushions of dark velvet. A bullet wouldn't even slow down going through a few layers of fabric and stuffing. They were trapped.

Over the screaming din of the audience, Nikolay heard the distant heavy boom of an automatic shotgun and the rapid staccato of multiple weapons on full auto. The sound was coming from outside the theater.

Nikolay's guard spoke over his shoulder. "Security forces are on scene, sir. They'll be here in two minutes. Hold tight, Mr. President, we're going to get you out of here, sir."

BOOM!

The door of the box disintegrated in the explosion of a breaching charge. Nikolay was thrown back against the railing and fell to the floor. He hit his head and a burst of color flooded his vision. His ears rang.

Somehow, the security man took the force of the blast and maintained his stance. He fired his weapon, the sounds registering as dull thuds in Nikolay's deadened hearing. But there was no one in the gaping hole that had been the doorway. A blast of gunfire from outside the box cut the guard down into a bloody twisting heap.

As Nikolay got to his hands and knees, a man appeared in the doorway, an AK-74 assault rifle at the ready as he swept the box. A smile traced his lips as he lowered the rifle and swaggered in. He spoke quickly into a throat mike, but Nikolay's deadened hearing could not make out what he was saying.

He wore a faded Russian Army combat uniform with the insignia of the Russian Federation removed. Atop his tactical helmet was a camera and a red light indicated it was recording. He gestured with the rifle muzzle. "Get up," he ordered.

Nikolay got to his feet, hands up, keeping Zave behind him.

A second man appeared in the doorway. He was younger, his face pinched with concern. "They're here, brother! We need to go."

Their captor seemed unconcerned. "Go. I'm right behind you, Sasha. I need to finish this swine."

His eyes bored into Nikolay's. "You're being livestreamed, Mr. President. On your knees."

Nikolay stayed standing, hands raised. "Leave the woman alone."

He regretted his words immediately. The comment sparked a light in the man's eyes. A crazy spark.

"Okay," Nikolay said, "I'm getting on my knees."

Still with his hands raised, he dropped to one knee, then the other, careful to keep Zave sheltered by his body. He could feel the heat of the terrorist's gaze on him and Nikolay Sokolov knew he was about to die.

"Brother!" the younger man said, his voice urgent with fear, "we need to go now."

Zave's face was between his shoulder blades, her hand on the back of Nikolay's neck. He could feel the cool touch of her fingertips on his fevered skin. She slid her fingers into his hair and Nikolay gasped with pleasure.

The terrorist half turned. The muzzle of his weapon drifted toward the floor. "Sasha, I said to go. I'm right behind—"

Zave gripped his hair, wrenched his head to the side, and Nikolay toppled to the floor. He felt the fabric of her dress drag across his face as she stepped over him.

When he looked up, Zave had a gun in her right hand. It was small and compact and it looked like it belonged there. The terrorist's expression went slack with surprise and his weapon came up, but he was too slow. She fired twice into the man's face, then shifted her aim and shot the younger man still standing in the doorway.

The muzzle of the terrorist's assault rifle was still in upward motion. The dying man squeezed the trigger and a three-round burst hit Zave's midsection at point-blank range. She stiffened, staggered backward, trying desperately to regain her balance.

She hit the railing and toppled over the edge.

The terrorist's body crashed down next to Nikolay, his head coming to rest a scant meter from the Russian President's face. There was a bloody, weeping hole where the man's right eye should have been.

Above his forehead, still attached to the helmet, the unblinking red light of an active camera stared back at Nikolay.

2

Emerging Threats Group, Tysons Corner, Virginia

Harrison Kohl wiped the steam off the mirror in the employee locker room. The weathered tan had faded, but his cheeks were still hollow. He had yet to gain back the weight he'd lost during his time as an embedded officer with the resistance forces in Central Asia. The mirror confirmed that his body remained toned and strong, ready for anything. But ever since he'd returned to the United States and his desk at Emerging Threats Group, he'd felt at loose ends. The unceasing adrenaline of his time in the war zone had faded into dull complacency.

But the last twenty-four hours brought it all back.

Harrison looked at his face in the mirror again. He looked tired, which was not a surprise. He hadn't slept since the assassination attempt on Nikolay Sokolov the previous day. The shower was his way of trying to wash away the fatigue. He yawned at his gaunt reflection. Mixed results so far.

As he lathered his face with shaving cream and filled the basin with hot water, his phone rang. The caller ID said Don Riley.

He used his pinkie finger to put the phone on speaker.

"Don, what's up?" His voice echoed in the tiled room.

"I need you at the White House in two hours, Harrison."

"I'm fine, boss. How are you?"

Don ignored the jab. "Bring the latest on the assassination attempt. Do we have attribution yet?"

"There's chatter about ISIS-K, but I think it's just them seeing an opportunity and jumping in to claim it. Nothing else points to them that I can see."

He could almost hear the gears turning in Don Riley's head as his boss processed the information. Beneath Don's doughy exterior was a first-rate brain. Harrison could tell by Don's tone of voice that he was on the scent of something.

"Bring everything you have on Bogdan Rabilov and the Russian succession planning for the office of the President."

"They don't have any succession planning, Don. You know that."

"Say it exactly like that when you brief the President, Harrison. Wear a suit."

Don hung up and Harrison's razor paused in mid-stroke as Don's words hit home: *When you brief the President.*

One hour and forty-five minutes later, as Harrison waited outside the Oval Office, he felt like a kid who'd been called to the principal's office. The ill fit of his only clean and pressed suit spoke to the twenty pounds he'd lost in Central Asia. He unconsciously kept pulling at the lapel as if that would somehow make up for the fact that there was just less body mass filling out the pressed material.

Don, on the other hand, had gained a few pounds since Harrison had last seen him and he looked as tired as Harrison felt. Still, he smiled as he shook his old friend's hand.

"You ready for this, Harrison?"

Of course not! Harrison wanted to scream, but he smiled back. "You know me, Don. I was born ready. Anything you want me to avoid in my brief?"

Don's glance cut to Carroll Brooks. The CIA Director had her arms folded, studying Harrison. She raised an eyebrow at Don.

"Honesty is the best policy," Don replied. "Give it to her straight and we'll take it from there."

Brooks rolled her eyes. "You're gonna be the death of me, Riley."

Harrison watched the interplay between the two. Once bitter rivals, they'd rebuilt their relationship into a high-functioning leadership team. Harrison attributed that transformation mostly to Don. Somehow, Don Riley had healthy ambition without an overpowering ego—a rare combination in the elite political circles of Washington, DC. Brooks, to her credit, recognized that trait and played it to her advantage, giving Riley a long leash as Deputy Director of Operations, where he ran the Agency's field operations all over the world.

From behind her desk, the executive assistant spoke up. "The President is ready to see you now, Director." The heavy padded door next to her desk swung open silently.

Harrison had never been in the Oval Office before and he'd never met President Eleanor Cashman. He'd seen her on TV, of course. He recognized the stylish cut of her ash-blond hair, the square shoulders, and the firm jawline, but the television could not replicate the probing quality of her eyes as they raked over him. He felt like he'd just been x-rayed.

"This is Harrison Kohl, one of our top Russia experts, Madam President," Don said.

Cashman shook Harrison's hand, her grip cool and firm. He experienced another probing scan.

"You were the embedded officer in Central Asia," she said.

Harrison nodded. "Yes, ma'am."

"And now you're my Russia expert." Her eyes flicked to Riley. "Explain, Donald."

"Harrison's tour in Central Asia was an assignment of opportunity, ma'am. His day job has always been Russia."

Harrison felt an unaccountable urge to laugh. Assignment of opportunity? He'd been there investigating the death of his best friend and got caught up in a resistance movement against the Chinese invasion of the region. When Don ordered him to come home, he'd refused. Don should have fired him on the spot for disobeying a direct order, but that was not the Riley way. Instead, he put Harrison to work as an embedded operator, serving as the liaison to the head of the resistance movement.

Cashman inclined her head. "Welcome back, Mr. Kohl. I hope you can put my mind at ease about this Russia situation."

She led the way to a pair of opposing sofas where the Chief of Staff waited. Cashman took a seat in the armchair at the head of the table. Harrison eyed the silver coffee service on the low table between the sofas. He could use a pick-me-up right now, but no one else seemed to be paying it any attention, so he pushed the thought aside.

Don took the lead in the discussion, passing out briefing tablets and giving a quick update. He ended his introduction by playing a video.

Bogdan Rabilov, leader of the ultranationalist New Dawn party, was being interviewed by a morning talk show host. The woman had glossy black hair and wore a well-cut dark suit over a crimson blouse with a plunging neckline.

Bogdan, on the other hand, looked like he'd just rolled out of bed. He was a big man who'd run to fat and his tentlike wrinkled suit jacket did little to modify his bulk. His short gray hair was as gnarled as a thicket and his gray beard needed a trim. Harrison knew he was seventy-three, but he looked older. Years of heavy drinking left red splotches on his baggy cheeks. As was usual for a Bogdan interview, he was ranting and his eyes flashed with anger.

The source of the anger was contained on the television screen between them.

Russian President Nikolay Sokolov was on his knees, bleeding from a cut on his head, looking dazed. As they watched, a stunning woman in a golden dress pushed him aside, stepped over his body and raised a small pistol. It spat fire at the camera and the video shot reeled to the side, briefly showing the ceiling of a concert hall, then crashing to the floor.

Nikolay Sokolov was on the floor, his face a few feet from the camera lens. On the screen, he blinked owlishly, turned his head and cried out. Tears ran down his face.

Bogdan and the interviewer watched the video together, then it looped and Bogdan went off.

"Can you give us a rough translation, Harrison?" Don said quietly.

"He's calling President Sokolov a wom—" Harrison caught himself.

"He's calling him weak, a terrible leader who cannot keep the country safe. This is why the New Dawn party needs to be elected in the fall."

Don stopped the video. "That's enough for now. Thank you." He turned to the President. "Ma'am, it's unclear if the New Dawn movement had anything to do with this assassination attempt, but they are certainly benefitting from it."

Cashman looked from Don to Harrison. "I don't understand. Sokolov's not up for reelection this fall, right?"

"That's true, ma'am," Harrison said. "President Sokolov is only two years into a six-year term, but the Duma—their equivalent of the US House of Representatives—has an election in mid-September, four months from now."

President Cashman pointed at the tablet screen. "And you think this guy is a threat to Sokolov's presidency?" Her tone was derisive.

"Bogdan Rabilov is not running for office," Harrison replied. "For the last thirty years, he's been climbing the ranks of the far-right movement in Russia. Hardcore ultranationalists, real post-Soviet types. His New Dawn party think only ethnic Russians truly matter, and that all other ethnic groups inside the Federation should serve the true Russian people. They're anti-West, and especially anti-America.

"They typically get twenty percent of the seats in the Duma, but the assassination attempt this close to the election has shifted things. With the number of seats up for election, some unexpected resignations, and this latest news, Rabilov's party could get a majority this time around."

Cashman sniffed. "So Sokolov has to deal with an unruly House. Welcome to the real world. He'll figure it out."

"It's not that simple, Madam President," Harrison said. "If Rabilov's people had a solid majority, they could try to remove him from office. Remember Boris Yeltsin? That could happen again."

"So Sokolov gets removed?" Cashman replied. "This is a problem for Russians to solve."

"Ma'am," Harrison said, "Russia is not like other countries. They do not have a succession plan. If Nikolay Sokolov is removed, we have no idea who will take over." He pointed at the tablet, which still showed Rabilov, eyes flashing, mouth open in mid-shout. "It could be him. Or worse."

Cashman pursed her lips, stared at the tablet for a long beat. "I'm listening."

"The New Dawn taking power in the fall could lead to a cascade of events that are not in our national interest," Harrison continued.

The Chief of Staff interrupted with a snort of derision. "I think that's an overreaction, Madam President."

Don started to speak, but Harrison beat him to the punch. "Is it? The last time we forced Nikolay Sokolov's hand, he cut a deal with the Chinese over Kazakhstan."

Harrison felt Don's body go rigid next to him. The President's face reddened. The China-Russia Kazakhstan Accord was still a policy black eye for her administration.

"Enough!" the President said sharply. She eyed Harrison keenly. "Considering your service in the region, Mr. Kohl, I'm not going to take that last remark personally—and neither will anyone else in this room." She placed a hand on her Chief of Staff's arm. "William, would you pour coffee for us, please? I think we all need a moment to cool off."

Don passed Harrison a cup of coffee and a stern look. *Be careful.* For Harrison, the more interesting reaction was from the Director. As he passed her the cream, she leaned close and murmured into his ear. "I thought Riley was the troublemaker."

But she said it with a small smile. What the hell was going on?

The President stirred her coffee, then placed the silver spoon on the saucer. "Let's start Round Two, Mr. Kohl. Explain to me why I should care if Nikolay Sokolov gets removed as President of the Russian Federation."

Harrison took a deep breath. Keep your cool, he told himself. Let the facts speak for themselves.

"Thank you, ma'am. Russia is the only nuclear power on the planet without a clear line of succession for the transfer of power, but it's actually worse than that. Sokolov's uncle, Vitaly Luchnik, established himself as the sole authority in the Russian Federation. Luchnik ran the country like an organized crime ring with himself as the Godfather. We're still living with that situation today. Checks and balances are gone."

President Cashman's eyes probed from over the rim of her coffee cup.

"We have credible intel that says the only thing that prevented a nuclear strike by Russia during the Ukraine invasion was the fact that Sokolov overthrew his uncle. We were that close. Whatever you think of Nikolay Sokolov, he is trying to reform his country, but he's starting from scratch, and rebuilding the infrastructure of government takes time. If yesterday's assassination attempt had succeeded, we have no idea who would assume the presidency. Best case is that a coalition of his cabinet would get behind the prime minister and stabilize things quickly."

"And the worst case?" Cashman asked quietly.

Harrison pointed at Bogdan Rabilov's image on the screen.

"Rabilov's party advocates taking back their country. By force, if necessary. We could be looking at a civil war inside a country with an arsenal of five thousand nuclear weapons."

"That's an exaggeration," the Chief of Staff said.

Harrison nodded. "Possibly, sir. Our best intel has the military split between far-right sympathizers and neutral parties. There's only one problem with that assessment, in my opinion."

"And that is?" the Chief of Staff said. His look told Harrison that he'd not been forgiven for the Kazakhstan remark.

"The Russian military is for sale," Harrison replied. "For the right price, they will fall in line behind Rabilov. One oligarch with a few million dollars to spare and we could be looking at a nuclear grudge match."

The only sound that broke the silence was the President stirring her coffee again. The spoon made a sharp ping as she returned it to the saucer. Cashman sighed.

"Thank you, Mr. Kohl." The President turned her gaze to Don Riley.

"Congratulations, Donald, you've convinced me that I should give a shit about Nikolay Sokolov. Knowing you, I suppose you came here with a plan?"

"Yes, ma'am," Don replied. He touched his tablet and swept his finger to advance to the next page. Harrison saw it was a draft Presidential Finding authorizing a covert action. He scanned down the page as Don continued.

"I propose we launch an influence campaign against Bogdan Rabilov immediately." Harrison could sense that Cashman was already skeptical, but Don plowed on. "This is a hands-off operation, no direct American involvement. The objective is to discredit Rabilov enough to slow the far-right momentum in the upcoming election."

Cashman smiled without humor. "There's a certain symmetry to that, considering the kind of disinformation they've injected into our politics." Her eyes cut to her Chief of Staff. "William, what do you think?"

"I think four months is a very short window to make a difference, ma'am." His lips twisted as he scanned the screen. "But I agree it's worth a shot."

Cashman nodded. "My thought as well." She leveled her gaze at Don. "Given the time constraints, I assume you have someone in mind to lead this operation."

Don tilted his head toward Harrison. "You just interviewed him, ma'am."

3

Moscow, Russia

The Moscow Central Clinical Hospital, better known as the Kremlyovka or Kremlin Clinic, lay nestled in a two-hundred-hectare wooded park some fourteen kilometers west of Red Square. It was, simply put, the premier source of top-notch medical care for the Russian political and monied elite.

Yuri Andropov and Mikhail Gorbachev had both died there, as had Ravil Manganov, the chairman of Lukoil and one of most outspoken critics of the Ukraine invasion. But while the two former Russian leaders had died of old age, Manganov had died of injuries sustained from a fall out of a sixth-floor window. The fact that Manganov's unfortunate accident had taken place shortly after a visit from Nikolay's Uncle Vitaly never made it into the contemporary news accounts.

Nikolay waited impatiently as his driver navigated the multiple layers of security surrounding the elite facility and pulled up to the front entrance. He exited the car gingerly, still sore from the multiple blasts his body had endured in the assassination attempt less than forty-eight hours ago.

His eyes lighted on a female plainclothes FSB agent waiting to greet him and his thoughts flashed to Zave. He recalled her beautiful body sprawled like a broken doll on the seats beneath his box at the theater, the front of her golden dress blackened by blood. His breath caught in his throat.

He still didn't know how to feel about the woman who had shared his bed for months. She'd said she loved him and he'd told her the same. But he hadn't known she was also an FSB operative, secretly assigned to his personal protection detail.

It doesn't matter, he decided. She's just as dead either way.

He'd known without even asking who had assigned Zave to the task of bedding the Russian President: his oldest and most trusted confidante, Vladimir Federov.

Nikolay ignored the pain in his side as he took the steps of the entrance two at a time. Now Federov would personally answer for that insult.

The woman FSB agent led the way to the elevator and pushed the call button. Nikolay's two bodyguards trailed after them. When the doors opened, he held up his hand.

"Take the next one," he ordered his men, and he followed the woman into the elevator. The air inside was stale and smelled of disinfectant.

She pressed the button for the seventh floor and the doors closed on his unhappy security team. The agent stared straight ahead. She was mid-thirties, dark-haired, and solidly built, the opposite of Zave's elegant body.

"How is he?" Nikolay asked.

The agent half turned her head. "I'm in charge of security, Mr. President. I don't interact with the doctors except to screen them for access."

That was a lie, they both knew it. There was no way Federov would permit his lead agent to act as a simple guard dog. He expected his team to know everything about their job.

Nikolay wanted to press her further but the elevator doors opened again. The agent stepped into the hall, looked both ways, then nodded to Nikolay to follow her. The lights in the hallway were dimmed for the evening, leaving isolated pools of light on the dark carpet.

They passed a nurse's station, where a trim young woman sat behind a modern desk with a battery of monitors arrayed in front of her. She stood when Nikolay passed by.

A security guard in civilian clothes posted outside the door at the end of the hallway. His shaved head gleamed in the dim light as his eyes tracked their approach.

"Is he awake?" the lead agent asked.

"She's in there with him," the guard replied.

Before Nikolay could ask who "she" was, the agent knocked gently on the heavy wooden door and entered.

The interior of the room was dark and very warm. Nikolay felt sweat prickle on his brow as the agent closed the door gently and advanced to a pair of armchairs placed to maximize the view through the large picture window. She knelt next to one of the chairs and spoke softly. Then she stood and beckoned Nikolay forward.

He advanced slowly, his footfalls muffled by the carpet, his underarms dampening. Nikolay hadn't seen Federov in months and suddenly this visit felt like a terrible idea. His anger drained away. He'd planned to come here to rail at Federov for abandoning him, but now he regretted coming at all.

Nikolay rounded to the front of the chair and it took everything in him not to recoil in horror. Vladimir Federov had always been a large man, the type of man whose presence was always felt, even when he said nothing—which was most of the time.

But the man in the chair was just a husk of his former FSB Chief. The reflected light from the window cast an orange glow across his haggard features. His flaccid skin looked dry and brittle as aged parchment and his once robust body had wasted away. A translucent line of plastic tubing snaked under his nostrils, crossed his cheeks, and ran behind his ears.

His fingers, now more like claws, gripped the arm of the chair and the handle of a cane as the man scooted forward in his chair, trying to stand. Nikolay stooped to place a hand on his shoulder. It felt like he was gripping a skeleton.

"No need, old friend," he said. His nostrils caught a scent from the struggling man, a sweetness like rotting fruit, and a wave of sadness swept over him.

What a way to die, Nikolay thought.

The person in the adjacent chair turned on a light and stood. Nikolay straightened, glad to put some distance between himself and the dying man.

The soft illumination played over the striking figure of Iliana Semanova. Tall and lithe, for decades Iliana had served as Federov's madame and closest confidante. Plucked from the gutter as a runaway teenager, Iliana had been groomed by Federov as an operative who specialized in sexual blackmail. But those days were behind her, Nikolay knew. Today she taught her skills to young women and ran them as companions in an exclusive international escort service.

She owed her life to Federov and was fiercely loyal to him. More than a wife or a lover, she was an extension of the man who slumped in the chair between them.

"Mr. President." Iliana inclined her head in respect. "This is an unexpected honor."

Nikolay searched her tone for an implied insult, but found nothing.

"Leave us," Federov wheezed. His voice, which had always been high-pitched, came out as a gasp.

Iliana bent down and pressed her lips to his forehead. She whispered something to him and Federov nodded. Then she glided across the room and let herself out.

Nikolay took the empty seat and together the two men stared out the window where the lights of Moscow blotted out the stars. He tried to think of a way to start the conversation. In the limo on the way to the hospital his mind had been full of indignation and rage. The massive intelligence failure, his fall in the polls, the death of Zave...

"Are you well, Mr. President?" Federov asked with a rasp in his throat. Nikolay turned to find his former FSB Chief leaning on the arm of his chair. Bright eyes twinkled from sunken eye sockets. Perhaps the old Vladimir was in there after all.

"I am not well, my friend, but I suspect you knew that already."

"Tell me," Federov said, and leaned back in his chair.

So Nikolay did. He unloaded his burdens as if the man next to him was not on death's door, but was his old confidante sitting in his private office discussing strategy.

"I don't understand how this happened," Nikolay concluded. "How could a half-baked militia gain access to a presidential event? It's preposterous. It's—"

"Troubling," Federov finished for him. "But I took precautions."

"You mean Zave?" Nikolay's anger was back with a vengeance. "She was one of yours, right? Well, she died protecting me."

"That was her job, Mr. President." Federov's voice hardened.

"I suppose you paid her to sleep with me, too."

"No. No, she did that on her own." The tone lost its edge. "She was a good officer who gave her life in service of her country. I believe her feelings for you were real."

Nikolay felt a flare of returning anger. "I fired Lipovsky," he said, unable to keep the spite out of his voice.

Federov sighed. "I wish you hadn't done that, Mr. President. Anatoly was my first choice to replace me and he'd only been there a short time. This failure was mine, not his."

"I needed to make a show of strength. I'm getting killed in the polls!"

Federov nodded slowly. "*Da.*"

"That's all you can say? *Da?*"

"I find it refreshing that you are focused on the right problem."

Nikolay drew in a slow breath. He would not lose his temper with a dying man, but that same man was making this extremely difficult. "What is that supposed to mean?"

It took him so long to respond that Nikolay wondered if the old man had fallen asleep. Finally, Federov let out a long breath.

"You need to focus on the home front. The Duma election is only four months away and your biggest problem is Rabilov and his New Dawn idiots. If they win, they will crush you, slowly and painfully. They will take away your hopes and plans for a renewal of our nation."

Federov's clawlike hand scrabbled for a device hanging on the portable IV stand. He pressed a button three times and Nikolay heard a beep in response. The old man let out a sigh of relief. His body sagged.

Minutes passed and Nikolay wondered again if Federov had drifted off.

"You need to take action." The wispy voice was distant and breezy.

"What kind of action, Vladimir? I need a game plan."

His former FSB Chief sank lower into his chair and closed his eyes.

"There is opportunity in chaos, Mr. President. Stay the course...Remain alert."

Opportunity in chaos? His public approval was in the single digits, supporters were fleeing him and his policies, and the woman he loved was revealed as an undercover operative. By all rights, he should be dead. What possible opportunity could he find in this disaster?

Nikolay leaned closer, touched the old man on the shoulder. It was like poking a bundle of twigs.

"Vladimir? What does that mean?"

The only reply was a gentle snore.

4

Special Activities Center
CIA Headquarters, Langley, Virginia

Harrison rubbed his eyes, suppressing a yawn. He stole a glance at the clock above the door to the secure conference room. Quarter to seven in the evening, which meant that in fifteen short minutes they would have been at this problem for twelve hours.

The "problem" stared back at him from the line of photos taped to the whiteboard. Bogdan Rabilov, the seventy-three-year-old leader of the ultra-nationalist movement in Russia, was a despicable human being. His face told the story of his vices: sagging jowls hid a square jaw and piercing eyes were rimmed with red. His lips were twisted into a half scowl, half roguish smile—Harrison could not decide which. If he believed the dossier on Rabilov, it seemed that the Russian public couldn't decide what they thought of the man either.

After three decades in the public eye, opinions about Rabilov were set in stone. He had survived scandals that would have felled any normal politician by using a simple procedure: deny, delay, denigrate. Women, drugs, political kickbacks, lawsuits, he had weathered them all. The man was political Teflon.

"Maybe we should take another look at the daughter," said Genevieve Matcombe. A striking Black woman with shoulder-length dark hair, she was Harrison's banking expert for the operation. She was also the only member of the covert action team that he hadn't known in advance. Genevieve had been assigned to him by Director Brooks.

A personal assignment by the Director might be Brooks's way of keeping tabs on the operation without having to go through Don. Or it could mean that Genevieve Matcombe was good at her job and the Director wanted Harrison to be successful. Time would tell.

"We don't have time for that," Stellner replied. Next to him, Meyers nodded. Harrison had worked with both men for years. The pair were old hands at CIA but had originally been Green Berets in the US Army. They assessed for Special Operations Detachment – Delta, or "Delta Force" as the unit was more commonly known, and had served together until they retired on the same day. Moving to CIA was a natural fit for both men.

The pair, known collectively as S&M, had been assigned to the team by Don. Maybe his boss wanted an inside opinion on Harrison's leadership skills, too.

"I think Tom's right, Genevieve," added Michael Goodwin. At least he'd been allowed to select one team member on his own, Harrison mused, and he'd chosen well. Goodwin was a top-notch analyst and a superb computer geek. From the looks of his broad shoulders and trim physique, the young man put in his time at the gym, too.

Harrison had known Michael since he'd joined Emerging Threats Group right out of the Naval Academy and he'd watched the young officer mature into a seasoned analyst.

The dark skin of the young man's brow wrinkled as he studied his computer screen. Michael's skill was in spotting patterns, especially in computer code.

"There's no reason to believe that anything we do to discredit Dariya Rabilova will rub off on her father," offered Michael. "Even if there was, we don't have a way to get at her. She hasn't left Russian soil in a year."

That was their problem in a nutshell, Harrison thought. Everything had to be done at arm's length, outside the borders of the Russian Federation.

"What about the money man?" Harrison said, trying to steer the conversation to a new angle.

Genevieve read from her computer screen. "Yuri Balinovich, sixty-four years old, net worth estimated at $30 billion. Numerous business ventures, all with global reach. Connected to mining, oil and gas, banking, some tech companies, even football."

S&M exchanged a look, then Meyers leaned forward. "Which team?" His tone was interested.

Genevieve consulted her screen. "Newcastle."

The two former Delta operators nodded at each other and leaned back in their chairs.

Genevieve shook her head, then continued, "Former best pal to everybody's favorite dictator Vitaly Luchnik. The overthrow of Luchnik led Yuri to hitch his wagon to the New Dawn party and Bogdan Rabilov." She looked up with a wry smile. "Here's an unexpected gem. Our friend Yuri is a raging bigot and anti-Semite. What a surprise." Her words dripped with sarcasm.

"Surely he travels outside of Russia," Harrison ventured.

"He sure does, and get this," Michael added. "He travels with his own personal Swiss banker wherever he goes. Roland Buhler, thirty years old, Swiss national. Guy carries a personal satellite comms setup handcuffed to his wrist so Yuri can access his accounts wherever and whenever he wants."

Meyers studied his own laptop with a bleak expression. "Yuri has tight security, both physical and cyber. He'd be tough to get to, especially on a short timetable. Maybe we could compromise the bagman?"

Harrison grimaced. His own reading of the dossier told him that Yuri Balinovich was a paranoid son of a bitch. He undoubtedly had Roland's nuts in a dresser drawer. Besides, compromising the bagman to get to the oligarch to get to the crazy Russian politician felt like too long of a daisy chain for an operation that already had a tight timetable.

"Other ideas?" he asked.

"Yuri has a daughter," Genevieve said. "Thirty-six years old, estranged. Works for Doctors Without Borders in Paris as an operations coordinator." The banker's eyebrows arched. "She's the real deal. Been on the ground in Haiti, Pakistan, Somalia, and Sudan."

"Sins of the father," Stellner said.

"I think there's something here, Harrison," Genevieve said. "Her dossier says that she was left a $20M trust fund by her mother and she turned it into a foundation. She hasn't had contact with Balinovich since she graduated from college ten years ago." Genevieve raised her eyes to Harrison. "Maybe we could turn her."

Harrison blew out a breath of frustration. "All these ideas come back to the same roadblock: time. We need something we can pull off in a short amount of time outside the borders of Russia."

Even in the age of hyper-speed social media, most influence operations took at least a year to build. An effective operation needed to appear as if it had grown organically and that was difficult to fake, especially against a character as slippery as Rabilov. They couldn't just start some sort of internet rumor and power it into the public consciousness with bots like in the old days.

Harrison got to his feet. He was tired and he felt a headache coming on. "Let's take it from the top."

Harrison tapped the photograph of Bogdan Rabilov. "We need to find a way to turn him into political poison."

"Known quantity. Been the bad boy of Russian politics forever," Genevieve said. "Whatever we pin on him needs to be urgent and easily understood by the average Igor and Olga. So far, we've got squat."

"Agreed," Harrison said, "so let's look at close associates." He tapped the photo of Dariya Rabilova. "He has a thirty-four-year-old daughter. No known vices, mostly stays in her old man's shadow. Do we have anything useful on her?"

There was no answer.

"She's got a huge online following," Michael said finally. "I'll take a run at her and see if I can find something that's not in the dossier. I know a couple of analysts in the Russian shop who may be able to help."

"What else?" Harrison asked.

Genevieve spoke up. "I think we should look at the oligarch's daughter. She's not in Russia. I could work up an approach. There might be something there."

Harrison sighed. "Okay, develop a contact plan. I don't see a path back to the target, but we should explore all the options."

"What about Yuri Balinovich?" he asked. "Ideas?"

He saw Meyers elbow his partner.

"What?" Harrison asked.

Team S&M hunched over their tablets. They both looked up at Harrison.

"Balinovich is the majority owner of the Newcastle football club," Meier answered.

"What does that have to do with Rabilov?" Harrison tried to keep the irritation out of his voice.

"Bogdan is a minority owner of the Moscow Dynamo," Stellner said patiently, then added. "That's a Russian football club."

Harrison shrugged. "So?"

Meyers continued. "Since the Ukraine invasion, Russia was kicked out of the European league. They've been trying to get back in ever since."

Stellner turned his laptop around. "The two clubs are playing a friendly match in the UK in three weeks."

Michael hammered at his keyboard. "According to Facebook, Bogdan will be at the match." He looked up. "He'll be outside of Russia."

Harrison felt a glimmer of hope. "Okay, we have a place and time. What's the play?"

"We set him up," Genevieve said. "Record him taking a bribe. He goes back to Russia and we leak the story. Give the FSB an excuse to pick him up."

"We can set up a paper trail," Michael added.

"I like it," Harrison said. "A big fat bribe, from someone that the Russians will hate."

"We need a way to get close to him," Genevieve said.

"What we need is a rich guy who loves soccer," Stellner said. "Maybe someone who is part owner of a competing team so he has a reason to be there. It would also help if he was a world-famous asshole."

"Exactly," Harrison agreed. Then he realized who Stellner was talking about. "No," he groaned. "Not him."

"Yup," Stellner said with a grin. Meyers, also grinning, nodded in unison with his partner.

Harrison realized the pair had walked him right into their L-shaped ambush.

"You need to go see V-cubed," they said.

5

Starovo, Russia, 120 kilometers northeast of Moscow

Bogdan was drunk. Again.

If Yuri really thought about it, he had a hard time remembering a meeting with Bogdan Rabilov in the last year when the old politician hadn't been at least a little buzzed.

"This is my favorite part!" Bogdan roared, pointing at the television. "I could watch this all day."

Yuri winced as his gaze fell on the large flat-screen TV on the wall. A half hour ago, he'd convinced Bogdan to turn off the sound. That hadn't worked out as well as he'd hoped. Instead of a silent movie, the action on the screen was punctuated by the soundtrack of the drunk politician who seemed to feel the need to comment on every scene.

The TV was big enough that the people were almost life-size. On the screen, Nikolay Sokolov, President of the Russian Federation, got on his knees, hands in the air. The look on his blood-spattered face was one of dazed terror as if he could not process what was happening to him.

Still, it was hard to look away. Sokolov's lips moved in dumb show, eyes raised, chin quivering. Yuri wondered what was going through the man's brain at that instant. He was no fan of the President, but no man deserved to be humiliated like this.

Bogdan roared again and polished off another glass of vodka.

This national embarrassment would have never happened under Vitaly Luchnik, Sokolov's uncle and the former President, Yuri thought. Things were good then, stable. There was order to the country. And then there was the money…so much money. Under Vitaly's leadership, Yuri had a free hand to do what he wanted—as long as he paid up to the boss when asked.

But with Nikolay as President, all of that stability and wealth was at risk.

Sokolov wanted economic reforms and fair taxes. He actually wanted Yuri to pay taxes. That little pissant didn't seem to understand how the world worked. Yuri was rich. Yuri owned businesses that employed people so that those people could pay the taxes. He had little time for American ideals, but even *they* understood how the world worked. Trickle-down economics was the perfect model. Let rich people invest and some of that vast wealth would inevitably roll downhill to the rest of the world.

On the screen, the woman in the golden dress rose up behind Sokolov and fired the small handgun. The picture reeled and swung wildly, then crashed to the ground. The dazed and bloody face of Sokolov filled the field of view. The screen went black.

Bogdan leaped off the sofa, his big belly swinging loose beneath his untucked shirt. He seized the remote. "Let's watch it again!"

Yuri held up his hands. "Bogdan, my friend, please. Enough."

Bogdan's stubby index finger poised over the remote, as if considering whether or not to honor Yuri's request. A mischievous smile spread across his florid face, but before he could act, a slim hand plucked the remote away.

"Papa," Dariya said, "I think that's enough."

For a split second, Bogdan's face clouded with rage, then he plopped his considerable backside down on the sofa. He held out his empty glass. "Get me another drink, Dariya."

"Of course, Papa." She took the glass from her father and turned to Yuri. "Uncle Yuri, can I get you something?"

Yuri looked up at her. Behind heavy-rimmed masculine glasses, her deep brown eyes glinted with amusement. "I'll have a Coca-Cola, Dariya. Thank you."

"It is my pleasure." Her voice was low and held the promise of a smile.

Yuri followed her with his eyes. She was not a bad-looking girl. Apart from the trendy glasses, she was pretty in a wholesome way. He'd never cared much for the skeletal supermodel type. They were all there for his money anyway. He hadn't dated seriously in decades. When he needed a woman, he called a number and one showed up. Iliana knew the type of woman he preferred for every occasion, and she delivered every time. Even his pleasure was a business transaction. It was simpler that way, cleaner.

Bogdan belched, interrupting Yuri's stream of thoughts.

"What do you want to talk about, Yuri?"

The oligarch studied the politician. Bogdan had cut his teeth in the bare-knuckles world of Moscow politics following the fall of the Soviet Union. In those early days, it seemed like Bogdan was everywhere. A fixture of stability in a time of chaos, dispensing favors, controlling the action. An outsized personality, he outdrank, outfought, and outfucked everyone who opposed him—always to excess, always the winner in every contest.

By all rights, Bogdan Rabilov should have been a rich man. Indeed, he'd probably gained and pissed away ten fortunes in the last forty years. Ex-wives, shady business deals, outlandish spending, everyone had their hand in Bogdan's pocket. But Yuri put a stop to all that. Bogdan was Yuri's man now, bought and paid for. Uncle Yuri paid the bills and Bogdan delivered the votes in the Duma.

Dariya arrived with fresh drinks.

The exception was Dariya, Yuri reflected, as he accepted his drink. She was the only person who had stood by Bogdan through thick and thin. The only person who didn't seem to want anything from her father, only to make him successful.

The girl had been born to Bogdan's third wife—or maybe his fourth—Yuri couldn't remember. No matter, she'd left him like all the others.

But something odd happened with Dariya's arrival. Instead of putting the child up for adoption, Bogdan kept her. He took her everywhere, traveling with a nanny, then a governess. The child grew up steeped in the far-right politics of her father and sat at his side during many a backroom deal.

Somehow, the young woman had grown into her father's alter ego. Thoughtful when he was brash, intelligent when he was incoherent, tough when he was soft. She was the brains behind this brawny aging ideological warrior.

"The new polls are in, Father," Dariya said.

The words stirred the old man from his stupor. His head snapped toward her, red-rimmed eyes bright. "Well? Don't keep your old man waiting, girl."

Dariya caught Yuri's eye and again he sensed the hint of a secret smile. "Favorables for the party are up twenty points, and a solid majority now say they will definitely vote New Dawn in the election."

Bogdan thrust his fist in the air, spilling his drink. He let out a roar. "We will own the Duma! Nikolay Sokolov is fucked!"

Yuri sighed and strode to the picture window. The late afternoon sunshine lit the meadow outside. His dacha was on a game preserve and he squinted into the dark depths of the Taiga forest beyond the meadow. Behind him, Bogdan restarted the TV, with sound this time, as he rewatched the humiliation of Russian President Nikolay Sokolov.

Dariya appeared next to him, her reflection ghosting the glass next to his.

"I thought the polls would be good news, Uncle," she said.

He had asked her to call him uncle years ago, right in this very room, during a weekend strategy session with the leadership of the ultranationalist movement. Bogdan was just one of a number of leaders back then, though the most popular by far. He wasn't as intellectual as some of the others, but he had charisma, and that was a quality that could not be taught. It was in that meeting that Yuri first saw the New Dawn movement coalesce around Bogdan. One by one, the rest of the party elite either fell in line behind Bogdan or disappeared—sometimes permanently. Yuri saw the momentum, sensed the mood shift in the country, and when Nikolay Sokolov seized power, Yuri went all in on Bogdan and New Dawn. Together, they began to shape the political discussion in the Duma, forming a solid bloc of votes that every coalition wanted to own.

And now, we have a chance to be in the majority, Yuri thought. It had all started on that afternoon years ago.

"Do you remember when I first asked you to call me uncle?" he said to Dariya's reflection.

The secret smile formed on her lips. "Of course. It was right here, in this room."

Yuri felt a little surge of pleasure that she remembered the moment so clearly. It meant something to her as well, he realized. When he recalled that afternoon, he pictured her a lonely, awkward girl in that room full of loud men, and he remembered feeling protective of her.

Dariya was different now. Mature, confident. A woman in her own right.

"If the election were held today, we would win in a landslide," she prompted.

"That is good news, my dear."

"You're troubled, Uncle. What is it?"

Was he that transparent or was she that perceptive? Yuri wondered.

"Did your father have anything to do with the assassination attempt, Dariya?" Yuri said finally.

"Absolutely not." Her answer was firm, definitive. She used the reflection to make eye contact with him. "I give you my word, Uncle."

"What if your father made arrangements without your knowing?"

Behind them, Bogdan shouted at the television and they turned. On the screen, Nikolay Sokolov begged for his life. Bogdan grabbed his crotch, thrust his hips at the TV. "Fuck you, Mr. President."

As Yuri and Dariya turned back to the window, Dariya met his gaze. Her face had the strained expression of a parent excusing an unruly child. "My father doesn't do anything without my knowledge, Uncle."

Yuri nodded, but his mind shot forward. If they took the majority in the Duma, it would be another four long years before the presidential election. As leader of the New Dawn, Bogdan would be the obvious candidate for the party. Bogdan whooped again and shouted another obscenity at the television.

Dariya gripped his arm. "Look," she said, her voice a breathless whisper.

On the far side of the meadow, an elk emerged from the forest. It was a huge bull, at least two meters at the shoulder. His antlers had already grown considerably, curving over his head like a velvet-laden crown. The animal stopped at the edge of the conifer forest, the muscles of his thick neck rippling as he swiveled his gaze toward the dacha.

"It's beautiful," Dariya whispered. Both of her hands gripped his arm. She pressed her body next to his. Her lips parted and she breathed in short, excited bursts that left a haze on the window, clouding their twinned reflections.

"Beautiful," Yuri agreed.

6

50 kilometers northeast of Roswell, New Mexico

The one thing Harrison hadn't expected to see in New Mexico in May was wildflowers. He stared out the window from the back seat of the SUV as the landscape flashed by in a blur of color.

Stellner, who was driving, noticed Harrison's attention. He pointed his chin at the scenery. "You see, Harrison. Climate change is a good thing." In the passenger seat, Meyers nodded.

Harrison said nothing. Right now, climate change was the least of his worries. It was hard to believe that the success or failure of his covert action against a Russian politician came down to whether or not he could convince an eccentric American billionaire to back his plan.

Victor van Valkenberg preferred to be called by his nickname, "V-cubed." Thirty years ago, V^3 had emigrated to the United States from Argentina as a college student on a full scholarship to MIT. Whoever sponsored young Victor got their money's worth. The kid graduated from the four-year program in three years and left the prestigious institution for California, where he founded a B2B tech company that specialized in interfacing software that allowed companies to fully integrate their legacy computer systems.

Never one to follow a script, Victor reveled in contradictions. Fiercely libertarian in his business practices, he also advocated for a strong social safety net and a view that employees were family. His company hired only the best and offered world-class salary and benefits. In Silicon Valley, it was common knowledge that if you were talented enough to get hired by V^3, you stayed for a career. On his fortieth birthday, V^3 sold his company for $30 billion and retired to pursue his real passion: aviation.

In the world of politics, V^3 defied political categorization. Like many immigrants, he was outspoken about his love for his adopted country, but dismissive of the American two-party political system. In interviews, V^3 often said that he liked to speak loudly and carry a big wallet. He gave money only to individual candidates who aligned with his values and woe be the politician that let him down.

Yet, for all his outspokenness on social, economic, and political issues, V^3 stayed strangely silent about national security. Harrison had been unable to find a single opinion from the man on the military, the CIA, or even the intelligence community in general.

I'm flying blind, he thought.

Stellner turned left off the 380 and headed north along a two-lane paved highway. Fifteen minutes later, a large silver-gray object rose out of the landscape, shimmering in the midday heat.

"Do you think this is it?" Stellner asked sarcastically.

A restored B-52 bomber occupied a field next to a turn off the highway. The massive aircraft, as tall as a house, with a wingspan of nearly two hundred feet, dominated the flat land around it, gleaming like quicksilver in the desert sunlight. Underneath the cockpit, an angled landscape of manicured native plants formed the words: *V^3 Aviation.*

"I wonder if he's compensating for something," Meyers asked wryly.

Stellner made the turn, drove past the bomber, and stopped at a guardhouse. A twelve-foot fence stretched to their right and left as far as Harrison could see and three metal bollards blocked their path.

A man emerged from the guardhouse, carrying a tablet. "Can I ask all parties to exit the vehicle and stand behind the painted line, please?" He had the physique of a linebacker and a high-and-tight haircut. "We're going to image your vehicle, Mr. Kohl. Do I have your permission?"

Harrison caught a glimpse of his photo on the tablet. "Yes, of course."

"Thank you, Mr. Kohl." He tapped the tablet and Harrison heard a low hum. "I apologize for the inconvenience, sir, but I need to secure all of your electronics at the guardhouse."

Stellner and Meyers exchanged glances, then handed over their mobile phones. "I'm a little low on juice," Stellner said. "Can you charge it for me and update the IOS?"

The guard offered a thin smile in return. His tablet beeped. "Your vehicle is cleared, Mr. Kohl. Be advised that your GPS navigation system will not work on the property. Drive straight ahead for five miles. V^3 is expecting you at the big house. Please do not leave the main road. We have drones monitoring your progress, sir."

Stellner got behind the wheel and started the engine. "Guess I can skip my colonoscopy now," he groused.

To call the van Valkenberg mansion a "big house" was like calling Downton Abbey a country cottage. The edifice was enormous, and yet somehow Harrison got the sense that the structure belonged in this environment. The sleek roofline followed the curve of the mountains to the west and the colors complemented the natural surroundings. They followed the road as it curved around the eastern side of the building and ended in a courtyard where a man stood waiting for them.

Victor van Valkenberg was medium height with a stocky build and wispy brown hair that showed gray at the temples. Silver dusted his stubbled chin. He was dressed plainly in a khaki work shirt with the sleeves rolled up and faded blue jeans with cowboy boots. As the car rolled to a halt, he stumped over and opened Harrison's door.

"Harrison Kohl," he boomed as if they were old friends, "I'm V^3." He stuck out his hand. He had a firm grip and he used it to pull Harrison from the vehicle. "Welcome to my compound."

Interesting choice of words, Harrison thought, as V^3 turned his attention on S&M.

"You're Tom Stellner," V^3 announced as Stellner alighted from the vehicle.

"Guilty as charged," Stellner replied as he shook the man's hand.

"Andrew Meyers," V^3 said, turning on Stellner's partner.

"Andy is just fine," Meyers said.

V^3 frowned as if that was a piece of information he should have known.

"Can I offer you some refreshment?" V^3 asked, leading them from the courtyard into a shaded open walkway. Wildflowers spilled down the graded slope. "You've come at a good time of year. Lots of rain the last two months means wildflowers. Climate change, you know?"

Harrison watched Stellner and Meyers exchange a quick smile.

Despite the piston-like quality to his walk, V^3 set a quick pace. Harrison guessed the man only had one speed. The group turned a corner and entered a wide veranda shaded by manicured bougainvillea vines dripping with waves of crimson flowers. A table, set for four, had a large jug of milky liquid sweating in the heat.

"Margaritas?" Meyers asked with hope in his voice.

"Just lemonade for now," V^3 replied. "I'm hoping I can convince you gents to go flying with me this afternoon."

"I'm not sure we'll have time," Harrison said.

V^3 grinned. "We'll see." Harrison saw he had a gold tooth on the left side of his mouth.

The billionaire poured lemonade for his guests, then himself. He took his seat, drank the entire glass in one go, and placed it on the table. "Now, Mr. Kohl, please tell me why the CIA is visiting my compound."

Harrison cleared his throat. They had used third parties to set up the meeting and the topic of discussion was ostensibly about funding a solar project in the Midwest.

"I'm a big admirer of your work in Central Asia, Mr. Kohl," V^3 continued. "You did our country a great service working with the resistance over there."

Harrison exchanged looks with Stellner. While his presence in Central Asia was something that could have been discovered by a diligent researcher, his assignment as a covert CIA liaison with the resistance movement was highly classified.

"Money buys information, Harrison," V^3 continued, "and I have a lot of money. We don't need to do the dance. You can just ask me whatever it is you came here to ask me."

Harrison almost cracked a smile. Despite all his money, V^3 didn't know why he was here—and it was driving him crazy.

"You're right," Harrison said. "We're not here to talk about a solar project, we're here to ask for your help."

V^3's right eyebrow twitched up. A tell. He was interested.

"I'm listening," said the billionaire.

"We'd like to use your influence to get us into a football match in the UK in a few weeks."

V^3's eyebrows collapsed together in a frown. "Why?" Then they sprang upward again. "The Russia match. You want to get into the Russia match."

"That's correct."

V^3 scratched his chin. "What do I get out of it?"

Harrison assessed the man. There was no pretense, no foreplay, just cards on the table. "What do you want?"

V^3 leaned forward, resting his forearms on the table. "Tell me what you're trying to do."

"V^3, I can't do that. It's a matter of national—"

The billionaire waved his hand. "Bullshit. Without knowing the variables, I can't solve the equation. You want my help? The price of entry is information."

Harrison sipped his lemonade to give himself a few precious seconds to think. He wouldn't get a second chance with V^3. The man would see through the cover story in an instant.

Harrison glanced at Stellner and Meyers. Both men smiled at him. They were enjoying seeing Harrison squirm.

"We're trying to compromise a Russian politician," Harrison said finally. "We have a very short timetable and he will be in the UK for the match. That's our window of opportunity."

V^3 sat back in his chair, his eyes unfocused as he digested Harrison's words. A full minute ticked by. Suddenly, the billionaire stood up abruptly. "Let's go flying," he announced.

Harrison started to protest, but their host was already on the move with S&M in tow. Reluctantly, Harrison followed them off the veranda to a waiting electric Polaris XPedition UTV. Harrison had barely found his seat before V^3 took off at breakneck speed.

The vehicle rocketed over a rise, then down a long slope toward the wide entrance of an underground bunker. Above the door, the desert stretched away to the mountains. They blasted into the dark interior at full speed. The air was cool down here and smelled faintly of jet fuel. As his eyes adjusted to the low light, Harrison realized they were in an aircraft hangar.

The UTV ran down the center of a wide concrete road. At intervals, concrete pillars rose into the darkness. Parked between the pillars were various types of small aircraft.

There did not appear to be a theme to the random collection. Harrison spotted a series of Cessna prop planes, an ICON A5 amphibious aircraft, and a vintage BD-5 microjet.

The space was huge, easily four football fields in size, and quiet as a tomb. The Polaris skidded to a halt. V^3 jumped out and made his way to a metal box on the side of the pillar. He punched in a code and overhead lights came on.

The aircraft parked in the bay was unlike anything Harrison had seen before.

It was electric, that much was clear. A thick cable snaked from an outlet on the plane to a heavy gray box on the pillar. V^3 tapped a pad on the side of the aircraft, which turned on interior lights and opened the doors. The cabin was roomy—large enough to hold six adults with plenty of room for cargo.

Instead of wings, four struts extended from the fuselage, one on each corner, each supporting a turbofan engine the size of a kitchen table. Harrison peered inside the nearest circular housing to find five wide, curved blades.

Stellner let out a low whistle. "Me like."

"Gentlemen," V^3 said, "welcome to my latest venture: air taxis." His tone was that of a proud parent.

Harrison cleared his throat. He tolerated flying, but this was not like any plane he'd ever seen. "What are we looking at here?"

V^3 ignored the question as he climbed into the pilot's seat. Stellner and Meyers did rock-paper-scissors for the copilot spot. A clearly disappointed Meyers joined Harrison in the back. The passenger area was every bit as comfortable as a luxury automobile, with leather seats and wide windows. The only difference was the three-point harness instead of a seat belt.

It'll be fine, Harrison thought.

By the time Harrison buckled in, V^3 had the aircraft powered up and rolling forward. The low hum of the electric motor instead of the roar of a jet engine was disconcerting. V^3 entered the wide central corridor, turned right. He flipped a switch over his head and spoke into his microphone.

Up ahead, the ceiling split open and sunlight streamed in. V^3 rolled the aircraft into a lit circle directly under the opening in the roof. He turned, speaking in a conversational tone over the low hum of the engines. "Normally, we'd use the elevator, but this baby is vertical takeoff, so no need."

Outside the window, Harrison watched the circular housings rotate until they were parallel to the ground, then increase power. The aircraft lifted smoothly off the concrete, their upward progress slow and steady. Harrison could see V^3 at the controls, but he wasn't touching anything. The aircraft was flying itself.

They emerged into full sun with the desert spreading out all around them, dappled with splashes of color from the wildflowers. V^3's enormous house merged seamlessly into the landscape below.

"Okay, now that we're clear of the hangar, let me show you what this baby can do." V^3's voice was gleeful. He yanked on the throttle and the plane shot straight up.

The air left Harrison's lungs in a rush and he was smashed down into his seat. He felt like his stomach was still a few hundred feet below his body. Their upward progress stopped suddenly and they seemed to float, then Harrison saw the turbofans snap vertical and the aircraft shot forward.

Stellner let out a rebel yell. Meyers pounded the seat next to him. "That's what I'm talking about!" he shouted. Harrison craned his neck so he could see the dashboard. They were traveling at 250 mph.

V^3 narrated with the equanimity of a newscaster. "For safety reasons, the commercial models will all be completely autonomous, but this is a prototype, so we have freedom to explore the flight envelope."

They snapped into a hard right turn that threw Harrison's body against the three-point harness. He felt his stomach roil.

V^3 put the aircraft into a steep climb, then leveled off. "This aircraft will fly autonomously at 250 miles per hour with a range of 250 miles. I'm going to call this model the Victory 250."

He engaged the autopilot and spun his chair one-eighty degrees to face Harrison. "How we doing?"

Harrison smiled weakly. "Great."

"Outstanding! Let's talk about our operation."

Harrison started to protest that it was not *our* operation, but V^3 cut him off.

"I see it this way," he began. "You need to catch Rabilov in a corruption scandal. Something that will really piss off the average Russian. How am I doing so far?"

Harrison swallowed hard and nodded. Even though the flight was steady and level now, his stomach was still queasy. With the sound insulation of the luxury cabin and low noise level of the electric motors, it was possible to have a normal conversation. For Harrison, the near-silence inside an aircraft was disconcerting.

"Good." V^3 nodded. "This is your bribe." He patted the arm of his chair.

"You want to give Rabilov a plane?" Stellner said. "Sign me up."

V^3 laughed. "No, I'm going to convince him to give me the exclusive air taxi service contract for Moscow—in exchange for a big fat bribe, of course."

"That's brilliant," Meyers said. "An American company comes in and takes Russian jobs."

Harrison shook his head. "I can't have you involved. What if—"

The billionaire stopped him with a cocked eyebrow. "You need me, Harrison," he said in a matter-of-fact voice. "It's my air taxi service and my name that will get us inside the football club. It's a well-known fact that I do all my own deals. If anyone but me makes the offer, Rabilov will smell a rat. I make the deal and your team handles the banking side to make him look guilty as sin."

Harrison looked at Stellner and Meyers. Both shrugged. It *was* a perfect setup. V^3 was famous for making up his own rules, so no one, not even Bogdan Rabilov, would question the pitch. If Rabilov took the bait, they'd have the paper trail ready. He was still in control, Harrison reasoned, even with V^3 as part of the team.

"Okay," Harrison said. "You're in."

V^3 pumped his fists in the air. He spun his chair around and disengaged the autopilot. "Let's do some barrel rolls."

Stellner let out a whoop. Harrison tightened his shoulder harness and clenched his eyes shut. If he concentrated really hard, he might not throw up all over his new team member's brand-new aircraft.

7

Saratov, Russia

Yuri Balinovich heard a distant, rhythmic thumping. He'd rolled the window of his limousine halfway down and the sound drifted in on the flow of the warm night air.

Some idiot playing his car stereo too loud, he thought. Normally, that kind of thing annoyed him, made him feel like the Russian youth of today were vapid sheep who listened to rap music and took drugs.

But not tonight. It was impossible to be angry on a spring night like this. Outside the window of the limo, the Volga River drifted by like dark glass in the silvery moonlight. He felt the dampness of the river on his skin and smelled the earthy scent of freshly turned soil. Yuri relaxed into the soft cushions.

After all, this was a vacation of a sort. Bogdan had asked him to look in on Dariya, who was giving a speech at a rally this evening. Yuri didn't mind. It was a chance to get away from Moscow for a day and see the rest of the country.

He hadn't been to Saratov in twenty years and what he remembered as a backwater port city on the Volga was now a thriving metropolis. The sidewalks were choked with pedestrians and the traffic heading toward the stadium was stop and go.

Yuri surveyed the people around him. Being only a hundred miles from the Kazakh border, this place had more than its share of immigrants and mixed marriages from Central Asia, but those things could not be helped. Through the open window, he heard snippets of the Kazakh language mixed in with Russian. These were not the kind of people who would support the New Dawn party in the upcoming elections. Bogdan had confided to Yuri that he did not expect more than a few thousand to show up for the rally, maybe less.

Yuri smirked at his reflection in the dark window. It was just like Bogdan to push off a less visible campaign stop on his daughter.

The limousine turned the corner and the Lokomotiv Arena came into view. The lights were on above the open-air stadium and the plaza leading to the rally was thronged with people. Thousands of people. They were all here for the New Dawn rally?

He rolled the window all the way down and called out to a group of young men on the sidewalk. "What's going on?"

A tall, young man wearing a tank top that showed off sculpted arms looked at him coolly. "We're here to see Dar." He pointed up at the arena and turned his back.

Yuri looked up where the young man had pointed and read the arena billboard.

New Dawn Rally tonight, featuring Dariya Rabilova.

Yuri frowned. There were thousands of people here. All to see Dariya? He was suddenly glad he'd come. This would be a challenging moment for her. She would need his support before a big crowd like this one.

The traffic suddenly thinned and the limousine lurched forward through the gate marked VIP Area.

Yuri called to the driver, "I'll walk from here."

Ivan, his security man, was at his window before the car had even stopped, opening the door of the limo. Yuri stepped out of the vehicle and buttoned his dark blue jacket.

He cocked his head. The pumping bass line was louder here and in the background was a dull roar like the sound of distant surf. The music he'd heard a few blocks earlier hadn't been some nitwit with a loud stereo, it was the music from the rally. Even the VIP area was crowded with richly dressed men and women.

A young woman in a dark blue pantsuit, wearing a New Dawn pin on her lapel, approached Ivan. They exchanged words and the woman said to Yuri, "I can take you to the VIP box, Mr. Balinovich."

"No," Yuri said. "I want to go backstage. I want to see Ms. Rabilova before she speaks."

The woman glanced at her watch. "We'll have to hurry. She's on in ten minutes."

Yuri waved his hand impatiently. "Go, then."

The woman set off through the crowd with Yuri following and his bodyguard at his heels. They cut through the garage area beneath the stadium that smelled of dirty astroturf and gasoline and she led them to a stairwell. Yuri took the steps two at a time. He had to make sure Dariya was all right before she went onstage.

The young woman paused at a steel fire door at the top of the steps. Without a word, she handed Yuri and his bodyguard disposable ear plugs and pushed the door open.

What had been a distant bass line and murmuring crowd noise became a wall of sound. The beat of the music thumped against the soft flesh of his belly. Yuri hastily compressed the bright orange earplugs and thrust them into his ears. The roar of the crowd muted to a comfortable drone.

He moved forward to the edge of the stage wing and peered out.

The stage extended ten meters forward, underneath a two-story-high video screen, and it was empty save a podium raised up on a dais. The audience, a meter below the edge of the stage, was a seething mass of humanity. Yuri ran his eyes over the sight, transfixed. There was not an empty seat in the house and the entire soccer pitch was packed with people dancing to the music. Hands in the air, mouths open in song, faces uplifted.

He spied a pair of binoculars on a shelf and he used them to scan the crowd. He saw children sitting on their parents' laps, teenagers with tattoos and piercings dancing, and gray-haired grandmothers pumping their hands in the air. This was not a political rally, this was a rock concert.

Yuri beckoned their guide. "How many people can this stadium hold?" he shouted into her ear.

"About twelve thousand in the stands, but there are more on the field," she shouted back. "We think there's over sixteen thousand people here tonight."

Sixteen thousand people here for Dariya, he thought. Could she handle that kind of pressure?

A young man with a blond crew cut and tattooed arms danced onto the stage from the opposite wing. The crowd spotted him and upped the volume another notch.

"Are you ready, Saratov?" he screamed into the microphone, sounding like an emcee at a professional boxing match.

The roar of sixteen thousand people drowned out the music.

He thrust his arms out, leaned into the microphone. The cords in his neck stood out as he announced. "I give you Dar-i-ya!"

The crowd took up the chant. *Dar-dar-dar...*

Yuri looked up and saw a woman on the opposite wing. She strode onto the stage.

It took Yuri a full heartbeat to realize the woman was Dariya. She wore tight black pants and boots with a white silk shirt open at the neck and topped by a tight black leather bustier. Her dark hair flowed down her back in silken waves and her thick heavy-framed glasses were gone. She embraced the young man, who bowed to her with clasped hands and quickly left the stage. The audience went berserk as Dariya made her way to the edge of the platform, pointing and waving. Flowers launched out from the audience, landing at her feet.

Like a seasoned politician, Dariya took her time with the crowd. Blowing kisses, smiling, waving, until she had completed a full circuit and ended up behind the podium. Yuri edged forward so he could see the video screen.

A two-story-high version of Dariya looked out over the milling crowd. She lifted her face and laughed, arms spread. Then she flipped her palms over and lowered her arms slowly. The noise died down to a dull roar.

Yuri checked his watch. She'd been on stage for ten minutes and had not said a word, yet the audience was rapt to her every move.

Dariya began to speak. Her voice was pitched low with a husky note, as if she was having a personal conversation with each and every audience member. Her message was simple and direct, filled with details that mattered to everyday Russians.

The economy, personal responsibility, strong national defense, pride in their hard work…

Yuri had seen so many of Bogdan's speeches that he'd forgotten what great political oratory sounded like. Wherever he went, Bogdan was the headliner for the New Dawn party. His speeches were rough and ready, more style than substance. Rambling and discursive, he filled his time onstage with sidebars that made people laugh—or at least, they used to. He favored brash pronouncements that shocked people, made them feel like he was speaking truth to power.

In reality, Yuri knew, Bogdan was a double-edged sword. His style limited his appeal, making New Dawn a perpetual minority party in the Duma.

Until now, Yuri realized. Because of the assassination attempt on the President, the ultranationalists had a real chance at a majority. But with Bogdan as the party's messenger, was that possible?

As he watched Dariya speak, he saw the influence of her father, but she'd taken his message and elevated it beyond cheap laughs and grievance-filled rants. Somehow, this woman managed to take the coarseness of her father and smooth off the rough edges. The policies of the New Dawn party that seemed half-baked and illogical coming out of the mouth of Bogdan Rabilov made perfect sense when they emerged from the lips of his daughter.

How had he not seen this side of her? Yuri wondered. Dariya Rabilova was not her father's assistant; she was her father's legacy. This was a woman who could convince millions of new voters to support New Dawn, the party that would return Mother Russia to the policies of Vitaly Luchnik and leave the weakling Nikolay Sokolov in the dustbin of history.

She never denigrated the other political parties—another difference from her father, who was considered the czar of insults—but she linked them to Nikolay Sokolov and emphasized his weakness on the world stage and at home. The entire speech was devastatingly effective while at the same time forward-looking and hopeful.

Yuri had a sudden epiphany.

This woman could be our next President.

Dariya drew the speech to a close at the twenty-minute mark, but she could have gone on for another hour as far as Yuri was concerned. The crowd was with her the whole time, roaring approval at just the right moments. But she was smart. She knew how to leave the crowd wanting more.

"I am sorry that my father could not be here with you tonight," she said.

"I'm not," Yuri murmured, and the roar of the stadium suggested they were on his side.

"But I am here as his messenger for the New Dawn. Join me! Together we will rebuild Russia into a great country!"

She stepped back. Even with ear protection, the crowd noise was deafening. Dariya raised her arms, her fingers flashing V-for-victory, and the music came on again. The soccer pitch was a sea of waving arms and upturned faces. People—young and old, men and women—were crying with joy.

Dariya ran offstage, passing Yuri without seeing him. A group of six men and women armed with tablets clustered around her. Dariya listened intently as one woman spoke. Dariya nodded, flicking through the screens on the proffered tablet. One by one, the others showed her their tablets and she gave a thumbs up or down for approval.

Yuri drew closer until he was looking over her shoulder. She was approving social media posts of her speech while being briefed on flash poll results. Dariya, fully absorbed in the flow of information, made decisions like a battlefield general.

The briefer stopped and looked up at Yuri. He realized how close he was to the group and stepped back just as Dariya turned around. Her eyes widened and her lips curved into a smile.

"Uncle Yuri!" She threw herself into his arms, her full body pressed against his. He felt the heat of her flushed face as she kissed him on each cheek. Her light perfume filled his senses.

"I'm so glad you're here," she said in a low voice.

Finally, Dariya released him, but she put the palm of her hand flat on his chest. Yuri's skin tingled at her touch. "Wait right here," she said. "I'll just be a moment."

She turned back to her staff and immersed herself in the information again. Yuri found his eyes traveling down the length of her body. His gaze lingered on the leather bustier, the curve of her hips. How was it possible he had never noticed how beautiful she was before this moment?

She's your daughter's age, you lecherous old man. He looked away.

"Thank you for waiting, Yuri." Dariya was back. "I'm all yours now." She took his arm, pressed it against her leather-clad breast.

Yuri cleared his throat. "What do you want to do?"

Dariya dug her fingers into his arm, then parted her lips and gave a throaty chuckle. "I want to celebrate, Yuri. I want to celebrate with you."

8

London

Genevieve Matcombe had butterflies in her stomach. She liked to tell herself that she harnessed to her advantage the nervous energy that she felt, but that was a lie. As always, this was a fraught moment. She'd been a case officer for more than five years and had successfully recruited assets across the globe, but for her, first contact—the *bump*, as it was known—never got any easier.

No matter how much research she did up front, there were so many variables out of her control in that first meeting—and she hated not having control of any situation.

The target could be having a bad day. Maybe she just had a fight with her boyfriend or the taxi driver was rude or she read something on social media that pissed her off. Or maybe the target was fine and Genevieve said or did something right off the bat that made her wary. Some subtle sign that told the target to walk away—

Stop, she told herself. *You're spinning and that doesn't help anyone. Just focus.*

Her mobile phone gave a soft ping. She turned the screen face up and read the text:

Tgt departing Hyde Park now.

Genevieve tapped an acknowledgement with a slim index finger, drained the last of her coffee and left the Nando's restaurant where she'd been waiting.

Gloucester Street was thronged with people enjoying the warm May afternoon. American tourists with ballcaps and Nikes mixed in with hippie backpackers. A passing group of teenage girls wore the uniform of the nearby school.

For this meeting, Genevieve had chosen her outfit carefully. Faded blue jeans hugged her hips and the fitted white Oxford shirt showed off her lithe body. She'd rolled up the sleeves and added a lightweight crimson cashmere sweater draped over her shoulder for contrast. She knew that shade looked fabulous against her dark brown skin. She completed the ensemble with leather ankle-cut boots with a brass buckle. The whole outfit said this was a professional woman dressing down for an afternoon off.

She turned at Kensington Gardens, taking her time on the two-block walk. The road sign at the entrance to the alley read Weatherby Mews. The sunlight faded between the five-story buildings and the ground changed from pavement to cobblestones. Genevieve paused at a granite step beneath a wide black door with tarnished brass fittings. Next to the door, mounted on the brick wall, a plaque read: *Herringbone Rare Books. By appointment only.*

She pressed the button beneath the plaque and heard a muted *bzzt* behind the door. Genevieve looked up at the camera on the wall.

"Miss Matcombe?" The male voice emitted from the intercom was gruff.

Genevieve smiled. "That's me."

The door buzzed and she pushed her way in. The smell of books surrounded her like an old sweatshirt, the kind that clung to you in all the right places and brought back fond memories. Her boots echoed on the solid wide-planked oak floor.

"Hello?" she called.

It was a small room, eight meters square, with high ceilings. Rows of bookshelves ringed the walls and four waist-high shelves lined the rest of the shop floor. Books of all shapes and sizes filled the shelves in haphazard fashion, some stacked, some placed spine out. Carefully hand-lettered cards labeled the shelves.

Although the bookshelves along the wall extended to the ceiling and there was a brass rail with a rolling ladder, the books were only stacked to the height of Genevieve's shoulder.

The curtain covering a door on the back wall shifted and a man in a wheelchair rolled in. He had a round, cherubic face softened by gray stubble and topped with flyaway gray hair.

"Miss Matcombe," he said in the clipped tone. "I'm Herringbone. It's a pleasure to meet you. Remind me again, you're here about the Trollope?"

"Yes," Genevieve replied, "the *Framley Parsonage* first edition."

As the man spun his chair and rolled to the wall shelf, Genevieve scanned the store. She found what she was looking for sitting on a table next to the curtained door.

"You have a first edition of *Sketches by Boz*!" Genevieve crossed to the table but did not pick up the book. "I've been looking everywhere for this."

Herringbone's wheelchair appeared at her hip. His face had a tight smile, but Genevieve pretended not to notice. "May I?" She gestured at the book.

Herringbone handed her a pair of cotton gloves and she picked up the book. The green embossed cover creaked as she eased it open. "I love Cruikshank's illustrations," she said. "They really bring Dickens's writing to life."

"It's not signed," Herringbone said tentatively.

Genevieve laughed. "I couldn't afford a signed copy, Mr. Herringbone, but I must have this for my collection. How much do you want for it?"

"I'm sorry. I've set this one aside for another customer."

"Nonsense. How much do you want for it?"

Herringbone's face twisted with indecision. From her research, Genevieve knew that Herringbone's Rare Books had not made a profit in years and his rent had gone up again last month. The man needed the money.

"I'm sorry," he said again. "This copy is spoken for."

"I'll give you one thousand pounds for it," Genevieve declared.

Herringbone's mouth fell open, revealing a history of poor dentistry. "Well," he began, "I'm not sure—"

The door buzzer rang, cutting him off. Herringbone spun his chair and ducked behind the curtain. A few seconds later, the door opened and Anoushka Balinovich walked in.

Up to this point, Genevieve had only seen surveillance pictures of her target. The photos were a poor substitute for the real thing.

Anoushka wore her ash-blond hair in a thick braid down her back and she had deep blue eyes. She was dressed in blue jeans and a plain white T with a battered tweed jacket and Converse sneakers. Her skin was flawless and Genevieve would have guessed her age as closer to thirty than forty. Still, for all her dressing down and casual nature, it was obvious that she came from money. It was there in the way she strode into the room.

"Hello, Mr. Herringbone." Her accent was American, slightly New England, without a trace of her native Russian. "We spoke on the phone yesterday about the Dickens first edition."

She saw the book in Genevieve's hand and a slight frown creased her brow, then disappeared. She held out her hand. "Hello there. I'm Annie." It was awkward because Genevieve was still wearing the cotton gloves. Still, she had confirmed one piece of intel. Although she'd never legally changed her name, Anoushka Balinovich was still using the name Annie Baker. She apparently did not want people to associate her with her Russian oligarch father.

"Genevieve," she said with a demure smile.

Annie's grip was firm, commanding, and she held on for a beat longer than necessary. "You're gorgeous," she said.

In spite of herself, Genevieve blushed. She held up the Dickens book. "Are you the other buyer? I was just pressuring Mr. Herringbone to sell this to me."

Annie put her hands on her hips in mock dismay. "Mr. Herringbone! You promised Boz to me."

The proprietor's cheeks turned deep red. "I'm sorry, Ms. Baker, but this woman just made me a very handsome offer..." His voice trailed off suggestively.

"Oh, did she?" Annie turned her attention back to Genevieve. She was smiling, but her eyes had narrowed slightly. Genevieve guessed that Annie Baker was used to getting what she wanted.

"It would be a nice addition to my collection," Genevieve said. She weighed the book in her hands as if trying to decide. This was the critical moment of the first meeting. This woman had to believe that Genevieve was making a real sacrifice on her behalf.

Genevieve sighed heavily, then placed the book back on the covered table and stripped off the cotton gloves. "I want you to have it, Annie."

"Are you sure?"

She hesitated, allowing her longing gaze to slip back to the book. "Absolutely," she said, "you were here first."

Annie bit her lip to hold back the smile. "Thank you."

"What about the Trollope?" Herringbone was clearly disappointed. "Do you still want the Trollope?"

"Of course." Both women turned over their credit cards and the man left them alone as he ran the cards and wrapped their purchases.

"That copy is in very good condition," Genevieve said. "Are you a collector?"

"Not really." Annie shifted her feet, looked away.

"Oh." Genevieve allowed her disappointment to color her words. She already knew that the book was for a friend who was going to resell it. Time to set the hook. "Well, I hope you enjoy it, all the same."

"I'm sure I will," Annie lied. "It was awfully nice of you to give it up like that. Can I buy you a coffee?"

Genevieve smiled. "I would love that, Annie." She worked to keep the feeling of satisfaction off her face. She had a live one on the line.

Mr. Herringbone rolled back into the room bearing two wrapped packages and two credit card slips. Once back on the street, Annie turned right, heading farther down the alley with Genevieve in tow. Less than a block later, she turned into a tiny coffee shop. The signs in the window advertised fair trade coffee and an open mike night on Mondays.

After the bright May afternoon, the interior felt dim and stuffy. The small room was crowded with mismatched chairs gathered haphazardly around low tables. Annie ordered a macchiato and Genevieve did the same.

When Annie insisted on paying, Genevieve made a small show of resisting but relented.

She allowed Annie to select two chairs in a private corner. The shop was not crowded, but Genevieve noticed she took care to sit away from the other patrons and maintain a clear view of the entrance and the front window.

"Tell me about yourself." Annie sipped her coffee.

Genevieve laughed as if self-conscious. "Not much to tell." She slipped into her legend, which was mostly true. "I was a diplomat's kid. My father worked for the American State Department and we lived all over the world. Africa, Germany, South America."

"That sounds exciting," Annie said.

Genevieve shrugged. "I suppose it was, but for me, it was just my life, you know? After school, I started working for a shipping firm, international cargo, import-export, that kind of thing." She conveniently left off the part where she now worked for the Central Intelligence Agency as an international finance expert and sometimes case officer. "What about you?"

Annie expertly deflected the question. "You didn't want to follow in your father's footsteps and enter the foreign service? That sounds fascinating."

"Government service is not for me, I'm afraid." Genevieve laughed. "I'm a capitalist, through and through. Somebody has to pay for my book addiction. That Dickens edition is really nice. I've been looking for a copy of Boz for quite a while."

Annie put down her mug and sat up in her chair. "I have a confession to make."

Genevieve wanted to pump her fist in the air, but instead she cocked her head. "What do you mean?"

"The book isn't for me," Annie replied. "It's for a friend. She deals in rare books and asked me to pick this one up while I was in London. I confess I'm not much of a Dickens fan."

Genevieve folded her hands, mirroring Annie's body language. "Well, as long as we're being honest, I'm not much of a Dickens aficionado either. My dad was a collector and I inherited his collection when he passed. I guess I see adding to it as a way of honoring his memory." She picked up her cup again and toyed with it. "I much prefer historical fiction."

Annie's eyes widened. "So do I. Who's your favorite author?"

"You've probably never heard of her."

"Try me," Annie challenged her. "I read a lot."

"Kate Quinn? Ever read her?"

"*Read* her? I *adore* her work."

Genevieve allowed the self-satisfied glow to bleed into her smile. "No way," she said. They'd hacked Annie's online accounts as part of the targeting operation. Annie Baker had read all of Quinn's work, most of them more than once.

"Way." Annie laughed, at ease once again. She picked up her coffee cup. "Have you read her latest?"

"You mean *The Briar Club*?" Genevieve opened her purse and pulled out her copy. A bookmark protruded from the top of the novel. "Don't tell me how it ends. I'm only halfway through."

"I won't, but the ending is amazing!" She hesitated. "How long are you in London?"

Genevieve tried not to anticipate the invitation she hoped was coming. "At least another month. I'm on temporary assignment at the London branch, but it's looking like I'll be here awhile."

Annie put down her cup and sat up in her chair again. Genevieve emulated her actions in a casual way. Mirroring was a subtle means of building rapport in these kinds of early development meetings.

"I'll be back in London next week," Annie said. "Let's have lunch and talk about the book."

"I would love that," Genevieve gushed.

"Good." Annie stood and they embraced quickly, just two new acquaintances saying a friendly goodbye.

Genevieve watched Annie depart. The bell over the door rang. The sound of the street traffic filtered in and then cut off again. She pulled her mobile from her hip pocket and selected Harrison's number from recent calls.

"How did it go?" he asked by way of greeting.

Genevieve grinned. "We're in."

9

Newcastle Upon Tyne, England

Harrison watched the pedestrians as Victor's limo navigated the heavy traffic outside St. James Park, the football stadium of the Newcastle United football club. They were far from London, in the north of England, and Harrison was glad for that. Operating closer to London increased the chances that their actions might be picked up by the GCHQ, the UK's version of the NSA.

Still, he reflected, this had to be the strangest covert operation he'd ever been a part of.

For starters, the operation was based out of a castle. An actual, no-shit stone castle that looked like it had been plucked from a Hollywood screening of *Highlander*. Although Harrison was not clear about whether V^3 owned the castle or had just taken a long-term lease, the safe house was only one of the billionaire's contributions to Operation Snow Leopard. In addition to the castle, he'd offered free use of his Airbus ACJ private jet, set up high-speed internet access, and staffed the place with pre-screened housekeeping staff that kept the team fed and boarded in a manner to which Harrison was not accustomed.

But he could sure as hell get used to it.

That said, having a billionaire as part of the operation was not all good news. V^3 liked to improvise, and in his mind, all his ideas were solid gold. Harrison spent a lot of time saying *no*, a word that billionaires were not used to hearing.

The limo paused at an intersection to let a horde of fans pass. The light was green, but the pedestrians didn't care. Most of them were carrying cans of beer or paper bags molded around bottles of vodka.

Andy Meyers, who was driving, cursed under his breath. "Russians."

The Russian fans were everywhere, thousands of them. The way they dressed, and their swagger, made them easy to pick out in a city the size of Newcastle. Right now, they were all converging on St. James Park for the international friendly match between Newcastle United and Dynamo Moscow.

Harrison chuckled. *Friendly* was not the right word. The Russian football fans had a chip on their shoulder and they were out for blood. Ever since the Russian invasion of Ukraine, the Russian Premier Liga had been banned from the European football league play—and the visiting fans were not happy about being shut out.

Today's event was something only a Russian oligarch like Yuri Balinovich could have arranged. Instead of a sanctioned match, he was pitting his own team, Newcastle United, against a Russian team in a friendly non-league match. It seemed if you owned your own English Premier team and had access to your own stadium, you could do whatever you wanted.

If the Russians lost, Yuri would pocket the proceeds from a sold-out stadium. If the Russians won, he would still pocket the money and tell the media that the European clubs were afraid to let the superior Russian teams back into the league.

Win-win. Either way, the rich got richer and more powerful.

There was a break in the pedestrian traffic and Meyers shot through the gap.

"Testing, testing, can you hear me, Harry?" V^3's voice rang in Harrison's earpiece.

Harrison closed his eyes and took a breath. He hated being called Harry and this was the third comms check in the last half hour. "I can hear you, V^3. You don't need to keep checking."

He could hear Genevieve's soft chuckle on the open channel. She was back at the castle with Michael Goodwin. In the last two weeks, both of them had been working nonstop to build the financial legend behind Operation Snow Leopard, their plan to entrap Bogdan Rabilov.

What Genevieve and Michael had constructed was a thing of beauty: fake bank accounts filled with laundered money transfers, all tied back to shell companies based in Dubai, the Caymans, and the United Kingdom. In each case, they'd dropped just enough breadcrumbs of information that a reasonably skilled analyst would be able to make the right connections and tie everything back to Bogdan Rabilov. There was more than enough incriminating evidence for the Russian FSB to arrest Rabilov and charge him with corruption. Even better, the information was layered such that new revelations would emerge every few weeks, keeping the New Dawn leader's transgressions fresh in the minds of Russian voters for the foreseeable future.

Bogdan had survived a lot of scandals and Russian voters might have become numb to corruption over the years, but no one liked to be reminded constantly that they were being screwed by the man who was supposed to be on their side. Harrison was confident that Bogdan's public image would suffer. Rabilov was the beating heart of the ultranationalist movement in Russia. Bring him down and the New Dawn party would collapse in short order.

Badda-bing, badda-boom. American national security interests protected—mission accomplished.

Meyers put his blinker on and turned into the VIP parking area underneath the stadium. He rolled down his window and passed their invitation to the guard at the gate.

That was the best part, Harrison thought. They were there at the personal invitation of Yuri Balinovich himself. No fake identities or elaborate ruses needed to penetrate the inner sanctum, just an engraved invitation to join the oligarch in his private box to view the match as his guest. It just did not get any smoother than that.

"All right," V^3's confident voice came over Harrison's earpiece, as the car drew to a halt. "It's showtime, people. Follow my lead."

Before Harrison could say anything, V^3 had popped open his door and stepped out of the car. Harrison cursed. Okay, maybe not as smooth as he thought. There were still plenty of ways to screw this up.

The underground garage was noisy and chaotic, full of idling limousines and well-dressed people laughing and talking in loud voices. Harrison got to the billionaire's side. "We have a plan, V^3. I need you to follow the plan."

V^3 replied through grinning teeth. "You're in my world now, Harry, and you're my security detail. Follow my lead."

He raised a hand in greeting to a tall man with styled gray hair and a tooled leather jacket. "How are you, Roger?" V^3 stepped forward and Harrison followed with Stellner in tow. Meyers stayed with the vehicle.

Stellner grinned. "How's it feel to be the help, Harry?"

Harrison ignored the jibe in favor of a two-tone beep that signified a private channel. "That guy is a piece of work," Genevieve said into his ear.

Harrison grunted and toggled the tiny switch that protruded from his ear. "I'm glad he's on our side—I think." He changed the subject. "You have the keystone transaction ready to rock?"

"All I need is the amount and the currency. We're solid over here. You're the one with the problem on your hands."

"He'll deliver," Harrison replied with more confidence than he felt. He switched back to the open channel where V^3 was holding forth on some technical point of computing minutiae that Harrison did not understand. The two men entered the elevator with Stellner and Harrison following silently. V^3 treated his security team like furniture, which was probably their best cover, Harrison knew.

The elevator doors opened onto a foyer in front of the owner's private box. V^3 and Roger, still chatting, strolled across the team coat of arms inlaid into the tile floor and into the owner's private skybox.

The "box" was at least fifteen meters across. A bar of polished mahogany took up most of the mirrored right-hand wall. Bottles of liquor on glass shelves rose to the ceiling and a man with a white cloth over his arm was stationed next to a fleet of stemmed wineglasses and a table of open wine bottles.

Still following V^3 and his companion, Harrison and Stellner moved deeper into the room. The people were an eclectic mix. Harrison saw everything from a woman in an ultra-chic black sheath dress and stilettos clinging to the arm of a portly man who could have been her grandfather to a much younger couple dressed in matching oversized worn flannel shirts, jeans with ripped out knees, and work boots. Waitstaff circulated with trays of drinks and canapes.

At the front of the room, three rows of plush stadium-style seats lined floor-to-ceiling windows. The private box cantilevered over the stands so it felt like they were hanging in the air over the soccer pitch.

The stands on the other side of the stadium seethed with people, most wearing team jerseys and sporting black-and-white striped scarves. Everyone was on their feet, yelling, clapping, drinking.

As the teams took the field, most of the people in the room focused on the soccer pitch. Harrison used the distraction to find the man they were looking for.

Bogdan Rabilov was seated at the end of the second row of seats, drink in one hand, a plate with a sandwich balanced on his knee. His attention was focused on a young woman in a plaid miniskirt and tight white shirt that struggled to contain her considerable bosom. Bogdan's girth hung over his belt as he leaned forward to whisper something to the girl. Neither of them showed any interest in the game. Bogdan looked up and signaled a waitress. Harrison saw him put his empty glass on the tray and the waitress disappeared. She returned a few moments later, with a fresh glass of vodka and a healthy pour of white wine for the lady.

Patience, Harrison told himself. He leaned over to Stellner. "How long do soccer games last?"

Stellner tore his eyes away from the pitch. "Are you serious?"

Harrison rolled his eyes. "Just answer the question."

"They're called matches and they last ninety minutes, usually."

"Usually? What does that mean?"

"The ref can add time, if he wants—" Stellner, his eyes still on the field, let out an exasperated sigh. "Ninety minutes, with a break at halftime."

Harrison went back to watching. V^3 had moved on from Roger and was yucking it up with an ancient-looking gentleman in a bright yellow polo shirt and blue blazer. The billionaire's voice played like a low soundtrack in Harrison's ear as he worked the crowd.

Yuri Balinovich appeared at the railing above the seats with a dark-haired woman in her thirties at his side. Bogdan's daughter, Harrison realized. Yuri had a thin, pale face with a sharp, patrician nose. His thick gray hair was parted in the middle and brushed back. He was tall and lean, with the air of a man who valued economy of movement. Dariya was shorter and curvy, dressed down in tight jeans, a dress shirt and a fitted blazer. They watched the game, chatting casually.

The two made an interesting pair. They didn't touch each other or even stand close together, yet they seemed at ease with each other. Harrison noticed that the oligarch rarely smiled, but when he did, it was directed at Dariya. Interesting. None of the intel he'd seen to date indicated more than a passing relationship between the oligarch and the politician's daughter, but he sensed there was more than that.

Halftime came and went with no score. The afternoon dragged on for Harrison as Bogdan and the young woman got even more drunk. The guy must have a bladder like a camel, Harrison thought. V^3 appeared at his elbow and leaned in.

"Time to make something happen," V^3 said.

Harrison came alert. "What does that mean? Don't force this. We have a lot of time left."

"We have twelve minutes left in the game," Stellner muttered. "It's now or never."

"Exactly," V^3 said with a self-confident grin. "Watch and learn, G-man." He strode away, appearing a moment later on the other side of the room, descending the steps to where Bogdan and his date were seated. V^3 paused in front of them, his back to the soccer pitch. The pair stopped talking and looked up.

V^3 nodded at the girl. "I need to talk to your boyfriend, young lady. Business."

Harrison willed himself to keep his face still, but inside he wanted to scream. This was a disaster.

The girl looked from Bogdan to V^3, then stood up and made her way up the steps without another word. V^3 took her seat.

Bogdan finished his drink. "Business." The word rang in Harrison's earpiece.

"You know who I am?" V³ said.

Bogdan laughed. "Everyone knows who you are. What do you want, Victor?" Harrison could hear Bogdan's words slurring together.

"I have a proposition for you."

Bogdan gestured with his glass in the direction of his date's departure. "She had a proposition for me. I don't need another one."

"I've never known a politician to turn down easy money."

Harrison wanted to plant his hand on his forehead. This was the worst possible cold pitch: *Hello, I'm here to bribe you.*

And yet it worked.

"How much money?" Bogdan asked.

"Depends on how fast you can get me what I need. Money is not my problem; my problem is time."

"What do you want?"

"A taxi license in Moscow."

Bogdan's fleshy face split into a smile. "You want a taxi license?"

V³ leaned back in his chair and crossed his legs. "I want an *air* taxi license," he said. "An *exclusive* air taxi license for greater Moscow for two years, with an option to renew."

The Russian politician frowned. "Air taxi license? Does that even exist? I never heard of it."

"It will exist when you create one and award it to me, exclusively."

"It sounds like a lot of work," Bogdan said, but he had set down his drink and leaned forward.

V³ met him halfway. "That's why I'm going to pay you a lot of money."

Bogdan's thick lips curled. "I will need one hundred thousand euros to get started—"

"Done. What else?"

"This will take time."

V³ shook his head. "I told you: I have more money than time. I want my air taxis to be flying over Moscow in sixty days. Can you do it or not?"

Bogdan's gaze sharpened. He licked his lips. "I can do it."

"Good." V³ stood up. "My lawyers in Moscow will be in touch with the paperwork. You'll have your money by the end of the day."

Bogdan started to rise, but V³ put a hand on his shoulder. "Don't get up.

I was just leaving." Without looking in Harrison's direction, he strode into the crowd.

On the field, a roar penetrated the glass of the private box. Russian players raced around the field perimeter. One had stripped off his jersey. The Russians had scored a goal.

"Damn!" Stellner said.

"We're moving." Harrison spied V^3 headed for the elevator as he pushed through the people massing against the railing to see the on-field celebration. He caught up with V^3 just as the elevator doors opened. The trio entered and the doors slid closed, cutting off the noise of the celebrating Russian guests.

"Did you get it?" Harrison subvocalized into the microphone.

"Oh yeah," Genevieve replied. "I've got great video of the whole thing. V^3 deserves an Oscar for that performance."

In the reflection of the stainless steel elevator doors, Harrison saw V^3's lips turn up in a smile.

"Do you have the package ready?" Harrison asked.

"One hundred thousand euros ready to go into one dirty Russian politician's account in Sberbank on your command, boss."

When they reached the limo, Meyers held the door for V^3 and Harrison moved to the front passenger's seat. He slammed the door closed.

"Launch the package." He tried to keep the smile from growing. "And then see if V^3 has any decent champagne in that dungeon he calls a wine cellar."

"Bombs away," Genevieve replied.

10

Newcastle Upon Tyne, United Kingdom

From the railing in the owner's box, Yuri surveyed the men and women crowding around him. The dull roar of their voices filled the air, a sharp laugh or shout punctuating the drone every so often.

The combined wealth in this room was greater than the GDP of most small countries in the world. They gorged on his food, guzzled his booze, but it was for a worthy cause. A few more "friendly" matches like this one and the European owners would be begging to have the Russian Liga back in play.

It was all about the money, he thought. It was always about the money.

His gaze settled on Bogdan. Although he was seated in one of the plush spectator seats overlooking the pitch, his attention was on the woman—hell, the *child*—seated next to him. The old politician had a beefy forearm on the armrest between the seats, and he leaned into her personal space, his grizzled face centimeters from her smooth cheek. They spoke in low tones and his shoulders quaked with suppressed laughter. From this angle, Yuri could see Bogdan's stubby fingers stroking the inside of the woman's thigh. He sighed.

"She's been vetted," Dariya said from her place next to him on the railing.

Yuri met her gaze. Two tendrils of dark hair framed her face. Ever since the rally in Saratov, she'd stopped wearing her glasses, which made her dark brown eyes seem larger. Yuri knew intellectually that the age gap between the girl next to Bogdan and Dariya was much smaller than the age gap between he and Bogdan's daughter, but she *seemed* older.

More mature. More desirable.

Yuri turned his attention back to the field of play. What was the matter with him? He had a daughter the same age as Dariya and yet he could not stop thinking about her, picturing her—

"Yuri, it's all right." Dariya put her hand on his arm. Her touch gave him a delicious tingle, causing him to press his hips into the metal railing. After the night of celebration following her speech in Saratov, she had stopped calling him Uncle Yuri. He was just Yuri now. What did that mean?

"Some women are attracted to men like my father," she continued. "They find proximity to power an aphrodisiac." Her hand was still firm on his arm. Those dark eyes drew him in and Yuri felt his stomach drop. "How do you feel about that, Yuri?"

His mouth was dry. What the hell was the matter with him? He was acting no better than that child next to Bogdan. His brain was stuck in neutral. Dariya's hand slipped off his arm.

"Who is that?" Dariya asked. Her gaze was back on her father, but instead of the girl, there was a man seated next to Bogdan.

Yuri found his voice. "Victor van Valkenberg." His mind cleared, brain engaged. "American billionaire. Minority owner." Yuri shrugged his shoulders, then added, "He's a regular here."

"What does he want with my father?"

"What does anyone want with your father, Dariya? Access to power. I've heard it's an aphrodisiac."

The joke fell flat. Dariya had her phone out, typing. Yuri saw a picture of Victor appear on the screen, then scroll away.

"He's leaving," Yuri reported.

As Victor climbed the steps away from the seats, Russia scored. The spectators rose from their seats cheering. Dariya's face lit up with pleasure and she hugged Yuri. He felt the heat of her body and he responded with a kiss. Not long, not passionate, but definitely a kiss, directly on her full lips. Her eyes opened wider, her lips parted, and she kissed him back.

A little longer, with some heat, and he felt her tongue brush his lips.

Yuri's head swam. By the time he recovered his composure, Victor van Valkenberg and his security detail were gone.

Ten minutes later, the game was over. Russia won—and Yuri had kissed an extraordinary woman. His mind still buzzed from the feeling of Dariya's lips on his. His mind was leaping ahead to where this mutual attraction might end up.

In his breast pocket, his mobile vibrated. It was Roland. He felt a surge of annoyance as he answered the phone.

"*Da?*"

"I need to see you. I'm in the office." Roland's voice was tense, but then again, Roland's voice was always tense.

Yuri cast a sidelong glance at Dariya. Although she was involved in a conversation with the woman next to her at the railing, she leaned her hip against his. He did not want this to end.

"Now?" he said into the phone. "It's that important?"

"It's urgent, sir."

Yuri ended the call. "I need to go," he said to Dariya. Her dark eyes turned on him and Yuri made an impulse decision. "Come with me, please."

A slow smile spread across her lips. "Of course, Yuri. Anything for you."

Yuri's office at the stadium consisted of a low trophy case beneath a wall of signed photographs, a sitting area next to a small bar, and a vast mahogany desk with a commanding view of the rapidly emptying stadium. The soft blush of a summer evening warmed the distant horizon.

Roland sat behind the desk. His attention was riveted on the screen of his secure laptop. Three burner phones lay on the desk next to a yellow legal pad covered with notes. He had a fourth phone crooked in his shoulder as he typed on the keypad with one hand and wrote with the other. Roland's normally neat, thin blond hair was disheveled and his sallow face pinched.

He looked up when Yuri entered. "I'll call you back," he said into the phone and ended the call. A frown crossed his face when he saw Dariya. "I think we should talk privately, sir."

The comment irked Yuri. This pissant worked for him. He would decide who could be in the room when they spoke. "What is it?" he said testily.

Roland's eyes flicked back to Dariya. "Sir, I—"

"What. Is. It?"

The banker pursed his lips. "I've got a flagged transaction."

"Which account?" Yuri asked.

"Not one of yours, sir." The reply was clipped, guarded.

Then Yuri understood. Ever since the assassination attempt on President Sokolov, he'd ordered Roland to monitor Bogdan's accounts for suspicious transactions. It was just a precaution. He trusted Bogdan, but verification of that trust was prudent. In his mind, the timing of the assassination attempt was just too perfect to be a coincidence.

Yuri Balinovich did not believe in coincidences. He'd invested heavily in Bogdan and the New Dawn party. Protection of that investment was warranted. He could have told Bogdan, but he hadn't.

"I see," Yuri said, his face impassive.

"It's my father, isn't it?" Dariya said suddenly.

Roland's eyes widened and he looked at his boss. Yuri studied Dariya's face. Her dark eyes had a fierceness to them that intrigued him.

Extraordinary, he thought. Had something in his body language tipped her off, or was she just that perceptive? Either way, there were new layers to this woman he had yet to understand. Yuri nodded and turned to Roland.

"What has Bogdan done?"

The analyst squinted at the computer screen. "There's a large wire transfer into his personal account."

"How large?" Dariya asked.

"One hundred thousand euros."

Dariya crossed to the desk. "Show me."

Roland tilted the screen and pointed. Dariya frowned. "I don't know this account. This is not his. It's a mistake."

Interesting, Yuri thought. Bogdan is keeping secrets from his daughter.

"It's his all right," Roland said grimly. "I've been tracking it for months. He uses it for small payoffs and kickbacks, I think. Like a slush fund." He scrolled down the screen. "Here's the issue: It normally has maybe twenty thousand euros in it, never more than thirty. Today, along comes a one hundred thousand euro deposit from an international source."

"Who sent it?" Dariya demanded.

"A shell company," Roland replied in a grim tone. "The transfer originated out of a numbered account in the Caymans. I'll need time to figure who's behind it."

"This is wrong," Dariya said. "There has to be a mistake."

"Call your father," Yuri said.

Dariya stepped away and pulled out her mobile. A few seconds later, he heard her arguing with someone in Russian. Her voice was stern, commanding. "I don't care if he's banging Catherine the Great. Put him on the phone now."

A full minute passed. Dariya paced the floor, finally posting next to the window. Yuri admired her figure framed by the setting sun.

Her shoulders tensed. "Papa," she hissed into the receiver, then her voice dropped and he could not hear the rest of the conversation. Her back went rigid and she nodded once, then ended the call. She turned to face Yuri.

"It's a fake transaction, Uncle Yuri," she said. "You need to get rid of it."

Uncle Yuri, he thought. Dariya's eyes locked on his and he saw the plea in her gaze. She was covering for Bogdan. That fool had taken a bribe, a payoff from outside Russia. If word of that hit the news, it could sink the New Dawn movement. Russians taking money from other Russians was normal, but taking money from foreigners was a sin. How could the old drunk be so stupid? He was risking everything.

"Kill the transaction," Yuri ordered Roland.

The banker had read the room and he was already shaking his head. "I can't. It's in the account already. The bank flagged it for investigation. It's in the queue."

"Can't you send it back?" Dariya asked.

Roland nodded. "I can, but they won't process the debit until Monday and it will still show up on the ledger. He's accepted the money. Even if he sends it back, the evidence is still there."

Dariya took his hand. "Yuri, we have to fix this. Please. It's my father."

Yuri tried not to look into her eyes and failed. The softness of her lips on his flashed in his mind.

"Fix the ledger, Roland. Make this transaction disappear."

Roland stared at him. "Sir, I can't just alter the bank records. I would need to hack the system."

Yuri felt the heat of Dariya's gaze on his face.

"Then do it," he said.

"Yuri," Roland protested, "to make this transaction disappear for good, I would need to take down the computer network for the whole bank—"

"Do it, Roland. Make it go away. Now."

11

Washington, DC

Victor's Airbus ACJ jet touched down at Dulles just after eleven in the evening. Harrison rattled the ice in his glass, wishing it was a single-malt scotch rather than the plain old water he'd been drinking throughout the flight home.

There had been no champagne on ice when he and Victor returned from Newcastle football stadium to their operations center in the seventeenth-century castle. Instead, there was chaos.

Genevieve met them in the grand front hallway. The pinched look on her face made her next words unnecessary. She said them anyway. "There's a problem." Her voice echoed in the space.

"What sort of problem?" V^3 cut in. "What have you people done?"

Genevieve didn't even bother to look at the billionaire. "It's better if Michael explains it," she replied. "He's upstairs."

The operations center was set up in what had once probably been some grand lord's dining hall. The room was like something out of a movie set: a hearth the size of a sofa, stone floors and walls hung with thick tapestries. The mullioned windows looked out onto the courtyard below.

Michael's command post was six computer screens set up in two rows at a standing desk, curved around him in an arc. Michael stood with his arms folded, legs apart, staring at the screens. When Harrison looked at the monitors, all he saw was scrolling data.

"What's up, Michael?" Harrison tried to keep his tone light, but the effort fell flat.

"The bank's offline," Michael replied.

"Probably a maintenance period," V^3 said.

Michael's stare even managed to shut down the billionaire. "The bank was hacked. It was *forced* offline." His gaze cut to Harrison. "It wasn't us."

"Who?" Harrison said.

"That is not something I can tell you right now. I can say that they know their stuff. You gotta have some stroke to take down an international bank."

"Was this because of us?" Harrison asked.

Michael shrugged. "Right now, I'm still trying to figure out how they pulled this off. Then I can maybe figure out who was behind it and whether or not there's any connection to our operation." He glanced back at the bank of screens. "That could be days, maybe more."

"It has to be a coincidence," Genevieve began. "We released the transaction to Bogdan's account less than an hour ago. There's no way—"

"There are no coincidences," V^3 interrupted. "It's Yuri. It has to be Yuri."

Harrison felt like he'd been punched in the stomach. "What about the transaction? Do we know if it went through?"

Genevieve shook her head. "It went to the bank and got posted to the account. We know that much, but will it still be there when the bank comes back online?" She looked at Victor. "If he's right, then we're screwed."

"The bank is in recovery mode," Michael added. "With luck, they'll have the site back online by morning. We won't know any more until then."

When the bank came online ten hours later, their tainted transaction in Bogdan's account was gone. Any trace that the transaction had ever existed was gone as well.

Their operation was blown.

The jet slowed and stopped. Harrison puffed out his cheeks and closed his eyes. There would be a full investigation. Somehow, within minutes of execution, his carefully laid plan to entrap one Russian politician in a bribery scandal had come undone. Thousands of man-hours, millions of taxpayer dollars torched in the space of minutes.

Had they been sloppy in their execution? Had their operations been compromised?

Harrison's gaze rested on Victor van Valkenberg, who had just opened his eyes and was stretching. That bastard had slept like a baby from wheels up to touchdown, unconcerned about the shit storm bearing down on his CIA colleagues.

Harrison had convinced Don Riley to bring a civilian into a top-secret influence operation on short notice—that was a huge red flag. They had used Victor's resources in the operation. What had seemed like a good idea at the time, now seemed like a massive error in judgment. *His* judgment.

His mobile phone buzzed with an incoming call. The screen read: DON RILEY.

Harrison pinched the bridge of his nose. He checked his watch. 1123. By coming in late, he'd hoped to avoid meeting Don until the morning.

He tapped the screen and lifted the receiver to his ear. "Don."

"Harrison, welcome home. I need to see you immediately."

"Sure thing, Don."

Don rattled off an address. "I'm at home. I need you to hurry. It's time sensitive."

It took Harrison less than twenty minutes to get to Don's front door. He paused, gathering his thoughts. Don stuck his neck out recommending Harrison as lead for a high-profile operation in the Special Activities Center and he had repaid that trust with failure. Even now, a full day and a half after the disaster, they still knew next to nothing about how they'd been compromised.

No doubt, this meeting at Don's home was a prep meeting for him to get his story straight before the firing squad in the morning. Harrison was tired and his thoughts felt jumbled and disorganized. Don deserved better than this. He clenched his eyes shut and blew out a breath.

He raised his hand and knocked.

Don was smiling when he answered the door, and Harrison thought he heard the sound of a woman's laugh from inside. Don held out his hand. "Good, you're here. C'mon in. We don't have much time."

Harrison took his hand automatically, allowing himself to be drawn inside. What the hell was happening? He'd just made the worst mistake of his career—and that was saying something—and his boss was *smiling*?

He followed Don through the entrance hall and turned into a living room. A long leather sofa faced a wall-mounted TV, flanked by two overstuffed matching armchairs. On the coffee table stood an open bottle of red wine and two glasses. A woman was pouring wine into a glass. She paused when Harrison entered and got to her feet.

Don stood between them. "Iliana, this is Harrison. Harrison, Iliana. I'll get another glass." He disappeared into the kitchen.

The woman was dressed casually, but with style. Fitted blue slacks, a sleeveless cashmere sweater of white and high heels. A Hermès handbag lay on the sofa beside her. She tucked a strand of long, blonde hair behind her ear and extended her hand to Harrison. "Iliana Semanova." Her voice was pitched low and her eyes met Harrison's without hesitation.

Her fingers were long and elegant, with nails painted a deep red. Golden bangles on her wrists chimed gently when he shook her hand.

"You recognize my name." She phrased it as a statement, not a question.

Harrison nodded.

"And?" She arched an eyebrow. "Am I what you expected from Vladimir Federov's mistress?"

"I—I," Harrison began. Thankfully, Don arrived with the third wineglass and she turned her attention away from him.

Don played host, pouring wine for Harrison and topping off the other two glasses. The Deputy Director of Operations was entertaining a Russian spy in his home, Harrison thought. What rabbit hole had he fallen into?

Harrison suddenly realized Don was speaking and he tried to concentrate.

"Iliana has a very limited time window, Harrison," Don said, taking up his wineglass, "so I'm going to let her speak. I'll fill you in on the background later."

Iliana looked at her watch, a Van Cleef & Arpels. "I have just under ninety minutes before my flight leaves for LA." She smiled at Harrison. "A recruiting trip."

Harrison didn't need to ask what she was recruiting for. Everyone on the Russia desk at ETG knew that Iliana Semanova ran the most exclusive escort service in Eastern Europe…and she was sitting in Don Riley's living room sipping wine like an old friend of the family.

"From the beginning," Don said. "Please."

Iliana set her wineglass on the coffee table. "I'm afraid I am bringing you bad news. The situation in Russia has deteriorated badly. Nikolay Sokolov is in danger."

Harrison put his own glass down. "Political danger or his personal safety?"

Iliana's elegant eyebrow arched. "In Russia, they are one and the same. If he loses power, he is a dead man."

"But the next presidential election is not for another four—"

Iliana cut him off. "If the New Dawn party takes control of the Duma in October, there will not be another presidential election in Russia. Not a real one, anyway."

She let the statement hang in the air as if challenging him. Harrison resisted the urge to look at Don. "Could you elaborate?" he said finally.

"I have information that if the New Dawn party wins, Bogdan Rabilov is planning a coup. He plans to remove Sokolov and install himself as the new President of Russia."

"What is the source of this intel, ma'am?" Harrison asked.

Iliana's head cocked, her lips bent into a humorless smile. "You know what I do for a living, yes?"

Harrison nodded.

"Then let's just say that very powerful men like to talk and my girls are very good listeners. Men are especially vulnerable in bed. They often feel the need to unburden themselves to someone they can trust."

"Can you give us the names of these men?" Harrison pressed.

"No."

"Is one of them Yuri Balinovich?"

Iliana's spine stiffened, but she caught herself. If he hadn't been watching her, Harrison might have missed the flash reaction to the oligarch's name.

"My information is impeccable and verified from multiple sources. Of that, you can be sure." She dropped her eyes to her wristwatch. "And now, unfortunately, I must be going, Donald. Thank you for the wine and the conversation." She rose to her feet.

Harrison stood. He knew from her file that she was closing in on fifty, but if he'd not known that he'd have guessed mid to late thirties. She moved with grace, every motion efficient and fluid. The strap of her handbag looped over her forearm, she kissed Don European-style on both cheeks and extended her hand to Harrison.

"Good luck." The pressure of her fingers in his tightened for a second, then released.

Don escorted her to the door, then returned. He poured her untouched wine into his glass, then flopped down on the sofa. "Well?" he said finally.

"What the hell, Don?" Harrison burst out. "You can't be buying this. It's single-sourced intel from an unreliable asset—"

"It's not single-sourced," Don interrupted. "We've gotten intel that Yuri Balinovich is stepping up his outreach in the Duma. He's paying off vulnerable representatives to lose to the New Dawn candidate."

"Okay, let's assume that's true. What motivation does she have to come to the CIA—to you, the DDO—with this cockamamie story?"

"Federov and I go back. Way back." He took a long pull of his wine and peered at Harrison over the rim of the glass. The look told him not to press the issue.

Harrison took a different tack. "So, she's Federov's pet and that gives her access to you. That tracks, but what's her motivation? Why is she here?"

"Federov is on death's doorstep. If Sokolov is taken out, she has no one to protect her."

"What about Balinovich? Did you see her flinch when I mentioned that name?"

Don nodded. "I saw it. You hit a nerve, that's for sure, but was she reacting to the name because that was her source or some other reason?"

"Like what?"

"Fear," Don replied. "If Sokolov is out of power, Iliana is expendable, and she knows it."

Harrison picked up his wineglass and took a sip. It was a heavy red, laden with dark fruits and acidity. He fought against the exhaustion in his mind and body.

"The team believes that Yuri Balinovich took down the bank to make sure the bribe to Bogdan disappeared," he said.

"A dangerous man, with a lot of power," Don said. "I'd say Iliana has a right to be concerned."

Harrison drank again, savoring the wine, turning the problem over in his head. Fear was a strong motivator, but was it a strong enough reason to feed intelligence to the Americans? If Balinovich found out, Iliana was a dead woman. There was nowhere she could hide from the oligarch.

He swallowed his wine. "What now?"

Don stared into space, his gaze unfocused. Harrison knew enough to let him work the problem. Finally, Don set his wineglass on the coffee table.

"Your operation is not over," he said. "We can't sit on this information. Pull your team together and come up with a new plan. I'll get us on the President's calendar for tomorrow afternoon."

Harrison's wineglass paused halfway to his lips. "Tomorrow afternoon?"

Don plucked the wineglass from his fingers. "You're wasting time, Harrison."

12

Moscow, Russia

In the Soviet days, the Moscow Metro was known as the Palace of the People. The claim was pure propaganda, but like all good misinformation, there was a kernel of truth to it.

In Mira Prospect station, vaulted plaster ceilings were supported by pink marble pillars, the material imported to Moscow from the Oblants region of Karelia. Ornate chandeliers illuminated the checkerboard floor pattern of black and gray granite squares. Across the city, other Metro stations were decorated in similar high fashion, each displaying its own unique aesthetic, constructed from quality materials sourced from all over the vast country, from Siberia to Sochii. The high level of craftsmanship delivered a message about the prowess and power of the former Soviet Union.

On the television screen, the beauty of the Mira Prospect station was hidden behind a wall of protestors. They wore shorts and T-shirts in the June heat, carrying placards calling for a pay hike. There was even a sign in English that read *Rubles or Rubble? Your choice, Nikolay*.

Cute, he thought. He studied the screen carefully, letting the two men standing at attention before his desk wait for him to acknowledge them.

If he looked closely at the architecture in the background, he could see the decay. The cracked plaster in the ceiling. The chandeliers that once proudly displayed beautiful, handcrafted incandescent bulbs were now populated with square LEDs that shed a cold, harsh whiteness. The splash of graffiti on the pink marble walls. He could read a new message in this scene: The empire that built this magnificent structure was gone.

He looked up, met their eyes. "How did this happen?" he asked in a tone of tightly controlled anger.

Lev Parmentov, his new FSB Chief, cleared his throat. "It's a dispute over pay, Mr. President. The contract negotiations have been going on for months, but they've broken down..."

His voice trailed off. The man didn't dare voice the reason for the breakdown. The strikers saw weakness in the government position. They saw weakness in the head of the government, the President himself.

Now they were forcing his hand.

Nikolay ground his teeth. His FSB Chief should have seen this coming and stopped it. That's how it would have happened under Federov.

But Nikolay was left with this moron instead, a moron that he'd put in the job after he'd fired Federov's handpicked successor in a fit of frustration.

Parmentov had his head bowed, watching his boss from under heavy-lidded eyes. Was he up to this job? Nikolay wondered.

He shifted his attention to the other man in the room. Gennady Abukamov was the head of the Rosvgardia, the Russian equivalent of the National Guard. Under Uncle Vitaly, the Rosvgardia had morphed into a private police force, used by the President to quell disturbances like this one.

But that kind of power had two sides. The Rosvgardia was a blunt instrument designed to solve problems through violence. Was that what was called for here? Was the New Dawn party trying to draw him into a bloody confrontation that they could splash across the internet as another example of his weakness?

"What do you say, Gennady?" he asked.

Abukamov was a wiry man with a shaved head and zero sense of humor. He shrugged. "I see this as a disturbance of the peace, Mr. President. I can have it cleaned up by tonight. My men are standing by." He bared his teeth in what passed for a smile.

Nikolay suppressed a sigh. Abukamov was a good man, loyal to a fault, but there was not a strategic bone in his body. The question *why?* did not exist in his vocabulary.

"Mr. President." Parmentov was sweating. "My information is that the strikers and management are close to a deal, maybe by the end of the day. Tomorrow at the latest."

"They're trash, sir," Abukamov interjected. "They do not respect you or your administration. We need to teach them a lesson."

Nikolay's gaze wandered back to the TV screen. The strikers were chanting something about fair pay, a call-and-response led by a middle-aged woman with red hair tied back in a ponytail. She wore a wide grin as she yelled into a bullhorn.

He surveyed the picket lines. At least half of the strikers were women, winter-white legs protruding from shorts and skirts. Some of them had children with them. Nikolay watched a bored girl of perhaps six years old on the edge of the front rank. She clung to her mother's hand. The red-faced woman was yelling, pumping her placard in the air in time with the chant.

Oblivious to the world around her, the little girl began to pick her nose. Nikolay smiled in spite of himself.

He raised his eyes to his FSB Chief. "You have until noon tomorrow to get this situation resolved peacefully. Do you hear me, Lev? Get. It. Done."

Parmentov's head bobbed in vigorous agreement. "I understand, Mr. President. It will be done."

Nikolay swiveled his gaze to Abukamov. "Keep your men on standby."

The head of the Rosvgardia did not argue, but he was clearly disappointed. "Yes, Mr. President."

He dismissed them and leaned back in his chair, studying the TV screen. The choice was made. Now all he could do was wait to see if he'd made the right choice.

His answer came at six in the evening. What should have been the height of rush hour was a gridlocked mess because of the strike. The unseasonable heat only added to the bad tempers on both sides of the picket line.

A female striker approached a male manager emerging from the Metro headquarters at Mira Prospect. There were angry words exchanged, and the woman slapped the man across the face. He pushed her, and she fell. Other strikers saw the altercation and tried to restrain the manager. The Metro security forces intervened and a melee ensued.

The police were on the scene in minutes, but the situation had already spun out of control.

Moments later there were gunshots. By the time the police cleared the area, three bodies lay on the gray-and-black granite checkerboard floor of the Mira Prospect station.

Within the hour, Nikolay was watching the flushed, bloated face of Bogdan Rabilov crowing on national TV.

13

The White House

"Ma'am, we're here today to brief you on the status of the Russian influence operation. At the conclusion of the briefing, we'll be asking for an upgrade to the Presidential Finding." Don's tone was brisk and professional.

Harrison's fingers felt slippery against the cool frame of the briefing tablet. Identical tablets had been distributed to the President, Director Brooks, and National Security Advisor Todd Spencer.

But no one was looking at their tablet, they were watching Don.

Cashman sniffed. "What do you mean by *upgrade*, Donald?"

"Ma'am, I think the brief will address your—"

"I think you should answer the question, Mr. Riley." Todd Spencer's tone suggested that he knew what was coming, even if his boss hadn't gotten there yet. "A direct question deserves a direct answer."

"At the conclusion of the briefing, I'm going to ask you for a lethal finding for this operation, Madam President," Don said.

Cashman's face clouded and she shot a look at the Director. "You agree with this?"

Carroll Brooks did not flinch. "I think you should listen to the brief, ma'am, before we discuss our options."

There was a moment of silent tension between the two women. Harrison's stomach did a flip-flop. This was going every bit as badly as he'd expected—and they hadn't even gotten to his blown operation yet.

Cashman flicked her fingers. "Proceed, Donald."

Don Riley was an experienced briefer. He'd seen more than his share of unfriendly audiences and it showed. Harrison admired how he dispensed facts in bite-sized pieces that helped the President make sense of the situation.

After two background slides, he announced, "The influence operation was unsuccessful."

Spencer barked out a laugh. "That's an understatement if I ever heard one. The influence operation was an abject failure. Do you have an explanation?"

Harrison's heart lodged firmly in his throat. This was where he got thrown under the bus.

Don met the National Security Advisor's derision with a mild expression. "We are dealing with forces much more capable than we anticipated, sir."

"You brought a civilian into a covert operation," Spencer countered. "I never would have approved that."

"It wasn't up to you, Mr. Spencer," the Director said. "It was up to me. I approved the use of a civilian."

Spencer barked out a laugh. "Victor van Valkenberg is not just any civilian. How do you know he's not the reason the operation was compromised?"

"Excuse me?" the President interrupted. "Victor was part of the operation?"

Spencer tried to hide a smirk. His point was made. Now he could sit back and watch the fireworks.

But still Don Riley seemed nonplussed. "Yes, ma'am. Given the timetable and the access we needed, he was the best option. He also helped us realize the scope of the opposition."

"What does that mean?" Cashman said.

"I mean that we're dealing with an opponent who was willing to take down an international bank just to hide a bribe to a Russian politician.

That's not normal, ma'am." He shot a look at Spencer. "That's also why we're here this afternoon. The scope of the threat has increased dramatically since this operation was authorized. We need to respond."

Cashman narrowed her eyes. Her gaze shifted between the CIA personnel. "I'm listening, Donald."

"We have new intelligence," Don stated. "If the New Dawn party wins a majority of seats in the Duma in October, they will remove Nikolay Sokolov from power and replace him with their own candidate, Bogdan Rabilov."

"A coup?" Spencer scoffed. "You're telling us that Rabilov's people will launch a coup?"

Don nodded as calmly as if he was discussing a lunch order. "That's exactly what I'm saying. We have an asset inside Yuri Balinovich's orbit who brought us the intel and we can corroborate it in part with other separate events."

"Can they do that?" Cashman directed the question at the National Security Advisor.

Spencer seemed flustered to be taken out of his role as opposition to Don's briefing. "It's Russia, ma'am. The question isn't *can* they do it, it's *will* they do it."

"And will they?" Cashman pressed. "Assume the New Dawn party wins a majority in the Duma in October, will they depose Sokolov and put Rabilov in power?"

When Spencer did not reply, Cashman sniffed.

"No answer is an answer, Todd," she said in a hard voice. She turned back to Don. "Explain to me again why this is my problem, Donald."

"Rabilov represents a massive unraveling of the Russian power structure, one that is dangerous to the United States and to our allies. This would be a throwback to the days of the Soviet Union except that the USSR had a Politburo to keep control of the country. This could be control by one man, one very unstable man. We're talking about five thousand nuclear weapons, Madam President. Once Bogdan Rabilov seizes power, he will not give it up, no matter the consequences."

Cashman's red lips pursed in thought. "And your conclusion is that we need to"—she paused, as if searching for the right word—"*eliminate* Bogdan Rabilov?"

"I'm getting there, ma'am, but, yes, that will be the recommendation."

"Surely there are better ways to change this situation in our favor, Donald. Why not just tell the Russian people what's going on? Or leak it to their security services and let them deal with it?"

Don queued up a video on the briefing tablet. Harrison watched a clip of the transit strike in Moscow that had devolved into riots overnight. He finished with a clip of Bogdan Rabilov being interviewed on a Russian morning talk show. His beefy face was ruddy, his dress shirt open at the neck, revealing a mat of curly gray chest hair. He leaned toward the female interviewer, his eyes locked on hers.

"Niko is a weak woman," the translation at the bottom of the screen read. "A real leader would have ended this strike before it even started. Instead, we have blood in the streets of Moscow." He turned his burning eyes on the camera. "The blood of the Russian people is on your hands, Sokolov. You do not deserve to be our leader."

Don let the video sink in before he continued. "At this moment, support for President Sokolov is low. Any public attempt to paint him as a victim is likely to backfire. It will make him seem even weaker."

"What about the Chinese?" Cashman pressed. "We can leak it to them, ask for their help to support Sokolov."

Don was shaking his head before she'd even finished the question. "Assuming the Chinese even believed us, they'd be more likely to see this as an opportunity. While the Russian President is consumed with his internal problems, they could seize the other half of Kazakhstan."

Harrison saw Don's words land with effect. The Russia-China occupation and division of Kazakhstan was an international miscalculation that the Cashman administration still had not recovered from.

Cashman's jaw tightened. "I didn't take this job to save the world, Donald. If the shoe were on the other foot, would you see Nikolay Sokolov lining up to help us?"

"He already did, ma'am," Don said gently. "When President Serrano asked for Russian naval coverage in the Pacific to deter the Chinese, he answered the call and he delivered."

Harrison held his breath. Don was baiting the most powerful person in the world, but he was doing it calmly and professionally. It didn't feel like the rebuke that it was.

The President considered her tablet, where Bogdan's red face stared back at her. His mouth was agape and there was a sheen of sweat on his jowly cheeks. Cashman nodded at the untouched coffee service. "Would you pour us all some coffee, Todd?"

The National Security Advisor's head ticked up. "I—uh, of course, Madam President."

Cashman said nothing as Spencer poured cups and passed around cream and sugar. She took her own cup, sipped, then sighed. "All right, Donald, you have my attention. Tell me what you want to do."

Don nodded crisply. "The New Dawn party is a populist movement, ma'am, and Bogdan Rabilov is the leader of that movement. It's basically a political cult that feeds off grievance and outrage. Rabilov is a master of manipulation. He taps into that outrage and turns it into political power.

"But the New Dawn party has always been a party of opposition. They only know how to attack, which is what makes them so dangerous, but Rabilov has no idea how to govern. Without chaos, he has no political energy."

"I understand how populist movements work, Donald. What is your solution?"

"Bogdan Rabilov must be stopped, ma'am. Without Rabilov, the party will fall apart."

"And by *stopped*, you mean..."

"I mean a lethal finding, Madam President."

"You want me to authorize the assassination of a Russian politician because he *might* win an election and then *might* launch a coup?"

"We're out of time and options, ma'am. We have a few months until the election. It's the only way."

Harrison felt frozen in his seat. Cashman stared at Don for a full minute, then shifted her gaze to the Director. "And you agree with this?"

Carroll Brooks nodded.

Cashman turned to Todd Spencer. "What do you think, Todd?"

Spencer shifted in his seat. "I came into this meeting ready to disagree with Riley's plan, but after hearing him, I have to say...I don't see another viable path, ma'am."

Cashman stirred her coffee. The spoon clattered back into the saucer. She took a deep breath and blew it out.

"No," she said.

"Ma'am—" Don began, but she held up her hand to stop him.

"You've made your case, Donald, and I admit, it's a good one, but I have to draw the line somewhere. Bogdan Rabilov is a cretin, a despicable human being and a dangerous man, but I will not act as judge, jury, and executioner to a politician in another country because of what he *might* do."

"Madam President," Don said, "we are running out of time. If we choose—"

"My decision is not up for debate, Donald. I will not authorize a lethal action. That said, you do what you have to do to make sure that Bogdan Rabilov never gets into power."

The President stood and Harrison scrambled to his feet alongside Don.

"I suggest you get started on a new plan," she said.

14

Starovo, Russia, 120 kilometers northeast of Moscow

It had been a long day, Yuri reflected, but then again, he'd planned it that way. After breakfast, there was skeet shooting in the back pasture, then horseback riding through the forest, where he'd put on a picnic lunch in a picturesque meadow that overlooked the valley and his estate.

In the afternoon, all of his guests went swimming and he'd arranged for massages for everyone before dinner. Dinner began at nine in the evening, the summer sun just beginning to fade on the horizon.

Yuri had debated about the seating arrangements at dinner. He wondered whether he should put Dariya next to him or mix her in with the other guests. In the end, he decided to put her in the center of the table, so that she was surrounded on all sides by his other twelve guests.

After all, he mused, this was a test of her ability to operate independently in a world of powerful men without Bogdan to clear the way for her.

It was odd how having Dariya's father absent changed the mood of the gathering. Bogdan was a force of nature—a hurricane, more accurately. He was loud and he drove the conversation in any direction he wished. He was not just the founder of the New Dawn movement, he was the beating heart of the party. Without Bogdan, there was no party.

But was that really true? Yuri wondered. Ever since he'd seen Dariya's speech in Saratov, he'd envisioned a different path for the future. A path where Bogdan was not leading the conversation. A path where Bogdan was not even part of the conversation.

And so, Yuri planned a test for Dariya. A weekend retreat at his dacha alongside the party leaders but without her father. How would the men—they were all men, all over sixty—treat her? How would she handle herself when she was on her own? Would Dariya stay in the background or would she become the woman he'd seen on stage in Saratov? The spellbinding speaker who had connected so deeply with such a diverse audience.

Whether she intuited that the weekend retreat was a test, he had no idea, but she exceeded his highest expectations. From the first moments at breakfast, Dariya had shone as the brightest star in the firmament. More importantly, she did something that he'd not anticipated: She'd managed to become part of the cohort without becoming one of them.

As the day wore on, Yuri watched her charm each of them individually. During skeet shooting, she relied on Igor to teach her how to handle a shotgun and instruct her on how to lead the clay pigeon. By the end of the tutelage, she was hitting the target with every pull.

During the horseback ride, she hung back to converse with the less experienced riders. On the way back to the dacha, she challenged the advanced riders to a race across the meadow. When she came in third, she laughed at the mistake that had cost her the race—which Yuri was reasonably sure was deliberate.

By the end of the day, she'd won over every man in the room. At dinner, she ran the conversation, delving into politics, economics, Russian literature, and history. Even the other women at the table seemed taken with her. Not wives, of course, no one brought their wife to weekends at Yuri's dacha. Yuri supplied companionship for the weekend, all personally selected by Iliana Semanova.

Again, Yuri noticed Dariya's uncanny ability to relate to an individual in a way that made the other person want to please her. It was Bogdan's gift of connection, but without all the baggage that came along with the aging politician. His daughter was a younger, cleaner, smarter version of her father.

The kind of politician that could define the future of the New Dawn party for decades to come.

It was nearly one in the morning when the dinner party broke up. Even as he plied his guests with delicacies and drink, Yuri ate and drank sparingly all evening. He needed to be sharp for the coming interview. Finally, he ground out his cigar and stood. The rest of the room followed suit.

"Thank you all for coming, gentlemen"—Yuri nodded at Dariya—"and lady. I'll see you in the morning."

After the activity of the day, the massages, and the rich food and wine, most of the guests were already half asleep. Their dates helped them to their feet and led them out of the room. There would be more snoring than sex in his dacha tonight.

The room emptied until only he and Dariya were left. She gazed at him across the table littered with glasses and plates, the room hazy with cigar smoke. Dariya wore a sleeveless navy-blue dress of shimmering material that reached to the floor. It rose to her collarbone in the front but plunged down her bare back. She turned away from him, her curves shifting under the dark material, the white skin of her back rippling with movement.

"A nightcap, Yuri?" she called over her shoulder.

He followed her into the study, the same room where he'd watched her drunken father revel in the humiliation of Nikolay Sokolov following the assassination attempt. The lights were turned low, pools of soft yellow on the plush carpet. Dariya went to the bar and poured two drinks before she returned to the sofa.

She handed one tumbler to Yuri and sat. He sniffed the glass. Macallan scotch, single malt, thirty year.

"How did you know this is what I wanted?" he asked. The default drink for any Russian was vodka and there were at least six different brands in his bar. But she'd gone to the back of the shelf and poured him his drink of choice.

Dariya sipped her drink, her eyes steady on his. "I've been watching you my entire life, Yuri. You'd be surprised at the things I know."

He took a seat next to her. Not at the other end of the sofa, but in the middle, their knees only a few centimeters apart. He leaned back, letting the whiskey slide down his throat and warm his belly. He felt the tightness in his shoulders ease.

"I noticed there was no woman for you at dinner, Yuri. Why was that?"

He shrugged. "Numbers. I wanted an even number of guests at dinner. It makes the seating less awkward."

Dariya raised a dark eyebrow in reply.

"Besides," he continued, "I wanted to spend more time with you." He regretted the words as soon as they left his lips. This woman was the age of his own daughter. What the hell was he thinking?

Dariya seemed to read his mind. "Relax, Yuri. I enjoy spending time with you as well." Her knee touched his. "Don't make it weird."

Yuri drank again to still his pounding heart. All he could think about was how her lips had felt against his in that brief kiss at the football stadium. He hadn't reacted to a woman like that since...before his wife died. He realized he was breathing heavily and he fought to regain control.

"So how did I do?" Dariya asked.

Yuri focused on her words, but the heat of her knee next to his was distracting. "What do you mean?"

She shifted her body on the leather sofa and her hip slid closer. She stretched her bare arm across the back of the sofa, waving her free hand in the air. "This whole weekend. Arranging to have my father held up in the Urals. You have something in mind. Tell me." Her lips parted in anticipation.

Yuri stood to refresh their drinks. He needed a clear head for this part of the conversation. When he returned to the couch, he sat away from her.

"You're right," he began. "This weekend was a test. And you passed with flying colors."

Dariya closed the distance between them. "And what are you testing me for? What office? Party secretary?"

"For President," Yuri said.

Dariya stopped cold, blinked at him. "What are you talking about?"

"I'm talking about you as the future leader of the New Dawn party and our candidate for President."

"But Papa..." Her voice trailed off.

"Your father is the leader of the party *now*, but he's old and he doesn't have the skills that you have. I saw you with those men today. You had the party leaders eating out of your hand. They would do anything for you."

"Papa built the New Dawn movement, Yuri," she said. "He is the party. You cannot separate them."

"We *have* to separate them, Dariya." He took her hand. "Your father is the past. You are the future. Surely, you can see that."

But she didn't see it, he realized. Her father was her blind spot. He'd been searching for her weakness, but it had been in plain sight all along. He'd just missed it.

Dariya had drawn her hands into her lap, cradling the tumbler of scotch. She stared into the dimness, her eyes soft.

Yuri cursed to himself. He'd made her uncomfortable. If he wanted to secure the future of the New Dawn party, he had much work to do.

"Maybe this is all too much, too soon, Dariya."

She shook her head. "It's okay, Yuri. I just never considered the idea of a world without Papa. Silly, right?"

Yuri moved close. His hand slid across the bare skin of her back as he put his arm around her. "Not silly at all, my dear. You love your father. For all his greatness and his faults, you love him. That's a good thing."

"I do love him, but..."

"All I ask is that you think about the future, Dariya. Sleep on it. We'll talk again tomorrow."

Dariya's hand moved to his thigh, sending a jolt of pleasure coursing through Yuri's body. He felt himself respond to her touch.

"Yes, Yuri," Dariya whispered, turning toward him. Her face was close enough that her breath painted his cheek. "Let's sleep on it."

15

Paris, France

The St. Germain neighborhood of Paris was packed with tourists on this Friday evening. In the space of half a block, Genevieve heard five different languages being spoken.

Above her, the summer sky slowly faded into darkness. Diners spilled from the cafes onto the broad sidewalks. The warm air carried the smells of food and cigarette smoke. Genevieve turned the corner into a narrow street and checked the address again. A few steps later, she was in front of the restaurant.

Augustin Marchand d'Vins was a narrow storefront, barely five meters across. It didn't look like a restaurant, but this was the address. Genevieve mounted the steps and entered the building. A bell above the door announced her arrival.

She paused. The interior was dim and cramped. On both sides of the room, racked wine bottles reached from floor to ceiling. To her right were two tables occupied by two couples.

A middle-aged man, balding, with an apron tied around his ample waist, approached. "You are Genevieve, yes?" he inquired.

"Oui," she responded.

He pointed. "Your date is waiting for you at the back table."

Genevieve edged past the dining couples and took the ten or so steps to reach the rear of the restaurant, passing the bar and a tiny kitchen along the way. She counted eight tables in the restaurant, plus a pair of stools next to the tiny bar. Annie Baker rose from behind a two-person table to greet her.

"I think you have the best table in the house," Genevieve said as she air-kissed each of Annie's cheeks. "And on a Friday night in June. You must be sleeping with the chef."

Annie's laughter was genuine. "I do have a connection here," she said. "It's impossible to get a table here in the summer. The tourists book the place out for months in advance."

Genevieve took her seat. "And yet here we are. I'm intrigued, Annie. You are a woman of many layers."

Annie brushed away the probing comment, busying herself with pouring a second glass of champagne. Genevieve noted the bottle was already half-empty. That was a good sign. She raised her flute of bubbling champagne.

"A toast," she announced.

Annie raised her own glass. "To friends."

Genevieve touched the rim of her glass to Annie's. "To friends who trust each other."

For a second, Genevieve thought she had pushed too hard. Annie's face froze, then cleared. "To trusting friends," she agreed, and downed her glass.

Genevieve drank deeply to cover her concern. She sensed she was pushing Annie too hard, but ever since the disaster in Newcastle, Harrison was on her case for results. He wasn't wrong, she knew. They were running out of options and time to access Bogdan Rabilov's inner circle.

Since their first meeting in London at Herringbone's Book Shop, the women had met twice. The next encounter was a walk and talk in Hyde Park. They'd strolled in the beautiful sun-drenched park for two hours, eating ice cream and talking about books they'd read.

Genevieve decided that she genuinely liked Annie Baker. The problem was that her job required her to meet Anoushka Balinovich. Until Annie admitted who she really was, Genevieve was failing in her assignment.

Their third meeting was a lunch date when Annie had been in London for the afternoon. Genevieve knew that the real reason for Annie's visit was a meeting with her lawyer about her trust fund, but the young woman made up a lie about seeing an old friend.

Harrison was not happy with Genevieve's progress in developing her asset. "She needs to open up to you, Genevieve. You've got to get through to her. Make her trust you."

And that led to tonight's meeting. Genevieve had called Annie on Monday evening.

"I'm coming to Paris on Friday," she said. "Are you free?"

"Bien sur." Annie seemed genuinely glad to hear from her. "What is the occasion?"

"I have a surprise for you."

Annie's face lit up on the screen of Genevieve's phone. "I love surprises. What is it?"

"You have to wait. I want you to buy me dinner first."

"I know just the place," Annie said.

As a meeting place, Augustin Marchand d'Vins was everything Genevieve could have hoped for: small, intimate, and dark, with lots of fine food and alcohol to encourage sharing.

Annie leaned forward. "Tell me the surprise."

Genevieve held out her empty champagne glass. "Dinner first. Then surprises."

The champagne led to a bottle of chilled Chablis and appetizers. The restaurant had a daily menu, featuring fresh ingredients from the local markets. There was no wine list. Instead, the waiter—there was only one for the tiny restaurant—heard what they wanted to eat and made wine recommendations based on their food choices. He used his mobile phone flashlight to search the wine racks, then brought three bottles to the table for them to choose from. Each bottle came with a description of the grape, the region, and the individual winery that had produced the vintage—all done without notes, of course.

The experience was wildly inefficient and utterly unique and charming. Genevieve noticed that Annie paid no attention to the prices that were written on the bottle in white grease paint. For their main course, she selected a pinot noir that cost 350 euros. It paired perfectly with the roasted lamb they both ordered.

Their table was deep in the far corner of the room and surrounded by velvet wall hangings that deadened the noise of the other diners. It felt as if they were completely alone.

Genevieve's head swam from all the wine. The main courses came and went and the level in the bottle of pinot had dropped to less than a third. Annie had consumed nearly two entire bottles of wine over the last four hours. By the time dessert arrived, a chocolate mousse that melted on her tongue, Genevieve saw her opening.

"Now," she announced, "I can tell you the surprise."

Annie's smile was loose, and she leaned heavily on the tiny table. "Tell me."

"I know that you're a fan of Kate Quinn," Genevieve began. "How would you like to meet her in person?"

Annie's eyes widened. "You can't be serious."

"I *am* serious. She's coming to the UK on holiday and I have a friend of a friend who has asked her to come to a luncheon at his estate in the south of England. He told me I can bring a plus one, so"—she paused dramatically, reaching across the table to grasp Annie's hand—"will you be my date?"

"Of course." Annie's fingers clenched hers and she let out a little squeal. "This is so amazing. Who is hosting?"

Genevieve waved her hands. "Some rich guy. Oh, that reminds me, I'll need your personal info so that his private security can pre-screen you. I think a picture of your passport is all they want."

Annie's hand slipped from Genevieve's grasp. "Is that necessary?"

"The event is on a personal estate. Those are his rules," Genevieve said, keeping her voice light. "Is that a problem?"

"I—I don't like giving out my personal information is all." Annie folded her arms.

"I can send it in by secure email," Genevieve said, pressing against Annie's resistance. This was the moment of truth, if she hadn't gained this woman's trust by now, she'd never have it.

Annie finished off the wine in her glass. "Who's the rich guy?"

"Victor van Valkenberg," Genevieve replied. "A software billionaire. He does—"

"I know who he is," Annie interrupted. She signaled the waiter for the check. Genevieve's heart beat faster. She was losing her.

"Annie, what's the matter? Did I do something wrong?"

"No, it's not you." Annie hugged her arms tighter to her chest and began to tear up. "It's just—just…I know him."

"You know a billionaire?" Genevieve forced a note of incredulity into her voice. "How?"

"My father," she said shortly.

"Your father does business with a billionaire? That doesn't mean anything. I'm sure lots of people do business with Valkenberg's companies."

"No…" Annie hesitated.

Tell me, Genevieve thought. Please.

"My father *is* a billionaire." Tears made Annie's eyes glassy in the dim light. "I'm not who you think I am, Genevieve. I'm not Annie Baker. My real name is Anoushka Balinovich."

Genevieve wanted to shout for joy, but instead she produced a few tears of her own, reached across the table and took Annie's hand.

"Tell me everything."

16

8 kilometers northwest of Marbella, Spain

The Costa del Sol was in the midst of a stifling heat wave. A hot wind from the east, the Levante, raced through the arid hills above the Mediterranean coast. Harrison watched the long gauzy white curtains whip away from the open French doors as he sipped his drink. The view of the ocean from this height was magnificent, the Med a royal blue, speckled white with sailboats and yachts.

"You look tired, my friend." Despite the words, the voice gave Harrison a sense of comfort. It grounded him.

He turned his attention away from the view. Akhmet Orazov looked younger than when Harrison had last seen him. His gray hair and beard were freshly trimmed and his linen suit hung loosely on his trim figure.

Harrison forced a smile. "If it's any consolation, I feel worse than I look."

Akhmet chuckled at the joke, but his eyes narrowed. "You're sure you want to do this?" he asked, his tone serious. "These are not men to be trifled with. I urge you to reconsider."

"Thank you again for your help, Ussat," Harrison replied, addressing his old friend by the name the resistance fighters had given him. *Ussat*, the Turkmen word for *master*.

"Bah." Akhmet waved away the backhanded compliment. "That name is in the past. I am your servant now, my friend."

Harrison sipped his club soda. Was it wrong that he wished for those times when he fought side by side with this man? When he'd been Akhmet's shadow, his life was in constant danger, but everything seemed so simple then. He had a mission and he had a leader he trusted.

Not at all like his present condition. Now, he didn't know who to trust and his mission seemed like an unresolved blob of conflicting priorities.

Andy Meyers, dressed in a polo shirt and chinos, armed with a Glock on his hip, appeared in the doorway. "They're at the gate, sir."

"Thanks, Andy." Harrison got to his feet. God, he felt tired. Everything ached, including his brain.

"Harrison," Akhmet said. "There are other ways—"

He cut off his friend. "I've made my decision, Ussat."

They stood shoulder to shoulder in the circular courtyard as the black Mercedes SUV drew to a stop. The door opened and to Harrison's surprise, a dog, a Belgian Malinois, leaped out of the back. He landed gracefully, then immediately sat, eyes fixed on Harrison. A long pink tongue lolled out of the side of his open jaws.

A thickset man with a shaved head and wraparound sunglasses exited the vehicle and stood next to the dog. His meaty hand dropped to the animal's head, stroked its ears.

He looked, thought Harrison, exactly what he expected a leader of the Russian Bratva should look like.

The man stepped toward Akhmet and they embraced roughly, like old friends. Harrison was surprised when the Russian referred to Akhmet as Ussat.

"And this," Akhmet said, turning to Harrison, "is my friend, Harrison Kohl. Harrison, this is Semion Borisovich Artemov."

"My friends call me Semi," said the Russian, squeezing Harrison's hand in viselike grip. "You know, like the truck in America. The tractor trailer."

Harrison produced a smile. "Nice to meet you, Semi." His eyes dropped to the dog. "And who is your friend?" he said in Russian.

He felt Semi's eyes appraise him. "You speak Russian like a Muscovite."

Knowing Semion was from St. Petersburg, Harrison suspected the comment about his language skills was not a compliment.

Semi nodded at the dog. "Say hello to Luca in Russian," he told Harrison.

"Luca, *privet*," Harrison said.

The dog responded with one snapping bark, not friendly, but not threatening either. He looked at his master for approval and got a nod. Semi smiled and roughed up the dog's ears.

"Shall we get out of the heat?" Akhmet said, leading them back to the room with a view.

In their absence, Akhmet had ordered the room set with a small wooden table and three chairs positioned near the open window. Drinks arrived: club soda for Harrison, orange juice for Akhmet, an enormous gin and tonic for the Russian, and a bowl of water for the dog.

The three glasses sweated in the heat, leaving pools of condensation on the surface of the table. Luca drank noisily from the bowl, then lay in front of the French doors, head resting on his outstretched paws, eyes watching his master.

"I've heard of you," Semi said to Harrison. "You were Ussat's CIA man."

Akhmet had not revealed to Harrison his connection to the Russian underworld, but Harrison took a guess. "And you were Ussat's weapons supplier through Kazakhstan."

Semi raised his eyebrows and his drink. He took a long sip, then pulled off his sunglasses. "And now the CIA has a proposal for me."

"Yes." Harrison shot a meaningful glance at Akhmet. This was his cue to leave. There was no need to involve him in what Harrison was about to do.

Akhmet sipped his own drink and met Harrison's gaze. The message was clear: I'm not going anywhere.

"We are concerned about the New Dawn party," Harrison began.

Semi laughed with enough force that Luca's head snapped up. But there was no humor in the outburst. "The Novo Zorya." His voice dripped with contempt. "They're bad for business. When everyone is a crook, no one makes any money."

Harrison ignored the obvious irony in the statement. "I'm glad we have a mutual interest in the matter."

Semi considered Harrison over the rim of his drink. "What is the CIA's concern in Russian politics?"

"Stability," Harrison said. "We think the Novo Zorya represents a threat to US relations with Russia."

Semi's bald head swiveled in disagreement. "I don't buy it. Political parties come and go in Russia. There's something you're not telling me."

"We believe that the Russian President could be in danger if the New Dawn takes power in the Duma in October." Harrison parsed his words carefully, letting the Russian fill in the details.

Semi made a subtle hand signal and Luca shot to his side. The Russian's thick fingers kneaded the dog's ears as he thought. Luca rubbed his muzzle along his master's thigh.

"You're talking about a coup," Semi said finally. "You believe this will happen?"

Harrison nodded.

The tempo of the ear rubbing increased and the dog gave a low groan of pleasure.

"Bogdan Rabilov is your problem."

Harrison nodded again.

Semi's free hand gripped his glass. "You want him…" The ear rub stopped and he made a fluttering gesture with his fingers.

Harrison shot a look at Akhmet. "We want Rabilov put on notice. We want him to feel threatened."

"But not…dead."

"Threatened," Harrison repeated. "Not dead."

Semi's hand dropped to Luca's head again as he considered the problem. "You want to stay at arm's length—that is the right term, no?"

"That is the right term," Harrison agreed. "And, yes, we want to stay out of it."

"It is possible," Semi replied after another round of head scratching. He patted the dog one last time, then signaled him to return to the window. Luca complied.

"It is possible," he repeated, "but there is a price."

"I can pay."

Semi scowled. "I don't want your money, Mr. CIA. I need a favor."

Harrison felt Akhmet tense beside him. "A favor."

Semi bared his teeth, but the smile did not reach his eyes. "I have a business interest that needs some attention."

"I'm listening," Harrison replied cautiously.

"I have interests in Japan. Pachinko parlors—you know pachinko?"

Harrison knew pachinko. Entire businesses were built around the game. The noise, the flashing lights, the excitement all made for superb, legal entertainment, and the parlors printed money. They also served as fronts for illegal gambling, money laundering, prostitution and drugs, which was undoubtedly where the Bratva entered the picture. He nodded in answer to Semi's question.

"The police in Yokohama have increased enforcement. That is the area we control through our partners in the Yakuza. Our methods of compensating the police are not working anymore. We need some...outside influence."

Harrison stared at him. He had no idea how he was supposed to get the Japanese National Police to back off enforcement of pachinko parlors, but Yokohama was home to the US Navy's 7th Fleet. Maybe there were local contacts he could work to get something done.

Semi read the uncertainty in his eyes.

"Harrison, this is my price."

"I'll see what I can do," Harrison said cautiously.

Semi spread his arms. "That's all I ask. And I will see what I can do about your problem." He held out his hand. "Partners."

Harrison said nothing, but subjected himself to another punishing handshake.

Semi was on his feet now, Luca at his side. He embraced Akhmet again and man and dog walked to the courtyard. Luca bounded into the back of the SUV and Semi followed. The tinted windows closed, the car departed.

A searing wind blasted through the courtyard, kicking up dust and grit.

"I hope you know what you're doing," Akhmet said quietly.

So do I, Harrison thought.

17

St. Petersburg, Russia

Bobo checked his watch as the black stretch limousine entered the fenced lot of Signature Limousine of St. Petersburg. Ten after four in the afternoon.

Right on time, he thought.

He waved to Alex, the shop supervisor, who frowned down at the new arrival from the second-story office window onto the service bays. The shop had been slammed all day.

"I'll see what he wants," he called. Alex responded with a thumbs-up.

Bobo sauntered over to where the limo had stopped. The driver, a thin young man in his thirties, had taken off his black suit jacket. He'd sweated through his white dress shirt. He tugged at his tie and mopped his brow with a red bandana.

"I need help, man," he greeted Bobo.

"What's the problem?"

"The air-con. There's something wrong with it."

Bobo took his time answering. "Like what?"

"I turned on the air-con to cool down the back for my clients and there's a noise in the vent. Rattling noise." He looked at the clock on his phone. "I have to pick up customers in an hour. Can you look at it?"

Bobo turned toward the shop. The bay doors were open and all three service lifts had cars on them. "We're pretty busy." He checked his watch, "And we close at five."

"Please," the man pleaded. "I picked up the car from this shop at noon. Maybe something is just loose and you can fix it without putting it up on the lift. Can you look at it? I don't want to lose this job." He lowered his voice. "The clients are big-time."

Bobo grimaced. "Well, I'm done for the day—"

The driver seized the opening. "So you're free? Just take a look. Please, I'm begging you."

Bobo held up his hands. "I'll take a look, but no promises." He led the chauffeur into the shop and pointed to the lounge. "Wait in there. I'll come get you after I have a look."

As the chauffeur headed to the lounge, Bobo retrieved his tool bag and walked quickly to the car. After starting the vehicle, he turned on the air-conditioning and raised the glass privacy barrier behind the driver's seat. He climbed into the passenger cabin. Looking out the tinted windows, he made sure the chauffeur was still inside the shop, then he locked the doors and set to work.

The main air vent was located under the bench seat at the forward part of the cabin, directly under the privacy glass. A loud grinding noise emanated from the vent and the air flow was weak. He loosened the four screws and removed the screen covering the vent.

Bobo lay on the floor and reached inside the duct, extending his arm and feeling for the plastic container he knew was there. He wrapped his fingers around it and peeled it away from the duct tape securing it to the side of the vent.

The hard plastic container held a handful of BBs that rattled when he dropped it into his bag. Bobo raised his head to take another peek outside. The driver was still in the lounge.

He extracted a small metal thermos from the bottom of his bag and unscrewed the cap. When he tilted the container, a slim black object slipped into his palm. Cylindrical, about as thick around as his wrist, the object was blunt on one end and tapered to a point on the other. It looked like an oversized matte-black bullet.

Bobo had never served in the military, but he knew what a shaped charge was—and what it did.

A thick strip of adhesive ran down one side of the object. He peeled off the plastic and reached into the vent with the charge in his hand.

His instructions were simple: Place the device as far into the duct as you can reach, pointy side toward the passenger cabin.

Bobo lay on the carpeted floor and shoved his arm in up to his shoulder, then he pressed the device to the bottom of the duct. It held fast.

The knock on the window startled Bobo. He jerked his arm, cutting the skin of his bicep along the sharp edge of the vent.

The driver pressed his face to the glass. "Did you fix it?" he yelled. "Open up. The door's locked."

Bobo took a quick glance to make sure any incriminating evidence was hidden, then unlocked the doors. He smiled. "Good news. It was a loose duct connection. I just need to put the cover back on and you're good to go."

The chauffeur's face flooded with relief. "You're a lifesaver. I owe you one."

"Don't sweat it."

"No, really!" The driver dug into his pocket, pulling out a wad of cash. He peeled off a handful of bills. "You saved my ass."

Bobo took the money. "Good luck."

"With this guy, I don't need luck. They say he tips like a sailor in a whorehouse."

Bobo watched the limo drive away, the chauffeur smiling like a fool. He almost called him back, but bit his tongue instead. When Semion Artemov called you for a special job, you did what you were told and you kept your mouth shut. He pulled out his mobile and sent a one-word text.

Bobo got his jacket from his locker. As he headed out the door, Alex came out from the office and called down from the landing. "Thanks for taking care of that, Bobo. I'll make sure you get the overtime."

He forced a smile. "No problem, boss."

"See you tomorrow, Bobo."

He waved, but said nothing. In less than two hours, he'd be on a plane. Tomorrow, who knew?

18

Gazprom Arena, St. Petersburg, Russia

The first chants began about twenty minutes after Bogdan took the stage at the Gazprom Arena. Yuri's eyes found Dariya watching her father from the opposite stage wing. Either she didn't hear the chanting or she was too focused on her father's performance to notice.

She was dressed in what Yuri had started thinking of as her "sexy intellectual" look. Black leather pants with ankle boots and a white silk blouse topped by a leather bustier. Her hair was loose, spilling past her shoulders in waves, and her cheeks were still flushed with high color from her own turn at the speaker's podium. Her painted lips moved as she mouthed the words of Bogdan's speech, which she had written. Her forehead creased into a tiny frown every time he went off script—which was often.

The chants died away, but the capacity crowd in the 68,000-seat arena was restless. Yuri could feel it in the damp heat around him, an undercurrent of tension and shifting moods.

Bogdan leaned on the podium with one elbow, launching into an anecdote about something that happened twenty years ago in Siberia. Dariya's frown deepened. Now, even she could see that he was losing his audience.

The leader of the New Dawn party got a few scattered cheers from the crowd, which he took as encouragement to continue his wandering tale.

Yuri closed his eyes in frustration. Dariya had been the warmup act for her father. She'd been pitch perfect, even better than the night he'd seen her in Saratov. She built the tension in the crowd to the edge of hysteria. They went wild for Bogdan when the old man trundled onto the stage. Father and daughter worked the crowd together, holding clasped hands high in the air, blowing kisses, picking up flowers and stuffed animals that rained onto the stage.

Then Dariya departed and Bogdan started to speak. The first fifteen minutes went fine. Not great, but fine. He stuck to the script and got the expected crowd response. Then he veered away from Dariya's prepared remarks. Slowly, imperceptibly at first, the energy began to leak out of the huge stadium, like air out of a punctured car tire.

Yuri checked his watch. Bogdan had been on stage for forty minutes and the tire was flat. They were driving on the rims now.

The chant began again, stronger this time.

Dar-i-ya! Dar-i-ya!

Yuri scanned the crowd. It was coming from the main floor, a group of at least fifty people pumping their fists in the air in time with the chant.

Dar-i-ya! Dar-i-ya!

At first, Bogdan thought the chant was for him. He clapped along, unknowingly adding to the energy. Like a stone in a still pond, the chanting spread in ripples through the arena until the entire building rang with the sound of...

Dar-i-ya! Dar-i-ya!

Then Bogdan realized what they were saying and his face darkened in anger.

"Enough," he roared into the microphone. "Stop!" The chanting slowly died away, but now the audience was distracted, laughing and talking. Bogdan had lost them.

Yuri searched for Dariya on the stage wing, but she was not there.

Bogdan tried to recover the spotlight, but the moment was gone. Abruptly, he thrust his arms in the air and yelled into the microphone. "New Dawn will win in October! Vote for the New Dawn in Russia!"

The crowd cheered, but Bogdan was already storming off stage to loud music. Dariya appeared at Yuri's elbow. Her face was bone white, slack with worry, her jaw quivered. She gripped his hand, lacing her fingers into his. "This is a disaster," she whispered. "Papa will be angry."

Yuri took her elbow, guided her to the green room at the rear of the stage. He closed the door behind them and pushed Dariya gently into an armchair. There were a few servers and some of the other speakers lounged in the chairs or grazed at the buffet. Everyone had been watching the TV that now showed the empty speaker's podium on stage. Their eyes turned toward Dariya, locked on.

Yuri swept his hand in a curt gesture. "Everyone out," he ordered. "Clear the room."

The space emptied in only a few seconds. Yuri knelt next to Dariya, handed her a bottle of water. "It wasn't your fault."

Dariya shook her head. "That's not what he will think. It's—"

The door burst open and Bogdan stormed in. His fleshy face was dark with blood, and spittle flecked his lips. Sweat was slick on his skin, and underneath his jacket his white dress shirt was soaked through. His breath blasted out of his open mouth like a winded horse.

Yuri's first thought was that the man was having a heart attack. He leaped to his feet. "Bogdan, calm down."

"Fuck off!" Bogdan strode to the bar, ripped an open bottle of vodka from a bucket of ice, and drank straight from the bottle.

Great, Yuri thought, the only thing worse than an angry Bogdan was an angry *and* drunk Bogdan.

"You need to calm down," he said through gritted teeth.

Bogdan wiped his mouth with the back of his hand, fingers still wrapped around the neck of the bottle. "Fuck off," he said again. His glazed eyes found his daughter and his mouth twisted in anger. "You," he growled. "They were chanting your name."

Yuri stepped between them. He had to defuse this situation, separate father and daughter until the old man could cool off. And he had to do it before Bogdan got seriously drunk and made a bad problem catastrophic.

He racked his brain. The limousines, he thought. They were leaving in separate limos. It was the perfect way to get them separated without causing a huge fuss in front of the public.

Yuri crossed to the door and pulled it open. Roland was outside, briefcase clutched to his chest, as was Yuri's security lead, Ivan. "We're leaving, all three of us. Hold the elevator."

Ivan nodded and set off for the lift.

Yuri took Dariya's hand and pulled her to her feet. He motioned to Bogdan. "We're leaving. Now."

The older man nodded, clutched the bottle tighter. Yuri started to tell him to leave the bottle behind, but decided against it. He'd deal with it in the elevator.

Three security men guided them across the crowded backstage area. The freight elevator doors were open and there was plenty of room for the group. Bogdan's color had lessened, but he was still breathing heavily. Yuri stayed close to Dariya, his back to Bogdan. He heard the swish and swallow of more vodka.

The elevator doors opened on the crowded underground garage. Over the heads of the VIPs waiting for their cars, Yuri spied their destination. Three idling vehicles at the head of the queue, lined up one behind the other.

Bogdan's black stretch limo, a black town car for Dariya, and then Yuri's own armored Klassen Range Rover. All he needed to do was get Dariya and Bogdan through this crowd and into their cars without being noticed.

He scanned the vicinity looking for press or some idiot with a mobile phone. No one had noticed them yet. He nodded at his security team to move out.

"Let's go." Yuri took Dariya's hand and started forward.

He'd only taken a few steps when pressure from Dariya's hand forced him to stop. Yuri turned. "We need to go now," he hissed.

"It's Papa," she whispered.

Yuri looked past her pinched face. Bogdan stood in the elevator, clutching his bottle, not moving.

"Bogdan," Yuri said in an urgent tone. "We need to go. Now."

In his peripheral vision, he could see people turning toward them. They'd been noticed. Any second now, the mobile phones would come out.

Bogdan's eyes traveled over Yuri, then dropped to where he held Dariya's hand. He wasn't holding her hand as if to lead her away, their fingers were interlaced. The way lovers held hands.

Bogdan's lip curled in disgust.

"Papa…" Dariya released Yuri's hand, moved back into the elevator. She knew the warning signs of her father's rage and she wanted to make sure it didn't spill out in public.

She held out her hands, palms out. "Papa, it's not what you—"

"You whore!"

Bogdan's hand whipped out and Yuri heard the smack of flesh on flesh, saw Dariya's head snap to the side, heard her sharp exhalation.

Yuri caught her as she spun toward him. He passed her limp body to Ivan. "Put her in the lead car now. Get her out of here." His eyes found the other two security guards. "Take every mobile phone in the area. No exceptions. Do it now."

The two men went into motion, snatching phones, pushing bodies out of the way. Yuri cast a look over his shoulder in time to see Ivan pushing Dariya into the stretch limo at the head of the queue.

He turned on Bogdan.

"You fool." He slapped the bottle out of Bogdan's hand. "She's worth ten of you, you stupid drunk."

His body raged with adrenaline. Yuri gripped Bogdan's lapel and swung his fist at the big man's face. When his knuckles connected, the whole world exploded.

Yuri felt himself thrown into Bogdan's chest. They crashed to the floor. He rolled off Bogdan's bulk onto his hands and knees and shook his head.

Yuri's ears rang, he saw spots in his vision. There was screaming all around him.

He staggered to his feet, looked out of the open elevator into a parking garage filled with dark smoke.

The smoke parted and he saw it.

The long black limo had stopped halfway up the ramp. Fire poured from the blown-out windows in the passenger compartment.

Yuri blinked, his brain trying to process what his eyes were seeing.

"Dariya!" he screamed.

19

The Kremlin, Moscow

"Tell me you have something," Nikolay said.

Although he'd taken two paracetamol an hour ago, his head still hurt. His eyes felt gritty from lack of sleep and his mouth cottony from the vodka chaser he'd downed at breakfast. Through the bulletproof glass of the large window behind him, the rest of Moscow was enjoying an absolutely gorgeous July morning.

But inside his private office, it was dark and stormy.

He glowered at the two men standing at attention before his desk.

"Tell me you have something," he repeated.

The two men shot furtive glances at one another as if trying to decide who would talk first. Which meant they had nothing. Nikolay's frustration boiled over.

"Parmentov," he barked, "speak."

Lev Parmentov, his second FSB Chief, cleared his throat. He was already sweating freely and he breathed heavily through his mouth.

"Information is sparse, Mr. President," he began. Noting the threatening look, he rushed ahead. "The Tajik separatists, the branch associated with ISIS-K, have claimed responsibility."

Gennady Abukamov, the head of Rosvgardia, rolled his eyes.

"You have something to add, Gennady?" Nikolay hissed.

"That makes no sense, Mr. President. This has all the earmarks of a gangland hit. My people are pursuing that angle of the investigation."

"The Bratva?" Nikolay responded. "Why would a syndicate want to kill Dariya Rabilova?"

The two men exchanged glances. "She may not have been the target, sir."

"Bogdan?" Nikolay asked.

They nodded together. Nikolay allowed himself a moment of fantasy. If they had managed to take out Bogdan Rabilov, this would be an entirely different issue. No, not an issue at all, a gift to him, the best gift of his political career.

"The car that was bombed was a stretch limo. It was there to pick up Bogdan, not the daughter," Abukamov explained.

"And she just got into the wrong car?" Nikolay was incredulous.

The Rosvgardia man shook his head. "We believe there was a fight between Yuri Balinovich and Rabilov. The daughter was put in the car to keep her out of harm's way."

Nikolay cradled his aching head in his hands. Talk about bad luck—for him and the girl. "Please explain what you are saying. This story makes no sense to me."

"People are reluctant to speak about what they saw," Parmentov said. "Balinovich's men have threatened them and taken their mobile phones."

Nikolay's rage erupted. "You are the fucking FSB. They should be afraid of *you*. Make them talk."

"Mr. President, I—"

"Shut up!" Nikolay was on his feet, his fist hammering his desk. "You are an incompetent fool and you are fired. Get out of my office. Now!"

Parmentov's mouth opened and closed like a gasping fish, then he turned and left. The door closed softly behind him. The room rang with charged silence.

Nikolay took his seat, pressed his palms flat on the desk to stop the trembling, and drew in a deep breath. He let it out and drew in another.

"Gennady."

"Yes, Mr. President?"

"You are in charge of this investigation. Tell me what you know so far. Facts only, Gennady."

"There was an argument between Balinovich and Rabilov. The daughter was put into the wrong car."

"What do you mean she was put into the wrong car?" Yuri said sharply. "How do you know that?"

"The video shows her being pushed into the car by one of Balinovich's security men."

"You have this on video? Show me."

Abukamov transferred the video from his phone to the screen on the wall.

"The mobile phone service in the arena was jammed with calls and Wi-Fi was down when this all happened. The only video we have is from a single CCTV camera on the ramp."

The image was black and white with no sound. The expanded picture was grainy, like an Impressionist's painting. The camera was positioned on the ceiling looking down a long row of idling vehicles, the first of which was a long, black limousine. People milled about next to the line of cars.

Suddenly, the people scattered and a man appeared in the frame, his movements jerky in the poor-quality image. He had his arm around a woman with long dark hair, but it was impossible to see her face with any level of detail. He yelled at the driver, who ducked behind the wheel, then he wrenched open the rear door and pushed the woman inside. The man went to the open driver's window and bent down. Then he straightened, slapped his hand on the roof of the car, and stepped back.

The limousine moved forward. Before it had traveled more than a car length, the rear windows erupted, fire spewed out. The car veered off the road, coming to rest against a concrete pillar. The driver's side door opened, and the chauffeur staggered out.

Nikolay looked up. "The driver's alive?"

Abukamov nodded. "Barely. He's in a coma."

"How did he survive?" Nikolay watched the screen.

The people close to the explosion in the waiting area, including the man who had put the woman in the car, were all moving. The man even got to his feet.

Nikolay looked up. "What are you not telling me?"

"It feels off, Mr. President," Abukamov said finally.

A fresh surge of frustration threatened his newfound stability. "What does that mean?" he snapped.

"The size of the blast is too small. Gangland hits are about power and overkill, not subtlety."

Nikolay looked at the burning hulk on the screen. "That's small?"

"By Bratva standards, yes. That car should be in pieces. Instead, it barely blew out the windows. The only reason why the girl is dead is because she was sitting right on top of the charge."

"What conclusions do you draw from that?"

"I don't, sir. The woman is dead, but I think we can safely say that she was not the intended victim."

"They were after Bogdan?"

Abukamov nodded.

"Then whoever they are, they're not going to succeed, Gennady. You are going to make sure of that."

The Rosvgardia man shifted on his feet. "I'm not sure what you're ordering me to do, Mr. President."

Nikolay rose to his feet again, put his knuckles on the desktop. "I am ordering you to take personal charge of the investigation into the death of Dariya Rabilova. Find those responsible and bring them to justice. Use whatever force is necessary."

Abukamov's eyes glinted. He understood that part of the order.

"Next, I am ordering you to put a round-the-clock guard on Bogdan Rabilov. As long as he is on Russian soil, he will be safe from harm. If you fail, it will be your head. Do you understand, Gennady?"

Abukamov's chest swelled with pride. "You can count on me, sir."

"Good. Dismissed."

Abukamov saluted, executed a precise about-face, and marched to the door. As the door closed behind the Rosvgardia Chief, Nikolay sank into his chair. He felt drained, his guts still jittery from the adrenaline rush. He spun around to look out the window.

The sun-drenched buildings across the courtyard looked like they were etched against a cobalt-blue sky. The beautiful view did nothing to lighten his mood.

He could feel the darkness out there—and it was coming for him.

20

Turkmenbashi, Turkmenistan

The walled compound stood on a bluff overlooking the Caspian Sea. Although the buildings were at least twenty miles from the nearest town, the straight road through the desert was paved smooth with neat yellow lines dividing the traffic lanes. Waves of heat rose from the black asphalt ahead of them, but the interior of the Mercedes sedan was cool and quiet.

They passed a private airstrip, a line of black in the sand. A red windsock next to the closed hangar stood parallel to the ground from the wind racing off the Caspian Sea.

The perfect safe house, Harrison mused. Escape routes by land, sea, and air.

The vehicle climbed a steep grade to the top of the bluff and paused at the closed gate. Harrison craned his neck to peer down the length of the thick, ten-foot-high stone wall. CCTV cameras flanked the gate and were posted on the corners. The two men at the gate were dressed like locals but carried small submachine guns, a model that Harrison didn't recognize. They all wore identical, brand-new wraparound sunglasses.

The driver spoke to the guards and they were waved through.

"I'm glad to see that Semi is not suffering during his exile from Russia,

Ussat," Harrison said to Akhmet, who sat next to him in the rear of the Mercedes.

"Do not judge a man by the house he lives in, Harrison," the older man returned.

"Shall I judge him by his deeds instead?" Harrison replied with acid in his voice.

"He said it was an accident. I believe him."

Harrison did his best to control his breathing. It would not do either of them any good to piss off a leader in the Russian underworld. But, for the love of Pete, this guy had screwed up. An innocent woman was dead, thanks to Semi, and he was left holding the bag. No, that wasn't true either. Don Riley was holding the bag that Harrison had filled to overflowing with shit.

He closed his eyes and counted to ten.

This is how careers end, he thought. In a fiery car bomb inside a Moscow parking garage.

When he opened his eyes again, he almost couldn't believe what he was seeing. The Mercedes moved slowly along a pea gravel drive, flanked on both sides by thick green grass and flower beds. Dead ahead, a pair of marble nudes played in a spraying fountain. A peacock strutted across the road, forcing the driver to stop. The scenery was something out of a wedding planner's notebook.

The car went around the fountain and stopped before the open front door. Semi waited for them at the top of the steps, flanked by two more armed men. All three wore identical sunglasses.

Semi looked distracted and his shoulders slumped forward. He came down the steps and opened Akhmet's door. The two men embraced and Harrison heard muffled whispering.

He took his time getting out the other side and making his way around the vehicle. The sun glared down on his bare head. His shoes crunched through the gravel until he stopped before Semi. He noted the cautioning look in Akhmet's eyes.

Semi put out his hand. Harrison hesitated, then took it.

"I'm sorry," Semi said. "It was an accident."

Harrison was not about to let him off that easily. "I need you to fix this."

Semi released his hand. "Let's go inside."

As they climbed the steps, the Bratva leader noticed Harrison's interest in the armaments of his men.

"Do you know them?" he asked.

Harrison shook his head, reluctant to let the Russian change the subject.

Semi grabbed one of the weapons from his men. "Honey Badgers. Made in USA, but illegal now. My dealer said it's an assault rifle in pistol form. Very powerful, but lightweight. Feel."

He handed the weapon to Harrison. It was light, less than ten pounds even with a curved AR magazine protruding from the bottom. The weapon had a pistol grip and a short barrel.

"A gift," Semi said. "You can keep it."

Harrison handed the weapon back to the guard. "I'm not here for an arms deal, Semi. I'm here to figure out how to get out of the situation you've placed us in."

To his credit, Semi looked cowed. He raised his hands in mock surrender and led them inside.

The front door opened into a foyer tiled with brightly colored geometric patterns. A huge brass light fixture hung from a chain overhead.

"This place belongs to the former President of Turkmenistan," Semi said as they entered an interior courtyard, designed like a riad with three stories of balconies overlooking a garden oasis of palm and citrus trees. Water splashed down from a multi-tiered fountain in the center of the walled garden.

"It looks like it's been here forever, but the place is only about twenty years old. It has all modern amenities." Semi continued through the courtyard and back into the main structure. They walked by a living room, a formal dining room, and a high-end kitchen before passing through open French doors to a patio that overlooked the Caspian Sea.

Sunlight glinted off cobalt-blue waves. A fresh breeze kept the shaded patio cool.

"Not a bad place to spend your exile, Semi," Harrison said. Akhmet threw him another warning look.

The Russian acted as if he hadn't heard the comment. He pulled a pair of chairs away from a heavy tiled table and indicated they should sit. "Wine? I have a Spanish Albariño on ice."

"Sure," Harrison said shortly, "why not?"

He accepted the glass, took a gulp of wine, and sat down. The wine was citrusy and sharp on his tongue. Perfect for the afternoon heat. But Harrison refused to allow himself to enjoy it. He took another swig and put the glass down.

"What happened?" he asked bluntly.

Semi put his own glass down. His free hand strayed to the side of his chair, then back to his lap. He looked at the water. "It was an accident. I am responsible."

Harrison wanted to scream, *You're damn right, you're responsible.* Instead, he took another gulp of wine. "What happened?" he repeated.

Semi's hand fluttered in the air next to his chair again. "We planted a small incendiary device in Bogdan's limousine. Start a fire, blow out the windows, but no one was supposed to be inside. It was supposed to happen before he got in the car. Send a message."

Harrison waited. Semi fidgeted.

"The device was on a remote trigger, set off from outside the stadium. We had a man in the garage to warn us when Bogdan came out of the elevator."

Harrison scowled. "But something went wrong."

Semi laughed without humor and his hand groped at the air next to his chair. "Fucking social media. The crowd at the stadium was so large that the mobile phone service was jammed. The elevator door opened and my man sent a text as soon as he saw Bogdan. But it didn't go through right away."

Semi rubbed his jaw. "There was a fight between Bogdan and Balinovich. They put the woman—Dariya—in the first car. Bogdan's car." He stopped.

"And then the text went through and your man on the outside pulled the trigger," Harrison finished.

Semi pulled off his sunglasses, drained his wine. "It all happened so fast."

Harrison resisted the urge to rub salt in the wound. "What now?" he asked.

Semi looked out over the water. "Now, I wait." His hand fluttered in the air again and Harrison realized what the motion represented.

"Where's Luca?" he asked.

Semi's eyes told of his anguish. "Home. I had to leave him. A Russian man traveling with a dog as beautiful as Luca is a dead giveaway for anyone looking for me."

"Will they find out what happened?" Harrison asked.

Semi shook his head. "No, not possible."

"I heard the driver lived," Harrison pressed.

Semi shrugged. "He did. He knows nothing."

"How many people know the truth about what happened?"

"Besides me?" Semi held up two fingers. "The mechanic who placed the device in the car. I personally gave him the bomb and instructions on how to install it. The man in the garage was a security guard. He had a number to send a text message. That was all he knew."

"You're sure the mechanic won't talk?"

Semi gave him a baleful glare. "I'm sure." He tipped his glass and finished his wine in one gulp. "We're done, Harrison. Rabilov is untouchable and I'm stuck here for a long time, I think. Russians know how to hold a grudge."

Harrison toyed with his empty glass. His mission was to make sure that nothing could be traced back to the CIA and his mission was complete. Then a final detail occurred to him.

"What about the trigger man? Who set off the bomb?"

Semi poured more wine and drank it down. His fingers fluttered in the air next to his thigh, searching for a dog that was not there.

"That was me. I killed Dariya Rabilova."

21

Red Square, Moscow, Russia

The Cathedral of Vasily the Blessed was not the largest Russian Orthodox church in Moscow, but it was by far the most famous. Built in the mid-1500s by Ivan the Terrible to commemorate a military victory, the Byzantine structure consisted of eight chapels arranged around a ninth central chapel. The nine onion-shaped domes over the churches were supposed to represent the flames of a bonfire rising into the sky.

Yuri Balinovich had heard that description for as long as he could remember, but as he viewed the cathedral from the back of his armored limo, he still didn't see it. In recent years the domes on the Cathedral of St. Basil, as the church was known in the West, had been refurbished to restore the bright colors on the exterior. In his view, the effort was a waste of government money.

Unique, yes. Memorable, of course. It was one of the most recognizable churches in the world. But beautiful? No. To Yuri, this famous building on the even more famous Red Square still looked like a mishmash of incoherent styles.

And yet Bogdan Rabilov had decided to hold the funeral of his only child in this church. It made no sense to Yuri. Bogdan was not a religious man and the Cathedral of St. Basil was more tourist attraction than church these days.

His question was answered three blocks from Red Square when his limousine was mired in traffic, both cars and pedestrians.

Bogdan wanted to create a spectacle.

Yuri's vehicle needed a police escort to navigate the crowds of mourners in Red Square. Jumbo TV screens had been erected on either side of the cathedral entrance and pictures of Dariya flashed in his vision. When the car stopped, Yuri took a moment to gather himself before he exited onto the cathedral steps. Once outside, the noise of the crowd laying siege to the funeral was deafening. Chants of *Dar-dar-dar* echoed in Red Square.

Yuri wore a dark suit, white silk shirt, and black tie. When he emerged from the limo, he put on dark glasses to complete the ensemble.

He didn't need the protection from the sun today. Clouds the color of pewter glowered down on the streets of Moscow. The air was hot and damp on his skin, adding to the feeling of oppression.

"Mr. Balinovich!" As dozens of photographers surged forward, Ivan, his security lead, moved his team to intercept them. The cuts and burns on his face had scabbed over, making him seem even more formidable.

"Scum," Yuri muttered. They were looking for pictures to put on the internet. Trying to make a ruble off Dariya's funeral was low.

He passed inside the building only to be stopped at a security checkpoint. The patch on the shoulder of their black uniforms identified the men as *omonovtsy*, a special branch police force of the Rosvgardia, the National Guard of Russia. They wore full riot gear except for their helmets, which were lined up on the floor against the wall.

"What is the meaning of this?" Yuri demanded. "This is a funeral."

The man who answered wore the removable rank insignia of an OMON major on a Velcro tab on his vest. "The cathedral is under the jurisdiction of the State, sir. We are responsible for site security."

"And Mr. Rabilov agreed to this?" Yuri asked, incredulous.

"He did, sir," the man answered.

Yuri could see he would get nowhere with this man. "I have a security team with me."

The man nodded. "As long as they are on the access list, they can enter. Unarmed."

"They have permits for their weapons," Yuri insisted.

"I don't care," the man replied. He gestured to the queue forming behind Yuri. "If you could step off to the side, sir. I will handle your situation personally."

Fifteen minutes later, Yuri entered the cathedral with Ivan at his side. After Yuri threatened to call Gennady Abukamov personally, they reached an understanding: Ivan would be allowed in—with his sidearm—as long as the remainder of his security team was unarmed. Yuri took it as a win.

The interior of the Church of the Intercession was exactly how one would expect the inside of a Russian church designed and built five hundred years ago to look.

The ceiling soared to the heavens—Yuri had read somewhere that the ceilings were more than forty-five meters high—but the walls were several meters thick and the floor space was minimal. An icon screen laden with gold leaf and pictures of saints dominated the front of the space, and every vertical surface of the walls was covered with some sort of painting or geometric design. A central chandelier provided illumination against the gray day outside.

Folding chairs were packed wall to wall into the limited floor space, leaving only a narrow central aisle clear. Although the funeral wasn't scheduled to start for another twenty minutes, the seats were almost all taken. Bogdan's access list included Moscow's political elite—and all of the media personalities. Yuri spied TV anchors from all the local stations as well as prominent reporters from the talk shows. He nodded at a woman wearing a chic black silk dress and a cloche hat with a fishnet veil. Even in the funeral wear, she oozed sex appeal. The woman looked away. Yuri had dated her once, slept with her, and never called her again. Apparently, she held a grudge.

He made his way up the central aisle, taking his reserved place in the second row. The air smelled of dust and incense, and undertones of women's perfumes.

At the front of the church, before the ornate icon screen, stood a mahogany casket on a black draped catafalque. Next to the casket, on an easel, a life-sized, black-and-white picture of Dariya looked over the assembly.

The image made his heart clench. His breath caught and he looked down at his hands. Although she had not been far from his thoughts in the two weeks since her murder, he'd had no physical reminders of her in his possession. Nothing, not even a toothbrush to remember the time they'd spent together.

They'd shared...What had they shared exactly? He'd been having an affair with a woman half his age, a woman he'd known since she was a child, a woman who once called him *uncle*. There had been mutual physical attraction—he felt sure of that—but there was more than just sex to their relationship. He considered himself her mentor as well. Yuri was convinced that he could have made Dariya Rabilova the first woman President of the Russian Federation.

Would their affair have lasted? Yuri wondered. He'd been infatuated with her, that was true. She had captured his affections like no other woman since Anoushka's mother, but could that be the basis for a lasting connection?

Painful memories of his daughter intruded on his thoughts. What would his daughter think of his actions? A dirty old man who lived for money and power. An affair with Dariya would be just another insult for her to add to the pile he'd already accumulated on her behalf.

Slowly, he looked up and confronted the photograph again. Dariya was smiling, her hair loose, a gleam in her eye that he knew well. *I know your secret...and it's safe with me*, the look said. Yuri felt his eyes sting with hot tears and he dropped his head. Moisture splashed into his clenched hands.

Yuri gritted his teeth until the moment passed. Then he leaned close to Ivan. "What is the latest on the investigation?" he murmured.

Ivan shook his head imperceptibly. "Our best guess is the St. Petersburg Tambovskaya Bratva. But no one has a direct link."

Yuri knew Ivan's methods. If there were links to be found, he would find them. "Then why do you think it's St. Petersburg?"

"Artemov is missing."

"Dead?"

Ivan shrugged. "Maybe. His dog isn't with him."

Yuri recalled the gangster with the guard dog. The man was famous for never going anywhere without his mutt by his side. If his dog was alone, that meant one of two things: Either the man was dead or the man was guilty.

"Is there a power grab among the Bratva families?" he asked.

Ivan shook his head. "We're looking into all angles. No one knows anything, but Artemov is still missing."

"I want answers," he whispered back to Ivan.

The security lead's response was lost when the entire room turned to watch the grieving father enter the cathedral.

Bogdan Rabilov stalked down the central aisle, his eyes fixed on his daughter's casket. Yuri had not seen or talked to Bogdan since the day of Dariya's murder and he immediately noticed changes. The leader of the New Dawn movement had lost weight and he wore a new tailored suit. He walked erect, none of his typical loose swagger and looser grin. There was no glad-handing here. He stared straight ahead as if the other people in the crowded chapel did not even exist.

He went to the front of the church, placed his hand on the casket and bowed his head, his back to the mourners. The historic chapel rang with silence. No one coughed or even shifted in their seat. Yuri felt himself holding his breath.

Slowly, Bogdan turned around. His eyes were clear, his gaze sharp, and Yuri could see now that he wore makeup and a lapel microphone. Yuri discreetly glanced to the back of the church to find the cameraman he knew would be there.

"Thank you all for coming today," Bogdan began. "We are here to honor the life of one young woman who was taken from us before her time. A young woman who was murdered..."

It was the most coherent speech Yuri had seen Bogdan deliver in years. Gone were the rambling asides and the inside jokes that sometimes only he seemed to fully understand. Instead, he was focused and sharp, each word placed for maximum effect. The audience—they weren't mourners anymore, they were audience members—was riveted.

Yuri had seen Bogdan speak hundreds of times over the last three decades, and as good as he'd been in his prime, this was better. Dariya, he thought with a sudden pang in his heart, would have been proud of her father.

After less than fifteen minutes, Yuri sensed Bogdan was building to a big conclusion. Was that possible? He'd seen Bogdan spend more time on a simple yes-or-no interview question than he was taking for his only daughter's eulogy.

"And so I ask you this," Bogdan said. "Who is responsible for my daughter's death? Who would have the most to gain? These are questions that deserve answers."

No, Yuri thought, don't make this about you, Bogdan. Please.

The cameraman crept up the aisle, crouching, the lens locked on a close-up of the grieving father.

Bogdan balled his hands into fists and held them out like he was about to be handcuffed. "The target was not my daughter. I was the real victim. I was the real target. Nikolay Sokolov tried to have me killed—and he failed."

A blunt finger stabbed at the camera, a bare meter in front of him.

"You missed, Little Niko, and now I am coming for you!"

Six men dressed in black suits emerged from the sides of the cathedral and lifted Dariya's casket off the pedestal. Bogdan strode down the central aisle, preceded by the camera, followed by the pallbearers. Yuri stood and fell into line behind the casket. None of it was planned, but it felt natural.

Bogdan's words electrified the audience. Yuri could feel the emotions in the air, raw and sharp.

"I don't like this, sir," Ivan muttered.

Yuri ignored him. He was here to honor Dariya, but if he was being honest with himself, Bogdan's speech had stirred something in him, too. He'd long considered himself above political manipulation, but here he was following a casket into an angry crowd of mourners.

They wound their way through the ancient halls of the cathedral to the main entrance. The same OMON major who had stopped Yuri on the way tried to block Bogdan's path. He held his helmet under one arm, but all his men were in full riot gear, face shields down.

"Mr. Rabilov," the policeman said, "we can't get the hearse up to the cathedral steps. I need you to wait."

"Get out of my way," Bogdan intoned. His voice was quiet, full of steely menace.

"I'm responsible for your safety, sir. I can't let you go out there."

"I don't need your protection," Bogdan snarled. "Those are my people out there."

If there was a signal given, Yuri didn't see it. A dozen men surged forward, overwhelming the police contingent. Bogdan and the casket followed in their violent wake, sweeping Yuri forward.

When the exterior doors of the cathedral opened, the roar of the mob was like a living thing surging into the church. Bogdan stepped aside and the casket propelled forward, shifting from the steady grip of the pallbearers to the grasping hands of the crowd. The mahogany box rose and fell like a ship tossed on the waves of an angry sea. It toppled to one side, righted itself, then flipped over completely.

He tried to shout for them to stop it. This was the remains of the woman he loved being treated like a beach ball at a rock concert.

Then he heard the laughing. He turned and found himself face to face with Bogdan Rabilov. He could see the pores of his skin, the red-veined jowls, but mostly he saw his gaping mouth and felt the warmth of his breath as he laughed with glee.

Then he felt Ivan's arm encircle his shoulders and Yuri was pulled away.

22

Moscow, Russia

"We have the situation under control, sir," Gennady Abukamov reported.

The head of the Rosvgardia stood at attention in Nikolay's private office in his home a few kilometers from the Kremlin. Nikolay swirled the glass of vodka and drank it off. The liquor was warm, but he didn't care. He'd drink a bottle of warm piss right now if it would just make the problem of Bogdan Rabilov go away.

He thumped the crystal tumbler down on his desk. He wanted another drink—hell, he wanted to take a bath in the stuff—but he knew he was already on the edge of dangerous.

He pushed up from the desk and began to pace in front of the map on the wall.

Abukamov sensed his mood. His back went rigid. He stood taller, eyeing Nikolay as he paced.

Nikolay noted the Rosvgardia man wore a bandage over his left eye and sported a purpling bruise on his jaw. Nikolay knew he would have been on the scene of the Red Square riot. Abukamov was a head-basher, not a manager. He was as much a part of the chaos as the demonstrators.

Chaos, Nikolay reflected. Federov's favorite counsel was about seeing opportunity in chaos. Well, Nikolay had chaos coming out of his ass, so where was the opportunity?

In the past, Federov would be there to help him see the big picture. But now? He cast a disgusted look at Abukamov. He had brawlers like this moron who had no use for strategy and the big picture.

It had taken six hours and three hundred riot police drawn from all over the city to clear Red Square. Hundreds were arrested. Hospital emergency rooms overflowed with injured citizens all claiming they'd been assaulted by the police. His security forces had lost three men and another thirty were among the wounded.

Nikolay went back to the bar and poured another drink. As he hefted the glass, an image flashed in his mind. His Uncle Vitaly standing in this exact spot, pouring a drink in his last hours as the President of the Russian Federation. A few hours later, Nikolay launched a coup against his uncle and seized power for himself.

Maybe history was repeating itself.

The glass trembled halfway to his lips as he recalled his uncle's state of mind in those last private moments. Paranoia, rage, rash decisions, all fueled by alcohol and stress.

Just like he was feeling now. His uncle had been too distracted to see the opportunity in that chaos. But Nikolay had seen it—and seized it for himself.

He placed the crystal tumbler carefully on the bar and stepped back. He would not make the same mistake as his uncle.

"What about Rabilov?" Nikolay asked. "Is he safe?"

"Yes, sir. Not a scratch on him."

That bastard probably would have liked a bruise or two, Nikolay thought darkly. Something to show off as he made his rounds of the talk shows going on and on about all of Nikolay's weaknesses.

"Too bad," Nikolay muttered. "I was hoping the motherfucker might have been collateral damage."

"Sir? If you want—"

"No!" Nikolay held up a hand. "I—I'm just frustrated by the situation."

Abukamov cleared his throat.

"What is it?" Nikolay said.

"The casket, sir."

"The casket? You mean the daughter's remains?"

"Yes, Mr. President. It's missing."

Nikolay was confused. "The casket is…"

"Missing, Mr. President."

Nikolay slumped into his desk chair. He stared at the wall-sized map painted on the wall of the office. As a kid, he'd loved that map. Now, as President, it seemed to mock him. The western, southern, and eastern borders of the Russian Federation were under siege and he couldn't even stop a riot in Red Square a few hundred meters from his office in the Kremlin.

He forced his mind back to the moment. What possible reason could Rabilov have to steal his own daughter's casket?

"You're sure it's missing?" he asked.

Abukamov shrugged. "It has not been interred at Novodevichy Cemetery."

"And has Rabilov asked for help in finding it?"

Abukamov shook his head.

Nikolay racked his brain. It had to be Rabilov, but why? Was he planning something? How sick did you have to be to use your own daughter's casket as a prop?

Nikolay blew out a snort of frustration. There were no depths to which Rabilov would not sink, of that he was certain.

"What do you want me to do, sir?"

Nikolay studied his Rosvgardia Chief, taking in the injuries and the determined set of the man's jaw. There was not a strategic bone in this man's body. If Nikolay gave him the task of finding the reason behind Rabilov's subterfuge with the casket, Abukamov would undoubtedly fuck it up. He needed a softer touch.

He picked up the card that had been delivered that afternoon to his home. It was plain cream-colored card stock folded once. Inside, written in Federov's hand, was a name:

Andrei Galenkov.

Nikolay had not been familiar with the name, so he looked him up. A steady, if unremarkable career in the FSB, one of Federov's middle managers. And yet this man was Federov's choice as the next chief of the internal security services for the Russian Federation.

Abukamov cleared his throat.

"You're dismissed," Nikolay said without looking up. "Send in Galenkov on your way out. I want him to handle the investigation for the missing casket. That task is beneath you."

Abukamov saluted, a smile on his face, did his crisp about-face, and marched out. There was a brief conversation in the hallway, then Andrei Galenkov appeared in the doorway.

Nikolay waved him to a chair, studying him as he carefully closed the office door and took a seat.

He was a thin man. Narrow face with round spectacles, thinning gray hair held securely in place with gel, and a slight frame. To Nikolay's eye, he looked insubstantial, more like an accountant than the potential leader of the most feared security service in the land.

But this was Federov's choice and Nikolay needed all the help he could get. If Galenkov was good enough for Vladimir Federov, then he was good enough for Nikolay.

"I am making you head of the FSB," he said without preamble.

The gray eyes behind the round glasses registered surprise, then delight, then something else. Something fleeting and quickly hidden. Nikolay tried to pin down the emotion and failed.

"Thank you, Mr. President," Galenkov said. He had a mild voice.

"Don't thank me yet. You are my third FSB Chief in less than three months. Don't fail me."

"I'll do my best, sir."

"Your first assignment is to find a casket."

"A casket? I don't understand."

Nikolay barked out a short laugh. "I don't either, that's why I have you. Abukamov has the details."

Galenkov sensed he was being dismissed and he got to his feet. "I'll keep you updated, Mr. President."

"Yes." Nikolay watched the door close behind the man. He was suddenly very tired and he closed his eyes.

That look in Galenkov's eyes still bothered him. It was not what he expected as a response to a huge promotion. It was…

Cunning. That was what he'd seen behind those round glasses. A sense of superiority.

He closed his eyes again.

"Vladimir Federov," he muttered, "I hope you know what you're doing."

23

Langley, Virginia

Harrison had never visited Don in his office at the CIA headquarters building. Every other time they'd met since Harrison had come back from Central Asia had been in a reserved conference room or some other location, like their visits to the White House.

Today was different. Normally, Don called him personally to schedule a meeting, but not today. Today, Don's assistant put the meeting on Harrison's calendar and then called him—twice—to confirm his attendance.

Today, Harrison had been summoned to the Seventh Floor.

I'm gonna get fired, he told himself as the elevator doors opened. What's more, I deserve it. The President never authorized a lethal action, and yet someone is dead. Someone important—and also innocent.

It was an accident, but no one wanted to hear that. Politicians wanted someone to blame and he was the guy in charge. He was responsible and he'd take whatever was coming his way.

Harrison squared his shoulders and marched across the expanse of blue carpet to the executive assistant's desk outside Don's office. The young woman with a short dark bob gave him a bright smile. "Deputy Director Riley is expecting you, Mr. Kohl. You can go right in."

Harrison gave her a wan smile, rapped once on the door, and entered.

Don looked up from his desk. His round face looked worn, but he gave his old friend a tired smile. He pushed himself to his feet and ambled around the desk, holding out his hand. "Thanks for coming."

"Of course, Don." Harrison shook the proffered hand. The handshake was normal and there was no hesitation in Don's manner. He took that as a positive sign.

The room, glowing with morning light from the southern-facing windows, had all the familiar trappings of a Don Riley workspace. Stacks of bound reports surrounded a drip coffee maker on the credenza behind his chair. The desk surface held an open report and a yellow legal notepad, both covered with thick scrawling from a black felt-tip pen. His laptop stood open next to a half-full coffee mug.

Don poured two coffees and led Harrison to a small round table that was piled with more reports. He consolidated two stacks of paper and moved them to the floor. He took a seat, waving Harrison to an empty chair.

His old friend sighed and the tired smile fell away from Don's face. Harrison got a heavy feeling in his chest.

"Don, am I fired?" Harrison said abruptly. There was no point in beating around the bush. If that was where this was going, then let's get it done and over with.

Don's eyebrows went up. "Why do you say that?"

Harrison shook his head. "Don't do that. Answer a question with another question. We go back a long way. If I'm getting the axe, just tell me."

"Fair enough." Don took a long pull of his coffee, which Harrison knew was just another way of buying time in a tough conversation. His heart sank further.

"It's okay, Don. I'm the one who screwed this up. It's my—"

"Harrison." Don put his hand on his friend's knee. "You're not getting fired. Not today, anyway." He tried to make the last bit a joke, but it fell flat.

"Why not?" Harrison pressed.

"You're arguing with me about whether or not you should be fired?" Don said. "Is this some kind of reverse psychology that I've never heard of?"

"This operation is a mess," Harrison said. "We managed to do the one thing that Cashman said—"

"Are you finished?" Don dropped his mug on the table. "Because I've got some real work to do that would be more productive than listening to you tell me how we've screwed the pooch."

Harrison gritted his teeth.

"You want me to tell you how much we've blown this op? Fine." Don's face flushed red. "We're in the bottom of the ninth, with two strikes and no runners on base. Thanks to us, Nikolay is weaker than ever and Bogdan is in an even stronger position. The election is a month away and the chances of a coup are higher than they've ever been. Does that about sum up our position?"

"Yes, sir."

"Good. Maybe we can get some actual work done now. I'd like to find a way to get back on track. Where are we with Balinovich's finances?"

Harrison cleared his throat. He felt like he owed Don an apology, but he also sensed that was the wrong move. "We've got about sixty percent of his financial empire mapped out, but it's like wrestling with a balloon animal. As soon as we nail down one area, he changes his position and we have to start over again."

Don nodded, let his gaze stray out the window to the hazy August morning. "He still has the bagman?"

Harrison nodded. "Roland Buhler. He's joined at the hip with his boss. He goes wherever Yuri goes. Whenever the mood strikes, Yuri accesses his finances and makes a change. We've seen transactions happen at two in the morning."

"Is there more to that relationship?" Don asked.

"Not that we can see. Both men appear to be straight." Harrison hesitated.

"What?" Don said.

"It could be nothing, but when I saw Balinovich with Dariya Rabilova in Newcastle, I felt like there was something there."

"A sexual relationship?"

Harrison shrugged. "I don't have anything solid, just a feeling I got when I saw them together. It could be nothing."

Don let his eyes stray out the window again. "When you meet with Iliana, ask her."

"I don't follow."

"I have a message out to Iliana asking for a meeting. I want you to use her to get us close to Yuri's bagman."

"And then what?"

"We look for an opening we can exploit. As of this moment, Bogdan is untouchable. Going after the money behind the man is our only play that I can see. Do you have another angle?"

"Maybe," Harrison said. "We've been developing Balinovich's daughter as an asset, but it's a long shot. She's been estranged from her old man for years."

There was a soft knock at the door and the assistant poked her head in. "Your eight o'clock is here, sir."

Don nodded, got to his feet. "Duty calls, Harrison."

Harrison stood. "Don, I don't have a plan and we're out of time."

"You sound like my boss, Harrison, so I'll tell you what I told her: I've got my best man on the job. You'll figure it out."

24

Moscow, Russia

The White Rabbit was a Michelin-star restaurant a block from the Moskva River in the Arbat District of Moscow. The name of the establishment, a reference to *Alice in Wonderland*, often attracted tourists. At night, the glass-domed roof offered a view of the stars and the tables next to the windows provided views of one of the oldest sections of the city.

But there was another part of the restaurant, known only to insiders, that catered to more discreet clients. CEOs seeking a private venue for a business dinner, government officials meeting with their foreign counterparts, and important men who wanted an intimate setting with women who were not their wives.

It was to this final category that Andrei Galenkov belonged. Yuri Balinovich studied the new FSB Chief on the CCTV monitor. The new surveillance system was state of the art and the quality of the video was excellent.

He used the tiny joystick to zoom in on the man's face. What did Sokolov see in this idiot? He looked more like an accountant than a leader of men. His thin shoulders barely filled out his suit jacket and his sallow cheeks needed a shave. Round glasses glinted in the soft lighting of the room.

The sound quality was good enough that he could almost hear the man panting. He zoomed back out and studied Galenkov's date. Iliana had outdone herself again. This entire arrangement—this restaurant, compromising Galenkov with a honey trap, the surveillance system—was her idea as a way to provoke Sokolov.

Yuri studied the couple on the screen. Iliana seemed to have a sixth sense about matching her women with powerful men. She'd decided that Andrei liked his women young and the woman seated next to Galenkov at the tiny round table looked barely eighteen. Her complexion was smooth, her skin white and dewy with youth. She threw back her head and laughed, tossing her blonde hair and placing her hand on Galenkov's thin arm. The new FSB Chief had to wipe his mouth to stop from drooling.

This was the problem with premature promotion, Yuri thought. Men like Galenkov had labored in anonymity for so long they were not ready for the big, bad world of political brinksmanship. Galenkov was about to learn a hard truth: Everything had a price. If you ate the meal before you knew how much it was going to cost, then the chef was free to set the price as high as he wanted.

It had been comically easy to entrap the new FSB Chief. On the Metro, the day after his promotion, Mila—that was the girl's name—approached Galenkov. She was a university student, a freshman, and wanted to interview him for her school newspaper. The man refused at first, but Mila was insistent. "Please," she begged him. "I'll do anything you want, meet you anytime, anywhere. I promised my editor I would get the interview."

Before Galenkov could say no again, she scribbled her mobile number on a scrap of paper, kissed him on the cheek, and disappeared into the crowd. Yuri learned later that she even signed her name with a little heart over the *i*.

It took Galenkov two nights to call Mila, but a date was set. Yuri had the phone recording. Mila suggested dinner and Galenkov made a reservation at the White Rabbit. The choice of restaurant was not an accident, of course. Iliana paid off Galenkov's assistant to make sure the reservation was made here.

As if on cue, the door to the private dining room slid open and their waiter appeared carrying a bottle of champagne in a bucket of ice. Dom Perignon was not Yuri's favorite champagne, but the name invoked an air of sophistication for the uninitiated.

The girl clapped her hands and squealed with delight. The waiter cocked an eyebrow at Galenkov and said, "Compliments of the house, sir."

He popped the cork, poured two flutes of bubbling liquid, and nestled the bottle in ice before he left.

"What do we toast to, Andrei?" the girl asked, leaning toward him.

Galenkov's eyes dropped into her cleavage. "Possibilities."

They clinked, drank, and Galenkov recharged their glasses. The girl was good, Yuri noted. The perfect blend of ingenue and sex appeal. She dragged her fingertips across the inside of his wrist. "I think we should get oysters," she whispered.

Yuri almost spit out his coffee he was laughing so hard.

After oysters, there were appetizers. In keeping with the theme of *Alice in Wonderland*, the tiny plates came with labels that said: *Eat me*. Mila took the label, licked it and plastered it to the white skin of her bosom.

She lowered her eyes. "You have to follow the instructions, Andrei."

Galenkov licked his lips, kissed her long and hard, then lowered his face toward her chest.

Yuri stood up. If he waited much longer, he'd be walking in on a live sex show. He opened the office door and strolled down the narrow hallway. He slid open the second door on the right and stepped inside.

Galenkov's head shot up like a surprised deer, eyes wide, moisture smeared on the lens of his round glasses. "What is—"

Yuri held up his hand to cut him off. To Mila, he said, "Leave us."

She stood, buttoned her shirt, and left the room without a word.

Galenkov seemed frozen in place. Yuri rapped on the door and the waiter opened it.

"A bottle of ITAR. Two glasses," he ordered.

Galenkov gulped the first shot of vodka. Yuri refilled the glass.

"I don't think we've been formally introduced, Andrei," he said.

"I know who you are, Mr. Balinovich."

"Good. Then you know why I'm here."

Galenkov drank again. His eyes wandered the room, then came back to the white linen tablecloth. "No."

"I'm sure you can guess, Andrei."

"No, sir. I can't."

"Look at me, Andrei."

Galenkov's pale eyes, a washed-out gray, widened. Fear made his eyelids quiver, but he met Yuri's gaze.

"You remember what it was like when the Soviet Union fell?"

Galenkov nodded slowly. "I was twenty. I remember."

"The chaos," Yuri continued. "The lack of direction, the waste of resources, the public distrust?"

Galenkov nodded again.

"I want to prevent all of that." Yuri pitched his voice low and soothing. "But I need men I can trust. Men like you."

Galenkov's lips moved, but Yuri stopped him.

"Don't interrupt me, Andrei," he said. "You are a smart man. You know what's going to happen. After all, you're the head of internal security." He nodded at the vodka. "Drink."

Galenkov drank. Yuri refilled.

"A few weeks from now, the New Dawn party will win the Duma in a landslide, and when that happens, there will be an uprising. The people will demand new leadership of the Russian Federation. Bogdan Rabilov will answer that call."

Galenkov's eyes pleaded with him. Yuri grinned. He loved moments like this, when the other party saw their future for the first time. A future where he held all the power and they obeyed his every command. It was such a rush.

"Rabilov will need men he can trust in positions of power. Men like you, Andrei. These men will be rewarded richly for their service. From this moment forward, you work for me, Andrei. Whatever the President knows, I want to know it. If he passes gas in the middle of the night, I want you to tell me what he ate. Do you understand?"

Galenkov's eyelids trembled, his chin quivered. For a moment, Yuri thought the man might actually weep, but then a change came over him. He sat up straighter, squared his shoulders, and nodded curtly.

"I understand, sir."

Yuri smiled. That was easier than he'd expected. He had not lost his touch. Yuri stood. "I'll send Mila back. I want you to enjoy your evening, Andrei." He touched the bottle. "I'd slow down if I were you. A man of your age with a woman like Mila…You don't want to have any issues in the bedroom later."

25

The Kremlin, Moscow, Russia

Nikolay's morning started with a plane crash. He was not in the plane, but the way the day was already going, he mused that dying in a plane crash was probably the only way he was going to get some positive press.

The plane was a Beriev A-50 Mainstay, the Russian version of an American AWACS, and it had gone down over the Russian-controlled part of Kazakhstan.

"Any indication that the Chinese were involved?" he asked his Defence Minister.

"No, sir," he replied. "It disappeared off radar. No Mayday, no indication of any trouble."

"Then how do you know the Chinese were *not* involved?" he pressed.

The Defence Minister shifted his feet and looked down before responding, "It's a very old aircraft, Mr. President, more than thirty years. Anything could have gone wrong." He paused, a sure indication that another shoe was about to feel the effects of gravity.

"What else?" he demanded.

"The news is out, Mr. President. It leaked to social media shortly after the plane was reported missing."

Great, Nikolay thought, military aircraft maintenance. Just another thing that the President is personally responsible for in the Russian Federation.

His security lead knocked once and entered. "He's here, sir."

Nikolay dismissed the Defence Minister. "Keep me posted on the search. Send my condolences to the families. I want you to attend the funerals for the aircrew. You know the drill."

The minister saluted. "Yes, Mr. President."

Nikolay turned his attention to the security lead. "Give me five minutes, then send Galenkov in."

Nikolay stood and stretched his back, feeling the vertebrae pop as he reached skyward. He picked up the tablet on his desk and swiped through the photos. His new FSB Chief with a girl that looked barely legal. His new FSB Chief with Yuri Balinovich, deep in conversation. Galenkov leaving the restaurant with the same girl, getting into a cab.

Why had Federov recommended this man to be his new head of internal security services? The man clearly had vices. While that wasn't immediately disqualifying, it didn't give Nikolay confidence that the man's first instinct after getting promoted well above his station was to go get laid.

And then there was the conversation with Balinovich. What had they talked about? More importantly, why hadn't Galenkov reported the meeting to Nikolay immediately?

There was a soft knock at the door and he heard Galenkov enter. Nikolay turned and made sure that the FSB Chief could see what was displayed on the tablet.

Galenkov wore a pale gray suit, slightly rumpled. His thin face showed a line of sweat beading his upper lip.

"I like this one the best," Nikolay said, flipping the tablet around. It showed the man with his face buried in the girl's bosom.

Galenkov swallowed hard.

"Did you enjoy yourself?" Nikolay asked with acid in his voice.

Galenkov nodded.

"A bit on the young side, eh, Andrei?"

The man smiled weakly.

His hands shaking with anger, Nikolay swiped to the picture of Balinovich and his new FSB Chief. He was about to turn the tablet around and confront Galenkov, when something made him pause. He hadn't ordered surveillance on the FSB Chief, he realized, so where had these pictures come from?

"Wait here," he ordered. Carrying the tablet, he left the room and found his security lead. "Where did these pictures come from? Who ordered surveillance on Galenkov?"

The man shook his head. "They came in as a tip, sir," he said. "Anonymous sender."

Nikolay wanted to slap his forehead with disgust. How could he have been so stupid? These pictures came from Yuri Balinovich. He couldn't prove it, but he knew it was true.

The oligarch *wanted* Nikolay to know that he'd already bribed Galenkov. He *wanted* Nikolay to fire the man—his third FSB Chief in as many months. He *wanted* Nikolay to know that no matter what he did, Balinovich was coming for him.

He returned to his office, where Galenkov still stood exactly where he'd left him.

"Go back to work, Andrei," he said.

"Sir?"

"You're dismissed."

Relief flooded the man's features, then that flash of craftiness that Nikolay had seen before. The little shit thought he'd gotten away with it.

Nikolay let him go. Let him believe whatever he wants, he thought. For now.

Nikolay used his mobile to call Abukamov. "Put a twenty-four-hour surveillance on Galenkov. I want a written report twice a day, with pictures of anyone he meets with and a full breakdown of his communications."

"It shall be done, Mr. President." The Rosvgardia head's tone was exultant. Everyone loved to spy on their peers. It gave them a sense of power.

Nikolay turned to the window. It was an unseasonably warm mid-August morning and hazy clouds hung over Moscow. He toyed with his phone while considering his next move. The surveillance was no more than a holding action against Balinovich. The real question was how could he turn the tables on the oligarch?

Balinovich had him boxed in. If he fired Galenkov, he would look like a weak leader, a man who could not make up his mind about one of the most important positions in his cabinet.

On the other hand, if he left Galenkov in place, he'd be hamstringing his own security apparatus. He had to assume that everything he did would go back to Balinovich. The internal security services were key to maintaining the State.

His mind kept circling back to one disturbing fact: He hadn't chosen Galenkov, Federov had.

His former FSB Chief, the man he trusted most in this world, had made this disastrous choice. No matter how sick he was, there must be a reason why Federov had chosen this man. If he knew the reason, maybe Nikolay would be able to figure out a way forward.

He called for a car, and fifteen minutes later, he was speeding through the streets of Moscow toward the Kremlin Clinic. Nikolay felt his spirits lift as soon as he entered the grounds of the hospital. The deep green of the trees offered shade from the scorching afternoon. The drive through the winding roads made him feel as if he'd left Moscow far behind.

Balinovich was a powerful man, but Nikolay was not down yet. An outing to see an old friend was exactly what he needed to reset his thinking about this problem.

Federov's security team was not in the lobby, so Nikolay bypassed the reception desk and took the elevator to the seventh floor. A young woman in nursing scrubs met him as the doors opened.

"Mr. President," she said. "We didn't know you were coming."

Nikolay stepped into the carpeted hallway and began walking to Federov's suite. The air-conditioned atmosphere was cool and dry. Sunlight flooded in through wide windows. Nikolay quickened his pace.

"Mr. President!" She hurried after him.

There was no security man outside Federov's room. Odd.

"He's not here, sir!"

"What?" Nikolay heard her, but the information didn't register in his brain. He opened the door.

The room was empty. The monitors and devices that had been keeping Federov alive were lined up along the wall in a neat row. The hospital bed was stripped and empty. The armchairs where they'd sat together now faced the bank of windows.

Nikolay felt winded. He dropped into one of the chairs. The air in the room was stale and still, tasted of dust. He stared out the window where the leafy treetops wilted in the afternoon heat, as still as a painting.

Vladimir Federov was dead. Nikolay's mind tried to absorb the information and failed. It seemed inconceivable to him that a man of such intellect and stature, his one true friend, was dead.

"He left a few days ago," the nurse was saying.

"What?" Nikolay asked.

"Mr. Federov left for Switzerland a few days ago, sir."

"Why?" Nikolay felt like his brain was gelatin.

"Hospice, Mr. President."

It didn't make sense to Nikolay. "Don't you have hospice here?"

"Of course, sir, but Mr. Federov said he needed to be out of the country."

"He said it like that? Out of the country?"

The nurse nodded slowly. "Those were his words."

Nikolay leaned back in the chair, deflated. He stared vacantly at the Moscow skyline.

A few days ago, Vladimir Federov had sent him his handpicked choice for FSB Chief. Then his only true friend in this city had left the country to die.

Nikolay wanted to laugh at the absurdity of his position. He wanted to throw up from the feeling of abandonment. He wanted to weep for the friend he'd lost.

He did none of those things. Instead, the President of the Russian Federation took a deep breath and held it for as long as he could. His face reddened, blood pounded in his temples, his lungs screamed for oxygen. When he blew it out, he imagined expelling all the deceit and hate in his life.

He stood, turned his back on Moscow.

For the first time in his life, he was truly alone.

26

Paris, France

Harrison stood on the balcony of his room at the Shangri La, the city of Paris sprawled at his feet. Although the sun had set, he could still feel the heat of the scorching August afternoon in the stone balustrade beneath his palms. Across the Seine, the Eiffel Tower, illuminated with golden lights, dominated the skyline. The rotating beacon swept across the darkening sky.

His mobile phone buzzed and he answered it.

"She's in the lobby, headed your way." Genevieve's voice. "She's clean."

He resisted the urge to ask *Are you sure?* His team knew how to assess surveillance on an asset, and if they told him Iliana was clean, then she was not being followed. Of course, if the Russian woman chose to leave her mobile phone on or carry some sort of tracking device, there was nothing he could do about that. He just had to trust her.

And that was the problem for Harrison. As much as Don assured him that she was working for their side, Harrison still had his doubts. He also knew he had no choice but to accept her help. All his other options had collapsed. Iliana Semanova was the only card he had left to play.

He reentered the hotel suite, closing the French doors behind him and drawing the curtains. The layout consisted of a sitting room, with a separate dining area and bar. According to the concierge who had shown him to his room, the space was decorated in the style of Louis XIV. The parquet floors with plush area rugs, the marble pilasters projecting from the walls at regular intervals, and the elegant gold-and-ebony furniture all struck Harrison as a bit too much for his taste.

To his right, the double doors leading to the bedroom stood open, showing a massive four-poster bed decorated in dark wood and rich red velvet tapestries. His cover for the evening was a romantic tryst with Iliana and this looked to him exactly like the kind of place a filthy-rich Russian oligarch might rent for a few hours in order to get laid.

There was a soft knock at the door. When Harrison answered, Iliana Semanova gave him a soft smile.

"Good evening," she said in Russian, and kissed him on both cheeks before brushing past him into the suite.

Harrison followed her, noting how she surveyed the room with approving eyes. "You weren't followed," he said.

She shot him a withering glance. "I was trained by the best."

"Still," Harrison replied, "one can never be too careful." He picked up a heavy plastic bag with thick copper wires interwoven in the exterior. "Would you mind?" He held it out.

Iliana looked from her purse to the bag in mock disbelief. "You still don't trust me? I'm the one taking the risk, you know."

Harrison held the EM-proof bag open. She dropped her purse into the bag. "Would you like to strip search me now? You never know where I might be hiding a transmitter."

"It's just a precaution," Harrison said.

"Tell Dariya Rabilova about precautions." Her voice leached acid.

"That wasn't us."

Iliana's glare told him she didn't believe him. "How are you going to get Bogdan Rabilov now?"

"We're not."

The answer made her stop pacing. "You're giving up?"

Harrison offered a thin smile. Finally, he had her attention. "First things first." He picked up the elaborate handset from the phone on the end table. "What would you like to eat?"

He kept the order simple. A bottle of champagne, a dozen oysters, and caviar—exactly what he figured a horny Russian with more cash than common sense would order.

Iliana played her role perfectly. She removed her light jacket to reveal a sleeveless top with a plunging neckline, and slipped off her shoes. When the waiter delivered the food, they spoke only in Russian and she made a show of placing a possessive hand on Harrison's chest as he signed the check. He tipped the waiter fifty euros. Russians were known to be lousy tippers, but he wanted this guy to remember him.

He poured two glasses of champagne and took a seat on the opposite end of the sofa from Iliana. In the soft yellow light of the lamp, she looked mysterious and alluring. She pulled her straight blonde hair over her shoulder so it spilled down the front of her dark shirt, and eyed him over the rim of her glass.

"Your target was Bogdan Rabilov," she said.

"The objective stays the same, but the plan's changed," Harrison countered.

Iliana sipped her champagne, said nothing.

"What can you tell me about Yuri Balinovich's travel plans for the next month?"

Iliana put her glass down. "You can't be serious. Yuri's protection is the best that money can buy. You'll never get close to him."

"Do you know his travel plans or not?" Harrison pressed.

She nodded.

Harrison topped off her glass. "Tell me."

He listened as she spoke from memory. Dubai...Munich...Geneva...Greece. Harrison held up his hand. "Where in Greece?"

"Yuri is hosting some friends on his yacht in Mykonos for a long weekend."

"When?"

"Three weeks from tomorrow," Iliana said.

"And you'll be there with your, um, team?"

Iliana smiled thinly. "Yes, I will be providing the entertainment for his guests, but if you're thinking you can put one of your people onto my team, that is out of the question."

"I agree." Harrison changed tacks. "What about Roland Buhler?"

"What about him?"

"Will he be there? With his briefcase?"

"Wherever Yuri goes, Roland goes, with the briefcase. You can consider it a law of nature."

"And where do Roland's sexual proclivities lie?"

Iliana sniffed. "Americans, so prudish. He's hetero, nothing kinky, no possibility for blackmail material on him. I told you, Yuri vets his people very carefully."

"I don't want to compromise him. On the contrary, I don't want him to even know we've accessed the briefcase."

Iliana sighed as she shook her head. "It can't be done. The case is biometrically locked and can only be opened by Yuri or Roland."

"No one said he had to be awake to open the case, Iliana."

"So, you want one of my girls to drug him and open the case?" She got to her feet, began pacing the room. "Then what? I already told you I'm not putting one of your agents on my team. It's too risky. If she were discovered, Yuri would kill all of them, and then he would kill me."

"If your girl can give us access to the case for ten minutes, that's all I need."

"Who is *us*?" Iliana leaned down, her face close to his. This close he could see the age lines around her eyes—and her desperation. "How are you going to get your agent onto his yacht?"

"I have a plan," Harrison said.

Iliana laughed. "Do any more innocent women die in this plan?"

Harrison bit back an angry response. She was under intense pressure and he did not need to add fuel to that fire.

Iliana resumed her seat at the end of the sofa. She topped off their glasses and the bottle was dead. She pushed it back into the ice.

"I came to you with information that Rabilov was about to launch a coup against Nikolay Sokolov. I made it clear that you needed to stop Rabilov. I risked my life to bring you that information." She gulped down some champagne. "Your attempt on Rabilov made the problem worse. Rabilov is even more popular now."

She got to her feet, then sat down again. She breathed deeply, set down her glass with a soft clink. "Forgive me if I seem skeptical, but I think your plan is shit."

Harrison licked his lips. There was no way he was going to divulge the details of his plan to this woman, so there was no way to convince her that he had any chance of success.

"All I need you to do is incapacitate Roland for ten minutes. A simple spray bottle. One pump in the face and he's out. He wakes up ten minutes later remembering nothing. I will handle everything else."

"And where will I get this spray bottle?"

"I'll provide it."

"You will bring it to me personally?"

Harrison shrugged. "If that's what you need to feel confident, then yes. I'll bring it to you myself in Mykonos."

Iliana shrugged as if she'd given in. She lifted her glass. "A toast then: To Bogdan Rabilov. May he rot in hell."

Harrison touched the rim of his glass to hers. "To hell."

27

Mapledurham, England

When Genevieve emerged from the tree-lined lane, she stopped the car and took in the sight.

"Wow," she said.

"It's like we just drove onto the set of Downton Abbey," Annie said from the seat next to her.

The van Valkenberg Mapledurham estate was a carefully preserved twelfth-century family estate and working farm located along the River Thames, in Oxfordshire, west of London. They'd driven less than two hours, but Genevieve felt as if they'd been transported back in time a century. From the historic mill in the tiny village of Mapledurham to the narrow country lanes with dry-stone walls to this stately manor house, it was the picture-perfect setting to meet a historical novelist.

Genevieve put the car in gear and followed the circular driveway up to the front door. The main house was an imposing, four-story mansion solidly built of some kind of reddish stone. The gray slate roof sloped steeply, punctuated by jutting dormers. Through the open car windows, the gravel driveway popped and crunched under the tires.

It was a glorious September afternoon, warm and breezy, the sun brassy in the cloudless blue sky. Once out of London, they'd rolled the windows down and sang along to power ballads at the top of their lungs. Annie—or Anoushka, as she had revealed herself—seemed at ease, showing no sign of regret that she'd entrusted Genevieve with her secret. That was a positive sign, and not a mood that Genevieve wanted to mess with. She would need all Anoushka's goodwill and trust for what was coming next.

The women got out and stretched. Annie pushed her sunglasses into her windblown hair. She turned in a full circle, taking in the view. "I feel like we're in an English country house murder mystery."

Genevieve opened the trunk. "The only thing missing is a line of servants waiting to greet us."

"No servants here, but I'll lend a hand," called a male voice from the open front door.

Before she turned around, Genevieve reminded herself that she had to act as if she'd never met Victor before. She put on a practiced smile and turned.

"Mr. van Valkenberg?" she said, "I'm Genevieve Matcombe, and this is my friend—"

"Anoushka Balinovich," V^3 finished for her. He took Annie's hand in both of his.

Genevieve held her breath. In the briefing, they'd agreed that V^3 would allow the CIA team to introduce Annie and he was off script already. Genevieve flinched as she saw Annie wince at the use of her actual name. But then she rallied.

"I go by Annie these days, Mr. van Valkenberg," she said. "Annie Baker. I've cut all ties with my father."

"First thing, call me V^3. Next, I've met your father and I agree he's a son of a bitch, so I respect your decision." He tucked her hand into his elbow and turned toward the house. "We've met, you know? In Sochii, many years ago. You were just a tot, maybe three or four, I don't remember…"

His voice faded as they entered the house, leaving Genevieve standing by the open trunk.

Harrison emerged from the house, looking over his shoulder. "Can I offer some help, miss?" he said with a wry smile.

Genevieve nodded. "I see our host didn't bother to read the mission brief." She yanked one of the suitcases out of the trunk and slammed it on the gravel drive.

"He has a way of worming himself into the center of the action. I'm treating it as a built-in mission risk."

"That doesn't bother you?" Genevieve studied her boss. "He could be throwing away all the developmental work I've done on her."

Harrison reached for a suitcase. "On the contrary, he's testing her for us. He just threw her Russian background in her face and she willingly told him that she hates her father. That's motivation we can work with."

Genevieve lowered her voice. "I don't know if she's ready."

Harrison hefted both bags. "I don't either. That's what we're here to find out. We're running out of time." He nodded toward the corner of the house. "You can park in the carriage house. I'll put these in your rooms. V^3 is serving drinks on the patio."

Fifteen minutes later, Genevieve joined the reception at the rear of the house. The sun was warm on the brick-paved patio, but a few strategically placed umbrellas offered shade. Over the balustrade, Genevieve saw a sea of green grass gently sloping to a glassy pond. A pair of white swans glided across the surface of the water. Beyond the pond, a forest of mature oak trees towered, shielding the estate from the outside world.

"Gin and tonic, ma'am?" A waiter dressed in a white shirt and bow tie offered her a silver tray.

Genevieve accepted the drink and took her time surveying the crowd. Victor's dinner in honor of American author Kate Quinn was a party of two dozen, most of whom were crowded around the author. There was an air of excitement and conversations buzzed as booklovers chattered about their favorite characters.

The whole thing was working well, Genevieve mused. The dinner and book discussion to follow were real, as were almost all of the attendees. Only she, Harrison and V^3 had other motives for being at the author event. She scanned the waitstaff, trying to pick out the security personnel that Harrison had provided.

Annie spotted her and excused herself from a small group standing next to a high-top table under an umbrella. Clutching a sweating glass, she rested her hip against the stone balustrade.

"This is so amazing," she said in an excited tone. "I actually shook Kate Quinn's hand! The hand that wrote my favorite novel." She took another sip from her drink and Genevieve could tell it was not her first one. Good, she wanted Annie to be relaxed tonight.

"I was surprised when Victor called you by your actual name," she ventured.

Annie's brow creased, then cleared. "It's fine. I tend to overreact about my background, assuming that people will hate me because of who my father is."

"And do they? Hate you, I mean?"

Annie shrugged. "Sometimes. It's complicated. I guess it's not that they hate me, it's that I want to avoid their disapproval."

"I don't follow," Genevieve pressed.

Annie took another sip of her drink, her eyes unfocused as she answered. "Something V^3 said clarified it for me. He said that people expect you to do something about the problems of the world just because you have money. But he said that's BS. Money is not a reason, money is a tool. The only real reason to do something is because you want to, not because somebody else expects you to do it."

"Is that why you work for Doctors Without Borders?" Genevieve asked.

Annie sighed. "Sometimes I feel like I work there out of guilt."

Genevieve took a sip of her drink but she barely tasted the bite of the alcohol. "You don't feel like you're making a difference?" she asked casually.

Her Russian friend faced the lawn. "Annie Baker is making a difference," she said softly. "But Anoushka Balinovich is just hiding."

The dinner was a rousing success. Kate Quinn was a short, dark-haired woman with an effervescent personality. V^3 placed his guest of honor at his right hand, and Annie diagonally across the table. Genevieve was a few places down, between a bookshop owner from Kent and a BBC television producer.

After dinner, V^3 moved the party into the drawing room, with a loose semicircle of chairs placed around the author. Kate read from her latest book, *The Briar Club*, the same one that Genevieve and Annie had discussed after their first meeting at Herringbone's Rare Books. In the Q&A, it came out that the author had trained as an opera singer before she became a writer. She stood and sang a few bars from *The Marriage of Figaro* to prove her bona fides. The audience clapped as she took a bow.

When Quinn took her seat again, her cheeks were flushed and she took a sip of water. "Where's Annie?" she asked, scanning the faces.

Annie raised her hand.

"We had such an interesting talk on the patio about *The Diamond Eye*. Do you mind if I share it with the group?"

Annie nodded, blushing.

"Annie wanted to know how I captured the spirit of the Russian people in the book without making it seem grim and fatalistic."

"But the Russian people are grim and fatalistic, are they not?" Harrison asked. All eyes turned to him. "I mean, look at their history, their leadership, even today."

"I don't see it that way," Annie replied. "I think the Russian people are ready for a change."

Harrison scoffed. "How do you know that?"

"I am Russian." For the first time, Genevieve heard the accent in her voice and she saw that Annie was sitting up straight, glaring at Harrison. "I know what is in the hearts of her people—and it is not what you see on the news."

"What I see on the news is the New Dawn party rolling over a weak President," Harrison shot back.

V^3 intervened. "As this is not a political forum, I suggest we table this discussion for another time." He turned to Kate Quinn. "And it is also time that we let our distinguished guest get some rest." He stood, clapping, and the audience followed suit.

Harrison passed by Genevieve. "She's ready," he muttered. "Library in fifteen minutes."

Annie appeared at her side, staring after Harrison. "Do you know that man?" she asked. Her color was high and her eyes sparked fire.

Genevieve nodded. "I think you should meet him."

In the library, Harrison helped himself to some of V^3's scotch.

This is all moving too fast, he thought. *Maybe Don is right after all. I should close up shop and go home now before someone else gets killed.*

He let his eyes roam over the bookshelves, anything to distract his mind for a few seconds of peace. Like everything else in V^3's manor house, the library was designed to impress. Shelves extended from the floor up to the twelve-foot ceilings. On either wall, a brass rail supported an antique wooden ladder on wheels so that it could be moved along the stacks.

Asking the author to call out Annie had been a setup, as had his challenge of her response. And Annie had responded well. She had passion and conviction in her answer, but his instincts told him to slow down. Under normal circumstances, he would take weeks, maybe even months, to prepare Annie for what he needed her to do.

He had days, at best, and the price of failure was…Well, failure was not an option.

He walked to the French doors. Moonlight bathed the lawn and pond in silvery light, with the forbidding forest a dark backdrop. Behind him, he heard the door open and he turned around.

Annie entered first and Genevieve closed the door behind her. The young woman's gaze shifted between Harrison and Genevieve. She knew something was going on.

Harrison stepped forward and extended his hand. "Ms. Balinovich, my name is Harrison Kohl."

Annie took his hand. Her lips started to form a question, so Harrison cut her off.

"I work for the CIA," he said.

Annie's eyes widened in surprise, then narrowed. Her head snapped toward Genevieve, and Harrison spoke again. "Genevieve works for me."

Annie's jawline hardened. She turned toward the door, but Genevieve stepped in front of her. "Annie, listen to what he has to say. Please."

"I thought you were my friend," she hissed.

"I am your friend," Genevieve said softly, "but I also work for him." She tried to take Annie's hand, but the woman evaded her grasp.

"Don't touch me."

Genevieve held up her hands, palms out in a surrender gesture, and stepped back. Harrison held his breath. If Annie left now, they were done. Kaput. Finito. Don had been right after all.

Annie swept by Genevieve. Her back was rigid, shoulders tense. Her hand rested on the doorknob.

The door swung open, and V^3 stormed in. "Here you are! What did I miss?" He put his arm around Annie, escorted her back into the room, and deposited her on the leather sofa. "Have these two spies offered you a drink yet?" he asked.

Annie shook her head.

V^3 clapped his hands together. "What'll you have, Anoushka?"

The woman looked up at him. A slight smile traced her lips.

"Vodka," she whispered.

28

Langley, Virginia

"It can work, Don." Harrison's voice was full of confidence, but Don could tell it was strained. Harrison was trying to sell him.

"Oh, I agree," Don replied, "It *could* work, but the risk is greater than the reward. It's time to cut our losses."

"No!" Harrison gripped the backrest of a leather armchair, his fingers dimpling the shiny surface. "I need you to trust me on this one, Don. Please."

They were in Don's office, in the sitting area, but neither of them was using the furniture as intended. They were too anxious. Don glanced back at his desk, where the tear-off calendar showed the date. The Russian elections for the Duma were only days away. He studied his friend.

Harrison had lost weight. His face was gaunt and two bright spots of color showed high on his cheeks. It's my fault, Don thought. He'd asked too much and his friend was paying the price.

Harrison's eyes narrowed at Don. "What?" he asked shortly.

"When was the last time you slept?"

"When was the last time *you* slept?" he countered.

Don raised his cup of cold coffee. "Touché. But, Harrison, she's a civilian."

"Genevieve can get her ready," Harrison replied stubbornly.

"We're out of time." Don kept his voice calm, patient.

"She can do it, Don. She *wants* to do it."

Is that what's bothering me? Don wondered. That Anoushka had said yes to this dangerous operation without enough consideration of the risks? Overnight, she'd gone from hiding her identity as the daughter of a Russian oligarch to volunteering for an undercover mission to ruin her father. Was it too much to believe?

Recruited assets betrayed their country for many reasons: money, sex, patriotism, ego, hate. There were as many justifications as there were spies, but it was a case officer's job to figure out what made *their* asset tick. That process took time—and time was the one thing they didn't have.

"Why is she doing this?" he asked.

Harrison responded immediately. "She hates her father and what he stands for."

Don took one of the armchairs and gestured for Harrison to sit. He complied, but his butt was perched on the edge of the chair, and he leaned toward Don, elbows on knees. "What's the issue, Don? She's willing and we don't have another option. We're out of time." Harrison paused, gauging Don's reaction. "I can make this work."

Don sighed. "Walk me through it. Step by step."

"Anoushka reaches out to her father. She finagles an invite to meet him on his yacht in Mykonos," Harrison began.

"So long-lost daughter, estranged for years, reaches out to dear old dad and he just falls all over himself to invite her onto his yacht?" Don countered. "This guy is not father of the year. How do we even know he'll take her call?"

Harrison shrugged. "Anoushka says she can do it. If she can't, then we're done. You win."

"I win?" Don's cheeks flushed with anger. "I think you're forgetting yourself, Harrison. This is not about me winning. This is about protecting US interests. We're trying to stop a Russian coup and safeguard their nuclear arsenal. That's the desired end state." Don started to say more, but held back.

"What?" Harrison demanded.

Don gritted his teeth. Harrison needed to know everything that was at stake here. "It's also about your career."

Harrison went still. "What does that mean?"

"I'm sorry," Don said. "Look, I pushed this assignment on you and it has not gone well. Nobody wants to be associated with a failed operation. When things get dicey, everybody goes into cover-your-ass mode."

"Except for you."

Don couldn't tell if the pained expression on his friend's face was a smile or a grimace. "We go back a long way, Harrison. What kind of friend would I be if I gave you a shit assignment, then threw you to the wolves if it went sideways?"

Harrison licked his lips, thinking. "Did the Director tell you to kill this op?"

Don evaded the question. "I'm in charge of operations, Harrison. I put you in this job and I'll decide when, if, and how we end it."

"Answer the question, Don."

"She wants to kill it," Don admitted, "but she said the final decision was mine."

"And what do you want to do?"

Don deflected again. "Assume your asset gets an invite to Yuri's yacht in Mykonos. What happens next?"

Harrison eyed him. "She asks Daddy if she can bring a friend. Of course, he says yes. Anything to rekindle his relationship with his estranged daughter."

"And the 'friend' is Genevieve?"

Harrison nodded. "Iliana has agreed that one of her girls will use a knockout spray on Roland. We get access to the briefcase and clone it. Within fifteen minutes, we'll have Yuri's entire financial network mapped. Roland wakes up with his dick wet and figures he just had too much to drink and passed out."

Don sipped his cold coffee, grimaced, and set the cup aside. Even he had limits to what was acceptable to drink.

"And then?" he asked.

"Genevieve and Anoushka get off on the next island and we take down the Balinovich network."

"How do we get the spray to the girl?"

"I'll meet Iliana in Mykonos and brief her on how to use it."

Don frowned. "Why you?"

"Iliana insisted. She won't trust anyone but me."

Don walked to the darkened window and looked out. He had a partial view of the parking lot from his office. Yellow sodium lights bathed the empty lot in heavy amber tones.

He glanced at his watch. Nearly midnight. Again. He needed to set boundaries. Get better balance in his life.

"Is me meeting with Iliana a problem for you?" Harrison's question brought him back to the moment.

Don shook his head. "She needs to feel comfortable with the op. It's a reasonable request. I'm more worried about what happens once your assets are on the yacht. What if they're searched?"

Harrison stood next to Don. "The tech guys are geniuses, Don. The digital cloning device fits inside a mascara wand. It's inert until she activates it. It won't show up on a scan. And the spray bottle looks like perfume. It even dispenses perfume until you twist the sprayer head."

Don rubbed his face, bristles grinding against his bare palm. "Look, Harrison, our target from the beginning was Bogdan Rabilov. How did we get from taking down a dirty politician to using a civilian to compromise her own father? There's just too much risk here."

Harrison was silent for a long time. "If Rabilov is elected, Nikolay Sokolov is a dead duck and US-Russia relations go back to the bad old days of the Soviet Union. Is that what you want? Bogdan Rabilov with his hands on five thousand nuclear weapons? The way I see it, there's more risk in not doing it."

"No car bombs this time?" Don's attempt at humor was weak, but Harrison took it as an olive branch.

Harrison put his hand over his heart and attempted a smile. "Promise. No car bombs."

Don sighed. He could name a hundred ways this operation could go sideways, but it was always like that. These choices were never easy ones. What mattered was who was running the operation and their ability to think on the fly. Harrison was the best and he was invested in this option. If it was possible for this operation to be successful, he was the man to do it.

But at what cost? If he failed, his career was over. No one in the Agency would touch him again.

And I'll be the moron who gave the green light to the whole crazy operation, he thought. The Director had made it crystal clear: This was Don's choice. If the operation failed, Don was taking the fall. He liked to think he'd be able to survive it, but who knew?

Harrison put his hand on Don's arm. "Please. I can do this, Don. Trust me."

"Okay."

Harrison's tired face brightened with a smile. "You won't regret this one, boss. We will take these assholes down. I promise you."

Don shook his hand and looked his friend straight in the eyes. "Be careful, Harrison."

"I give you my word. If anything looks off, I'll pull the plug. Everyone is coming home. I promise."

29

Fetisov Arena, Vladivostok, Russia

The door of his armored limo closed with a solid *thunk*, cutting off the noise of the cheering crowd outside. The heavy car began to move. He heard the thin wail of sirens from his police escort.

"An excellent speech, Mr. President," said Gennady Abukamov, head of the Rosvgardia, from his position on the bench seat opposite Nikolay.

"You're a terrible liar, Gennady." Nikolay reached for a water and removed the cap with a vicious twist. "How many in the crowd were paid?"

"Mr. President, I—"

"Just tell me, Gennady. I'm not an idiot."

Abukamov shifted in his seat, then replied, "About a third, sir."

A third, Nikolay reflected, which probably meant half. The venue had held maybe five thousand, he guessed, so that meant that the President of Russia couldn't muster more than a few thousand supporters in all of Vladivostok.

Oh, how the mighty have fallen, he mused. Less than a decade ago, he'd been Commander of the Pacific Fleet, a decorated Admiral and much beloved in this city. He would have filled that stadium ten times over.

But now that the New Dawn was coming, people were afraid to support him.

He drained the bottle and twisted it in his hands, the flimsy plastic shrieking in protest.

Abukamov cleared his throat. Nikolay eyed him.

"More bad news, Gennady? You're like the fucking angel of death." His tone was bitter and full of self-pity, but he didn't care anymore. He just wanted this election to be over so he could get back to pursuing his agenda—what was left of it.

"There's been a development in the security arrangements for Bogdan Rabilov, sir."

"What sort of development?"

"We've intercepted some of Rabilov's phone communications. We think he's planning to leave the country," Abukamov said.

Nikolay stared at him. "That makes no sense. The election is almost here."

Abukamov nodded. "I agree, but indications are he's planning to leave tomorrow on Balinovich's private jet."

"To where?"

"We don't know that yet, sir. The communications are mostly encrypted and there is no flight plan yet."

"Where is Balinovich now?"

"He's on his yacht. In the Aegean Sea."

Nikolay sat back in his seat. "And you think that Rabilov is going to join him?"

"That's our working theory, Mr. President."

Nikolay stared out the window. His limo raced past traffic stopped by the local police, but none of it registered in his mind.

It was a little more than a week until the elections in the Duma, and the leader of the opposition party was leaving the country for a vacation. Nikolay wasn't sure that Rabilov had ever taken a vacation in his life. He was a politician's politician, always campaigning, always cutting a deal with someone somewhere at any time of the day or night.

And now he was about to leave the country? Why? What could possibly be more important than the upcoming election? Nikolay's supporters were behind in the polls, but only by a few points. Certainly not enough of a lead that Rabilov could declare victory and leave the country.

He could feel Abukamov watching him. He turned back to the Rosvgardia Chief.

"What does Galenkov say?"

Abukamov's face twisted with disgust. "The FSB is clueless, sir."

"Has Galenkov had any contact with Rabilov or Balinovich?"

The Rosvgardia Chief shook his head. "Not that we know of, sir."

Nikolay let out a long breath. At least a dozen times a day, he found himself missing Federov and the comforting certainty of the man's presence. But Federov was gone, probably dead by now. This was Nikolay's problem to solve.

"I could take Rabilov into protective custody, sir," Abukamov suggested. "If he leaves the country, my men cannot protect him."

Nikolay shook his head. That idea was so stupid it didn't even warrant a response.

Abukamov cleared his throat again.

"If you have something to say, Gennady, just say it."

"I think you should cancel all of your public appearances until after the election, Mr. President."

"That's absurd."

The car slowed and the Vladivostok International Airport came into view. High chain-link fences rose up from the grassy verge next to the highway. Beyond the fence, the flat expanse of the tarmac disappeared into the darkness, punctuated by runway lights. Nikolay's jet waited, the windows a long line of yellow portholes. The car slowed to make the turn into the airport gate.

Nikolay suddenly felt his energy drain away. It was an eight-hour flight back to Moscow. More than enough time to get a good night's sleep.

As he watched, three military vehicles roared up to the jet and skidded to a halt. Soldiers piled out, forming a cordon around the jet. Two working dogs emerged from one of the vehicles and their handlers led the animals up the jetway.

"What's going on?" Nikolay demanded.

Abukamov's face was profiled in the lights of the airport. "I've ordered a sweep of the plane for bombs. It will take an hour, Mr. President. I apologize for the delay." The limo halted next to the President's plane and the Rosvgardia Chief got out, leaving Nikolay alone.

He understood what Abukamov was saying now. Rabilov wasn't leaving the country for a vacation or because he was certain of the outcome. He was leaving the country so that he was far away from Russia, so he had an alibi if something happened to Nikolay.

Nikolay watched the military teams open the cargo bay and start to remove crates and luggage. This was going to take more than an hour. He wrapped his arms around his rib cage and settled deeper into his seat.

Nikolay's tired mind sifted through the possibilities.

A bomb on his plane…another assassination attempt…a massive demonstration that spins out of control. There were so many possibilities, too many to count.

Too many to care.

Nikolay closed his eyes and slept.

30

Mykonos, Greece

Harrison planned to leave no later than eleven thirty for his meeting with Iliana Semanova at two in the afternoon. He wanted plenty of time to run a full surveillance detection route before he met with the Russian madam.

Was he being paranoid? Absolutely, but he'd promised Don an operation where everyone came home safely, and he intended to keep that promise.

He surveyed the command post they'd set up in the large dining room of the safe house in the Faros Armenistis neighborhood of northern Mykonos. Michael Goodwin had set up four workstations. The first station monitored a high-flying overwatch drone. From fifteen thousand feet above the island, the UAV not only gave them a bird's-eye view of the town and the crowded harbor, but it also hoovered up all the electronic communications within sensor range.

The second workstation used an AI program to sort and catalog the electronic data. Ninety-nine percent of it was useless, and the one-tenth of one percent that they cared about—comms from Balinovich's yacht—was almost all encrypted. A bored operator scrolled through any communications that had been flagged by the AI for further investigation.

"Anything?" Harrison asked the operator.

She shook her head. "Target is still on the yacht. One outgoing call this morning to a Russian burner phone. Thirty seconds, all encrypted."

"Where was the phone?"

"Athens, near the airport. We don't have ID on the recipient."

Harrison returned to the first workstation and studied the yacht on the screen. The custom-built ship was forty meters long with a crew of eight and room for a dozen passengers. They'd gotten a copy of the specs from the original manufacturer, but they'd been warned that Balinovich had made aftermarket modifications in the ten years he'd owned the yacht. The crew were all long-timers, tight-knit, not easily turned in the short amount of time they had to work with.

He studied the tinted glass that wrapped the three levels above the waterline. If everything went according to plan, his case officer and their asset would be on that ship by this afternoon. Then it was out of his hands.

"Where are Genevieve and Annie?" he asked.

Michael led him to the third workstation. The screen showed a map of the city and two red dots in the Paralia Panangka waterfront area on the south side of Mykonos.

A second screen contained a running history of their electronic communications since they'd landed in Mykonos last night. Texts to each other, outbound mobile phone calls, and social media posts. They were tracking the phones of the two women, even though it was possible their phones would be taken once they boarded the yacht. Additional electronic trackers were too risky.

"Still at the beach," Michael responded. He checked his watch. "They'll be heading back to the Belvedere in the next half hour to get ready for lunch."

"Do our people have eyes on them?" Harrison asked.

Michael nodded. "Guy on the beach and a watcher in a café have visual contact. Number three is in the room across the hall at the hotel."

"Anyone search their room?" Harrison asked.

Michael shook his head. "As near as we can tell, they're clean."

Harrison chuckled to himself. Yuri Balinovich was covering the cost of the rooms at the Belvedere for Annie and Genevieve, but Uncle Sam was picking up the $5,500 per night tab for the security team across the hall. Don would have strong words about that expense, but when Harrison nailed Balinovich to the wall, all would be forgiven.

They assumed that the Russian oligarch had people watching the women since they'd left Paris together twenty-four hours ago. Genevieve and Anoushka had been advised to document the trip with as many pictures as possible. Michael's team ran facial recognition analyses on the constant stream of photos to see if they could match faces in the background and suss out the oligarch's security people. They hadn't found any evidence that the women were under surveillance.

Harrison grunted. The news was unexpected, but not unwelcome. When it came to security, Yuri Balinovich was not a man who left things to chance. Michael seemed to read his mind.

"Look, boss, either the target is playing three-dimensional chess or the women are clean," he said. "All evidence points to the latter."

Harrison glanced at the fourth workstation, which sat unmanned at the moment. "We're all set for data capture?"

Michael nodded with confidence. "I'll be handling that part myself. You get me a connection to the briefcase for thirteen minutes and I'll give you the world." He grinned broadly.

Harrison wished he felt that confident. He checked his watch and saw it was already past time to go. He regretted promising Iliana that he would deliver the knockout spray personally, but there was nothing he could do about that now. He needed her to be confident, and him acting as errand boy was a small price to pay.

With the tiny pump bottle in the breast pocket of a reversible jacket, Harrison set out from the safe house on foot. The house was located on a hill overlooking the harbor, surrounded by a maze of narrow streets. Mykonos was an old city with all different styles of houses mashed together in a hodgepodge of twisting lanes and alleys. He set off at a quick pace. It was only about three kilometers to his destination, but he'd cover at least twice that as he ran a full SDR.

He passed a one-story stone house that looked like it had been there since the time of Christ abutting a sleek modern glass-and-concrete structure. The only thing that tied everything together was color: Every structure was painted a blinding white that reflected the midday sun.

It was a pleasant afternoon, warm and breezy, but Harrison had work to do. He made a right at the first intersection, then another right as soon as possible. Halfway down the next block, he took a narrow set of stairs that let him out onto a commercial street at the bottom of the hill.

He ducked into a café and took a small table at the rear, ordering a coffee and pretending to look at his phone. For fifteen minutes, he watched the foot traffic on the street, studying the people as they strolled by, looking for familiar faces or people who seemed out of place.

Nothing.

That was a good sign, but not conclusive. A good surveillance team operated in a bubble around their target, rotating the "eye" of the team through multiple watchers.

Harrison stepped into the bathroom next to his table, reversed his jacket, put on a ballcap, and left through the rear entrance.

For the next ninety minutes, he continued the process of surveillance detection and came up clean every time. Satisfied, he arrived at the side entrance of Villa Rubini Mykonos at five minutes to two in the afternoon. He took the narrow stairs two at a time, passed through the lobby without removing his hat or sunglasses, and made his way to suite 110 on the first floor. He rapped his knuckles on the door and Iliana opened it immediately. She shut the door behind him and threw the deadbolt.

"Were you followed?" she asked.

Harrison advanced into the room. His eyes swept over the sitting area that led onto the partly shaded patio. Iliana's purse and a floppy sun hat rested on the coffee table. He stepped into the primary bedroom, then the en suite. They were alone. Satisfied, he returned to the main room.

"Did you find what you were looking for?" Iliana asked without bothering to hide the sarcasm in her voice. "Any spies under the bed?"

She was wearing what Harrison would call elegant beachwear. A red silk wrap was knotted across her chest, leaving her shoulders bare. Her skin was smooth and tanned, and her arms rippled with toned muscle. Iliana's blonde hair was pulled back into a messy chignon. The silk wrap clung to her body, ending mid-calf. Her feet were clad in sandals. She was a rich woman on vacation in Mykonos.

"I don't have much time," she said. "I'm expected back at Yuri's yacht by three."

Harrison dug the spray bottle out of his pocket and held it between his thumb and forefinger. The sleek silver case was about the size and shape of a stick of lip balm. He popped the flip-top with his thumb to reveal a tiny nozzle.

"That's it?" Iliana asked, holding out her hand.

Harrison touched the top. "Twist this twice to arm the pump. It'll release a single dose. Otherwise, it's just perfume."

"And that's enough?"

Harrison nodded. "The dosage is calculated for a man of Roland's weight and build. He'll be out for about twenty minutes, max. When he wakes up, he won't remember anything. As long as he doesn't see a clock before he gets knocked out, that amount of time shouldn't be suspicious." He cocked an eyebrow at Iliana. "I'm assuming your girl can distract him?"

Iliana rolled her eyes. "You Americans and sex. You need to get out more."

Harrison ignored the barb. He snapped the cap back in place and handed it to her. "Once it's used, rinse it off with water and throw it away. The drug will decay rapidly. Within a few minutes, it's just an empty spray bottle."

Iliana took the device. "And that's all she has to do?"

Harrison shrugged. "That's it. Once Roland is dosed, you let my officer into the room and she'll take it from there."

"How long will it take?"

"By the time Roland wakes up, she'll be long gone and his computer will be turned off. He won't suspect a thing."

Iliana crossed to the sliding glass doors that opened onto the patio. A pair of lounge chairs faced a magnificent view of the sun-drenched old harbor. Harrison joined her at the window. It was easy to pick out Yuri's yacht. The *Svarog* was the largest vessel in the harbor and moored well apart from the rest of the ships. Harrison spotted two figures patrolling the deck. Next to him, Iliana seemed restless.

"Is there a problem?" he asked in a low voice.

"No." Iliana shook her head, but when he looked in her eyes, he saw an uneasiness. Something had cracked her icy confidence.

"What is it?" he asked. "Tell me."

"Nothing." She attempted a smile and failed. "It's a risky game we're playing."

"It's fifteen minutes, Iliana. You want Bogdan destroyed? This is how we do it."

Iliana drew a deep breath. "I understand. We all have our part to play."

"Stay focused. By this time tomorrow, this will all be over."

"I need to go," Iliana said. "Mustn't keep Yuri waiting." She crossed to the table, picked up her hat and purse, and headed for the door. She looked through the peephole, then threw the deadbolt.

Harrison would have liked to be the one to leave first, but she was on the clock. He followed her to the door. "I'll give you a ten-minute head start before I leave."

Iliana turned. She put her hand on the back of his neck and kissed him on the cheek, murmuring something in his ear before turning back to the door.

"What did you say?" he asked.

Iliana's hand turned the door latch. She did not turn around. "I said I'm sorry."

The door flew open. A man leveled a Taser at Harrison and pulled the trigger. Two electrodes lanced out of the weapon, buried themselves in Harrison's chest. His body convulsed with fifty kilovolts of electricity and he toppled to the floor.

31

Mykonos, Greece

They sat down to lunch at half past two in the afternoon, at a restaurant called Raya. The shaded patio opened onto a white sand beach that ran down to the crystal-blue waters of the Mediterranean. Fifty meters away, a concrete jetty ran out into the old harbor. Yuri's motor launch, a sleek Sacs Rigid-Hull Inflatable Boat, or RHIB, was tied up halfway down the pier. The craft took up two spaces and Genevieve noticed that Yuri had left a member of his security detail on the jetty to ensure no other boats got too close.

Out in the harbor, separated from the other boats, Yuri's yacht, *Svarog*, lay at anchor. The forty-meter craft was three levels, gleaming white in the Mediterranean sunshine.

The maître d' led them to a table set for twelve. A flight of wineglasses fronted the white plates and polished flatware. "Will this be to your liking, sir?" she asked Yuri.

The oligarch took the chair at the head of the table. "Please send the sommelier over immediately."

"Of course, sir." The woman accepted the proffered tip from Ivan, Yuri's head of security. Ivan's face was still healing from the injuries he'd sustained during the car bomb that killed Dariya Rabilova. The bruises were gone, but the healing cuts still showed as angry red scars on his face and neck.

Genevieve looked around the patio. Every other restaurant in the area was packed, as was the interior of this one, but the patio was empty. She realized Yuri must have bought the entire section out for their late lunch.

"Please," Yuri called out. "Please, everyone, take a seat." His eyes found his daughter and Genevieve saw the question there.

Anoushka waited while Ivan pulled out the chair at her father's right hand. She sat and scooted in. Yuri gave her an encouraging smile, then his gaze strayed to Genevieve, who sat to Anoushka's right, and the smile tightened.

Genevieve knew about Yuri's history of bigotry. She was prepared for whatever might come out of his mouth, but so far the oligarch had been nothing but coldly polite to her. She suspected that Anoushka secretly relished the thought of rubbing her father's nose in the fact that after years of separation she had returned to him with a Black friend at her side.

Anoushka took off her sunglasses and draped her arm over Genevieve's shoulder. "Do you know, Papa? Genevieve has never been to Greece before. She's never even been on a yacht, much less one as magnificent as *Svarog*."

Genevieve felt Yuri's cold eyes rake over her. "Is that so? Well, then I am happy to be your first, Genevieve." He cocked an eyebrow to see if she would react to the double entendre, but a witty response evaded her and she found herself blushing.

So much for grace under pressure.

The awkward moment was broken by a cry from the end of the table. "I'm parched, Yuri. What are we drinking?"

The sommelier arrived and Yuri issued a series of rapid instructions in a low voice. The man nodded and hurried off. Buckets of ice appeared on either end of the table.

"Champagne?" a voice asked in a hopeful tone.

Yuri shook his head. "Don't be so predictable, Marko. We're starting with a very young, very fresh Galician Albariño. I know the owner and he is a remarkable man." He chuckled to make sure everyone got the joke that he was the owner of the winery.

The wine arrived, was approved by Yuri, and served. Genevieve could smell the citrus long before she took a sip. The drink was cold and sharp on her tongue. She saw Yuri watching her.

"What do you think of the wine, Genevieve?" Yuri asked.

"It's wonderful. Refreshing. Perfect for a hot afternoon at the beach."

He nodded with approval. "What sort of food would go well with this, do you think?"

Genevieve tried not to focus on the fact that she was trading wine tasting notes with a Russian oligarch and said the first thing that popped into her head.

"Ceviche."

Yuri's eyebrows went up. "Ah! Well played, Genevieve."

The waiters arrived with martini glasses piled with seafood ceviche. While the food was being served, Genevieve surveyed the other guests.

Four men with their escorts. Yuri had introduced three of them as a group, calling them business associates but not offering any names. The men were muscled with sloping shoulders and thick necks, chests matted with dark hair, eyes hidden behind dark glasses. They spoke among themselves in Russian, laughed at their own jokes, and ignored the other end of the table.

Their escorts were all stunning women. Mid-twenties with long, toned legs and impressive breasts. The women moved with the grace of models on a fashion runway and dressed the same way. They ate little, drank a lot, and spoke almost not at all.

The fourth man was Roland Buhler, and he stuck out like a pig in a beauty pageant. His limp blond hair was damp with sweat and his thin, sallow face was flushed from the heat. But behind the glasses that kept sliding down his nose were a pair of alert blue eyes. His escort was different, too. Short and curvy, she had small breasts and a perky upturned nose. Her bobbed hair was curly while the rest of the escorts all wore their hair straight and shoulder length. Alexandra was the only one of the women who had introduced herself to Genevieve and Anoushka.

Genevieve considered Alexandra more cute than beautiful, especially next to the competition in the room, but Roland appeared utterly enthralled with her. He spoke with her in German as they ate and she responded in the same tongue, often placing her hand on his arm as if to make a point. Roland enjoyed it when she touched him.

Genevieve tried to assess if the young woman would be able to complete the task they'd assigned her. As if she'd sensed her question, Alexandra looked across the table. Genevieve caught a glimpse of steel in her gaze and the moment filled her with confidence. This woman was a stone-cold operator.

Genevieve had never met Iliana Semanova, but the woman knew her people. This very risky operation was going to work. Genevieve could feel it.

She let her linen napkin slip off her lap, then bent to pick it up. She stole a glance under the table. The briefcase—the goal of this entire operation—stood between Roland's skinny white calves.

"Anoushka, how did you two meet?" Yuri said as Genevieve sat up.

"We met in a bookstore, Papa."

Yuri's reptilian eyes flickered over to Genevieve, then back to his daughter. She half expected to see a tongue come flitting out of his mouth. "I remember you always loved to read. Just like your mother." His expression softened for an instant, then his jaw tightened again.

"I have many of Mama's good qualities," Anoushka said quietly.

It was a remark intended to hurt her father, but Yuri ignored it in favor of announcing the next wine. A French pinot noir, lightly chilled.

"Do you approve?" Yuri asked Genevieve after she had tasted the wine.

Genevieve nodded. It was the lightest of reds, fruity and refreshing in the heat. "Do you own this winery, too, Mr. Balinovich?"

He eyed her over the rim of his glass, then gave a wolfish grin. "Not yet."

Ivan appeared at his elbow, mobile phone in hand, and bent down to whisper into Yuri's ear. Taking the phone, the oligarch walked to the far end of the empty patio before he spoke a word. He gazed out over the water toward his yacht as he listened. Less than a minute later, he was back at the table, smiling, wineglass in hand.

His mood was lighter, Genevieve noted, and she wished she knew what he'd learned on that brief phone call. She decided to probe Yuri's mood a bit.

"Mr. Balinovich—" she began.

"Please, call me Yuri," he interrupted.

"Yuri. The name of your ship. *Svarog*. What does that mean?"

Yuri turned to look across the harbor. His voice took on a wistful tone.

"Svarog is the God of Fire in Slavic mythology. I have a library full of Slavic classics and I love folklore and mythology. Perhaps my daughter inherited her love of books from her father as well as her mother."

Anoushka's expression hardened and she looked like she was about to say something. Thankfully, more food arrived.

Grilled fish and octopus, followed by stuffed grape leaves, then moussaka, and bite-sized baklava for dessert. Their flight of wineglasses disappeared and a single elegant shot glass like a crystal teardrop appeared before her. Genevieve had monitored her alcohol intake carefully so as to stay alert, and now she was glad she had. She knew what was coming next.

"Ouzo," Yuri announced. A waiter made the rounds pouring chilled shots into each glass. He finished at Yuri's place and Genevieve noticed that their host had two shot glasses in front of him.

Yuri's gaze lifted toward the far end of the patio and his face broke into a smile. "My friend, join us."

Genevieve's head swiveled to see who Yuri was calling out to, and her heart skipped a beat.

Bogdan Rabilov lumbered toward them. He was dressed in a loud beach shirt and dark pants. His fleshy face was red with the heat and he panted like a bull. He opened his arms and enfolded Yuri in a bear hug.

The two men parted, gripping each other's shoulders, grinning like schoolboys who shared a secret. Yuri broke away, handed one of the shots to Bogdan, and raised his own drink.

"A toast!" he cried. The air was full of the sound of scraping chair legs and groaning men.

Yuri looked at Anoushka. "My darling Anoushka, it is so good to see you after all these many years apart. Your presence here this afternoon is a balm to my soul. I would do anything for my family."

"Hear, hear," Bogdan grunted. The shot glass looked tiny between his thick fingers.

Yuri placed a hand on Bogdan's shoulder. "To family," he shouted.

"To family!" The shots tipped. The ouzo flowed.

The liquor burned in Genevieve's mouth and all the way down her throat. She felt the warmth spread through her very full stomach.

Yuri threw his shot glass to the stone patio, where it shattered. His Russian friends immediately dashed their own glasses to the ground. Anoushka put her glass back on the table and Genevieve followed suit.

Yuri held up his hands for silence. "Unfortunately, duty calls. Our cruise this evening is postponed. Ivan has arranged for hotels and transportation for everyone—"

"Papa!" Anoushka said. "What are you saying?"

Yuri took his daughter's hands in his. He kissed her cheek. "Thank you for reaching out, my darling. It has been a joy to see you, but I must go. Urgent business."

He tried to pull his hands away, but Anoushka held on. "No. Take me with you. Take us with you."

Yuri's face hardened into a scowl. "Not possible."

Anoushka released her grip. She crossed her arms. "I won't come back, Papa. If you leave me now, I won't ever come back to you."

Yuri did not hesitate. "Everything has a price, my dear. Even your love."

Genevieve watched Yuri, Roland, and Bogdan leave, flanked by Ivan's security team. They hurried across the white sand, down to the pier, and into the waiting launch.

32

Langley, Virginia

Don found himself staring at the mission clock on the front wall of the operations center inside the Special Activities Center. The foot-high red numbers read: 05:45:36. The seconds ticked by with infuriating regularity.

It had been nearly six hours since Harrison Kohl had disappeared and Don knew about as much now as he did then.

At 1400 local, Harrison Kohl entered a hotel on Mykonos for a meeting with Iliana Semanova. At 1415 local, Iliana exited. She left the hotel alone and got into a black Mercedes.

Neither Harrison nor Iliana had been seen since. The last location on their mobile phones was the Villa Rubini Mykonos.

At 1520 local, Bogdan Rabilov arrived at the Raya restaurant on the south side of the old harbor in Mykonos, where Yuri was lunching with his entourage. At 1550, Yuri and Bogdan, with Roland and the briefcase in tow, departed the island on Yuri's yacht, *Svarog*, leaving his guests on the beach, including his daughter, Anoushka, and Don's case officer.

All these events were linked—Don was sure of that—but how? If he wanted to find his people, he needed to solve the riddle. And the clock was ticking.

He glanced at his watch. Although he had little to report since their last call two hours ago, he owed the Director an update. Don slipped on a headset and dialed the secure line in her office.

"Don," Carroll Brooks answered. "What's the latest?"

He resisted the urge to sigh. "Not much. We've had people inside the hotel, but the place is clean. No sign of Harrison or Iliana."

The Director put words to Don's greatest fear. "Do you think we're dealing with a Khashoggi situation?"

On October 2, 2018, Jamal Khashoggi, a US-based Saudi citizen in exile, walked into the Saudi consulate in Istanbul. He sought official Saudi papers that would confirm he was divorced, which would allow him to marry his Turkish fiancée. He never exited the building. An investigation later determined he was murdered, dismembered, and his remains cremated over a period of three days.

Don took a moment to gather his wits. "I've considered that," he said in a low voice, "but that would require preplanning and time. The meeting was set only a few hours in advance and we were inside the building within two hours of his disappearance. Even a team of professionals would have a hard time disposing of a body that fast and not leave a trace. We've accounted for every person in and out of the building."

"He didn't just disappear, Don."

"I know." He tried to keep the frustration out of his voice.

"What about the Russian woman?"

"Iliana got into a car and now she's gone. Michael is accessing traffic cameras and video feeds from the area but it's not a centralized network. He's having to pull the data from each site separately. It's slow going."

"Do the Greeks have a surveillance system we can tap into? I can make a call."

"It's a tourist destination, Carroll. The island has 12,000 permanent residents and 250,000 visitors—and that doesn't include the refugees that come in by boat. It's a facial recognition nightmare."

The Director switched tacks. "How did Rabilov get there and why is he there at all?"

Don gave a humorless laugh. "He came in by ferry from Athens. As to why he's there? We don't have a clue. For all we know, this could be a vacation. We're backtracking his arrival to see if we can shake anything loose."

"Do you know any politician who would take a vacation the week before an election? Whatever's going on, it was important enough for him to come to see Balinovich in person." The Director paused. "Did Rabilov seem worried when he showed up in Mykonos?"

"On the contrary, Genevieve reports that they both seemed excited. She said they were thick as thieves when they left for the yacht."

"What could make two raging assholes happy days before an election?" The words were light, but Don heard the concern there. "I don't think we're going to like the answer to that question."

"You're worried they've got something planned to take down Sokolov?" Don asked.

"Plausible deniability," the Director replied. "That's the only reason I can come up with that would make a politician leave the country this close to an election. He wants to make sure that everyone knows he was a million miles away when the surprise goes down."

"We're not seeing any chatter in the usual channels," Don said. "The NSA says it's all quiet, nothing out of the ordinary."

"That makes me even more suspicious. They've got something big planned. I can feel it coming like a migraine."

One of the operators signaled to Don. "Carroll, I have to go."

"Listen, Don, I've got people working on the Moscow angle. You concentrate on finding our people."

Don hung up and joined the operator at her screen. Michael Goodwin's face filled the ultra-high-definition screen. His normally handsome features looked haggard with worry.

"I think I have something," Michael said. Without preamble, he put up a video image of Yuri's yacht, *Svarog*, in the Mykonos harbor. A small boat was alongside the stern, where men unloaded plastic crates. The men looked local and the boat was a battered shallow-draft working vessel with minimal freeboard and a wide deck.

"The little boat belongs to the harbor delivery service," Michael continued. "They take supplies from local businesses out to the big yachts. This is about thirty minutes before Yuri left the restaurant." He froze the image of two men pushing a large white container up a ramp onto the stern deck of the *Svarog*. There was a picture of a smiling fish on the side of the white container. "This is from the local seafood supplier."

Michael changed the screen. A white van bearing the same smiling fish logo drove onto a street in Mykonos. "This is the seafood supplier's van leaving the loading dock at the hotel where Harrison disappeared."

"Okay." Don's voice sounded strangled. A twisting sensation slithered in his guts.

"I'll cut to the chase, Don. I was able to track the van on traffic cams and ATM video feeds. It went from the hotel directly to the Mykonos Port Authority docks. I don't have a camera in there, but ten minutes after the van arrived, the delivery barge departed for Balinovich's yacht."

"Go on," Don said.

Michael went back to the video of the yacht. The large white seafood container landed on the stern of the yacht. A man in sunglasses and a polo shirt unsnapped the latches on the white lid and lifted it a few inches. He shut it and relatched it. He stepped toward the sliding glass door, pulling a mobile phone from his hip pocket.

Michael's voice was somber. "We always assumed the call that Yuri received in the restaurant was from Rabilov. I don't think so, Don. I think the call that Yuri got was from this guy on the boat."

Don tried to say something and failed.

"We're running down the van driver and the guys on the delivery boat, but that's gonna take time," Michael said. "I think Harrison is on that yacht."

Finally, Don found his voice.

"I'll call you back, Michael." He turned away and redialed the Director's phone. "I have an update."

"Let's hear it."

"Not on the phone. I need you here, Carroll. Now." He hung up.

33

Aegean Sea, 35 kilometers southeast of Limnos

Harrison woke in the dark, his heart racing. In his dream, he was drowning, his lungs starved for oxygen, but when he tried to open his mouth, nothing happened.

There was no air, but there was no water either...just *nothing*.

His lungs burned. He tried to scream but there was no sound. His brain hit the panic button. Adrenaline surged through his body. He fought, but his hands and feet refused to move. His eyeballs felt like they were about to pop out of his head.

He passed out.

When he opened his eyes again, he had no idea how long he'd been unconscious. The dream was gone, but his new reality was worse.

There was tape over his mouth, but he could breathe through his nose. His brain wanted to scatter in a thousand different directions, but he fought for control of his emotions.

Breathe, he told himself.

Three deep breaths later, he gave himself a new order.

Think.

He forced himself to take stock of his situation. He was sitting in a sturdy metal chair, hands and feet bound to the chair frame. Tape over his mouth. He tried to shift his body and he felt a damp chill in his crotch. He'd peed himself, but it had been a while ago.

His head throbbed with every beat of his pulse. It felt like the worst hangover he'd ever experienced. He knew he was dehydrated, but this was more. He'd been given some kind of drug.

His chest burned like he'd been stabbed. The pain sparked an avalanche of fresh memories.

Iliana at the door of the hotel…the door opening…unbelievable racking pain in his whole body…then nothing.

Iliana's mouth moving. The words: *I'm sorry*.

Arriving at the realization that he'd been betrayed might have taken Harrison fifteen seconds or fifteen minutes. He had no sense of time passing. The pitch darkness was disorienting and his brain was foggy from the drugs. It felt like he had to excavate every thought from his consciousness.

Kidnapped. His brain formed the thought at the pace of freezing water. *Where am I?*

Even though it was dark, he closed his eyes again to help him focus his senses.

He sniffed the air. Moisture, salt water, and something else. A cloying undertone. He knew the smell, his muddled brain tried to put a name to the scent.

Diesel fuel.

Under the soles of his bare feet, his numb toes detected a slight vibration in the floor. His bound body swayed ever so slightly in a hypnotic rhythm.

His brain collated the variables into an answer.

He was on a boat. A big boat, considering the rhythm of the rocking motion.

His breathing kicked up again, his pulse hammered. He struggled against the panic that threatened to overwhelm his drugged brain.

He was on *Svarog*. He was on Yuri Balinovich's yacht.

His mind made the leap on instinct, without facts to back up his conclusion, but he instantly knew it was true. He felt it deep in his guts.

There was a sound behind him, a door opened. He heard the muted whine of engines and the door closed again. Harsh fluorescent light stabbed into his eyeballs and Harrison slammed his eyelids shut against the pain.

The sound of a chair being dragged across the linoleum floor, the creaking of chair legs as the weight of a body settled onto the seat.

Harrison cracked his eyes open.

The man wore an untucked Hawaiian shirt with a garish crimson-and-gold flower pattern spewed like vomit across the material. It was open at the neck and a thick mat of gray chest hair ran up to the man's collarbone. His face was flabby, red with heat and sunburn, and bathed in sweat.

Bogdan Rabilov studied Harrison through half-lidded eyes. He panted heavily, shifting his bulk in the chair. The room reeked with the smells of sweat and alcohol.

Harrison forced himself to meet the man's eyes and the rage he saw there made him want to puke. He tried to empty his brain of all emotions, especially fear. He focused on his breathing.

Steady in, steady out.

The staring contest lasted for a long time.

"Do you know who I am?" Rabilov said finally.

Harrison shook his head.

Deny, deny, deny.

Rabilov smiled. He looked over Harrison's shoulder and nodded.

34

Langley, Virginia

The mission clock read 12:04:28. Harrison Kohl had been missing for twelve hours.

Don found himself watching the seconds tick away, each one a silent reminder that he was running out of time.

He heard the door to the ops center open and the click of Carroll's heels on the linoleum floor faded as she reached the carpeted section. She came up behind him.

"How we doing, Don?" she asked. Her voice told the story he didn't want to hear. Empathy, concern, but a note of resignation.

"How did it go at the White House?" he asked.

"I saw the Chief of Staff and the National Security Advisor."

Don bit his lip. Not a sympathetic audience.

"Don't read anything into it, Don," Carroll said gently. "The President was in another meeting about a different crisis."

"Does Cashman know we have a kidnapped case officer?" Don pressed.

"The President knows what we can prove with facts," Carroll returned. "We have a *missing* case officer."

"Carroll—"

"Don, if Balinovich took him, he's probably already dead," the Director said. "You know that."

"I don't think so," Don shot back.

"Okay, then *prove* it. Give me something I can use, Don."

He took a deep breath and held it.

"Don? I'm waiting."

He let the breath out slowly, like air leaking from a balloon, and forced his mind to slow down. He needed to put aside his concern for his friend and be persuasive.

He needed to do his job.

The mission clock read 12:06:02. Two more minutes had slipped away. Time was his enemy.

"Let's agree that we have reasonable cause to think that Harrison was transported to the yacht," he began.

"I agree it's possible his *body* was moved to the yacht," Carroll replied.

"There was no blood in the room, Carroll. No evidence of poison. If they killed him there, they were meticulously clean about it. Remember, they had very limited advance warning of the meeting site."

Carroll nodded. "Okay. It's possible he was still alive and he was moved to the yacht. Circumstantial, but plausible."

"We've had eyes on the yacht since it left Mykonos. If he's dead and they planned to dump the body at sea, they would have done it before they hit the Dardanelles. No one has thrown so much as a cigarette butt overboard. In fact, almost no one has been seen on deck, at all, throughout their transit north."

"They suspect they're being watched," Carroll said. "They put the body in the freezer and they plan to dump it later."

Don ignored her. "These yachts are like floating houses for rich people. They need a lot of resources to keep going. Food, fuel, water, fresh flowers—"

"Is there a point here, Don?"

"There is. These yachts set up supply deliveries well in advance. The next scheduled delivery for the *Svarog* was in Naxos, tomorrow. Naxos is thirty miles *south* of Mykonos." Don looked at the Director, waiting for her to fill in the details.

"Instead," she said, "Rabilov arrives, Yuri kicks off all his passengers, including his long-lost daughter, and he heads north."

Don nodded. "With Harrison on board," he added.

The Director narrowed her eyes at him. "Now what?" she said. "Let's assume you're right. Harrison is alive and they have him prisoner on the yacht. Where are they going?"

Don pulled up a map on the workstation screen. "They've entered the Dardanelle Straits, which takes them to the Sea of Marmara and Istanbul, Turkey." He traced his finger on the monitor, resting on Istanbul. "By the end of the day, if I'm right, they'll be approaching the Bosporus Strait."

"And then into the Black Sea," Carroll said. "You think they're going home."

"I do," Don said.

"Why?"

"Last night, Yuri Balinovich placed a call to one of his assistants in Moscow. The call was encrypted, of course, but we tracked the movements of the assistant after the call."

"And?" Don could tell he had her attention now.

"The first thing he did was book a flight from Moscow to Sochii. The second thing he did was contact a PR firm in Sochii. They immediately reserved a ballroom at the Rodina Grand Hotel for an afternoon event the day after tomorrow."

"What kind of event?"

Don shrugged. "We don't know, but they only booked the room for two hours in the middle of the afternoon."

Carroll said nothing for a full minute, thinking. "And your conclusion?"

"It's one week before the elections for the Russian Duma," Don said. "I think this is their 'October Surprise.' I think they're going to put Harrison in front of TV cameras and have him confess to the car bomb that killed Dariya Rabilova. They'll probably try to make the case that Sokolov is an agent of the United States."

The Director stared at the map.

"Harrison is alive, Carroll. We have to get him back."

"Don, look at the map," she said. "The *Svarog* is in the Sea of Marmara. That's Turkish waters. There is no way Turkey will let us launch a military operation to take down a Russian oligarch's ship in their territory. Even just asking permission, we might as well send out a press release. The Turks leak information like a sieve. Balinovich will know about it before we hang up the phone. And then…" She let her voice trail off.

And then Harrison will be dead for sure, Don finished the thought in his head.

"The Black Sea, then," Don said. "That's international waters."

"Don." The Director spoke calmly, as if she was explaining something to a child. "We're talking about launching a military strike in the next twelve, maybe eighteen hours at the most, right?"

Don nodded.

"That timeframe and mission parameters," the Director continued, "means we're talking JSOC or a SEAL team, and even then, we're cutting it close. Assuming we could get Tier One operators in place, do you really expect the President of the United States to authorize a raid on the private yacht of a Russian oligarch in the middle of the Black Sea? We're talking Russia's backyard here. It won't happen, Don. President Cashman is one of the biggest Russia hawks I've ever known, but even she won't give this a green light."

"How do you know that?" Don demanded. "We have to try."

The Director put her hand on Don's arm and lowered her voice. "I just spent two hours with her closest advisors, Don. They will not take this to her. It's not going to happen."

Don felt his face grow hot with angry blood. He was not going to leave Harrison in the hands of Yuri Balinovich. Whatever the cost.

"What if there was another way?" he said. "What if I had a way to do the mission without directly involving the United States?"

Carroll Brooks eyed Don for what felt like a lifetime. "Define what you mean by indirect involvement."

"The strike team I have in mind needs a launch platform," Don said. "Like a big-deck amphib. We have ships like that in the Black Sea right now. A US Navy Amphibious Ready Group is on deployment there. Three ships. Any of them would do."

"Launch platform only? No direct US military involvement?"

"They'd stay at least thirty kilometers away from the yacht. In international waters the whole time."

"How much?" the Director said.

Don shrugged. "This op won't cost the US taxpayer a dime."

The Director's eyebrows went up. "Do I want to know the details?"

"I'm calling in a favor. Harrison Kohl is a man with many friends."

The Director sighed, then nodded. "You win, Riley. I'll get you the big-deck. You bring our man home."

"Yes, ma'am."

35

Dardanelles Strait, Turkey

The tape came off Harrison's face in one swift, painful motion. Harrison's eyes watered. He tried to lick his lips and tasted blood. The air on the skin of his raw mouth felt like his lips were on fire.

Ivan balled up the bloody duct tape and threw it into the garbage can. He smiled at Harrison. "Nothing but net," he said in halting English.

Bogdan was sitting in a chair like a hairy, sweaty Buddha. He laughed at the joke as he watched Ivan set up shop.

Harrison watched too, with much more fear and much less interest. His stomach, empty as it was, roiled with acid.

Ivan had an angry red scar across his right cheek and shiny red patches on his forehead where the burns had healed following the car bomb. He hummed to himself as he worked.

He removed a leather bundle from a small satchel. With a flourish, he untied the bundle and rolled it out across the lower bunk. Stainless steel tools gleamed in the harsh light. Pliers, knives, scalpels.

Ivan looked up at Harrison. "Don't worry. I always sterilize my tools," he said in Russian.

Bogdan roared with drunken laughter, slapping his knee.

Ivan's next dip into the satchel yielded a black hard plastic case the size of toiletry kit. He arranged it on the bunk next to the leather toolkit, but did not open it. He stepped back, folded his arms, and nodded to Bogdan.

The big man reached between his thighs and grabbed the chair seat, dragging it forward until he was in front of Harrison. Their knees almost touched.

Bogdan inspected Harrison's face, licking his own lips in involuntary sympathy at Harrison's damaged mouth.

"Do you know who I am?" he asked.

Harrison shook his head.

Bogdan shrugged. "Then I'll tell you. I'm a grieving father. My daughter was killed recently."

His beady eyes searched Harrison's face. Harrison creased his brow to show confusion. "I'm sorry for your loss," he said.

Bogdan's backhand came out of nowhere. Harrison's head snapped to the side like he'd been sideswiped by a pickup truck. Pain exploded in his head. His eyes bled tears and fresh blood spilled from his mouth. Bogdan's paw closed around his throat.

"You tried to kill *me*," Bogdan screamed, his face only centimeters from Harrison's. Breath that reeked of sour vodka washed over him. The hand closed tighter and Harrison's air supply closed off.

"You tried to kill me and you killed her instead. She was innocent. She was..."

All the color leached away from Harrison's vision, and his field of view tunneled down to a pinpoint. As his brain teetered on consciousness, he thought he heard distant shouting.

Then the pressure was gone. Air rushed into his open throat and he gagged with relief. Slowly, he lifted his head to find Ivan's back to him, holding Bogdan down in his chair with both hands.

Finally, Bogdan's shoulders sagged and he pushed Ivan's arms away. "Okay, I won't touch his face again. I get it."

Ivan's stance signaled indecision, but he finally stepped away.

Bogdan glared at Harrison. "They tell me I'm not supposed to touch your face. They want to make sure you look good on camera when you testify in court."

Harrison felt his insides seize with frozen dread. "I don't know what you're talking about."

"You will," Bogdan assured him. "We have some time to practice. I want to make sure your performance is perfect." The old man paused. "And I want payback for my daughter, you son of a bitch."

"I'm sorry for your loss, sir." Harrison tried again, trying desperately to hold down the panic he felt to his core. "But I don't know what you are talking about. I'm an American citizen on vacation in Greece. You've made a horrible mistake."

Bogdan's expression shifted. He put his hand on his chin. "An American citizen?" His eyebrows lifted. "Ivan, I think we've made a terrible mistake."

Harrison nodded. "Yes."

Bogdan touched Harrison's cheek where he'd hit him. "Does it hurt?"

"Yes."

"Ivan!"

"Yes, Mr. Rabilov?"

"Give this man something for the pain."

"Right away, sir." Ivan turned to the bunk bed and opened the black plastic case. He removed a syringe filled with yellow liquid. He pulled off the cap and turned to Harrison.

"You might feel a little sting." Ivan drove the point of the needle into Harrison's chest and slammed the plunger down.

Harrison screamed with the pain of the shot. Then the effect of the drug hit home.

His eyes snapped open. His arms and legs went rigid. It felt like every nerve in his body had been dipped in acid, every sensory organ turned up to eleven.

"How does that feel?" Bogdan asked with a vicious smile smeared across his face.

He might have been whispering, but it sounded like a bullhorn in Harrison's ear.

The big man placed his huge hand on Harrison's knee and he gasped with the sensation.

"Let's start over, Mr. Kohl."

The grip tightened, heavy fingers digging into the flesh of Harrison's thigh.

Deny, deny, deny...

Harrison began to scream.

36

USS *Fort Lauderdale* (LPD-28), Batumi, Georgia

Commander Brett Hardy had just finished his afternoon walk-through of the engineering spaces and he was preparing to do his topside tour. Given the weather, going outside would require rain gear.

"I'd be better off with a wetsuit," he muttered.

He stood in the open doorway of a watertight hatch, looking over the gunwale across the harbor. Rain came down in ragged sheets and the wind whipped up whitecaps in the open water. Swells rolled in from the Black Sea, crashing into the concrete pier and rippling down the jetties.

The *Fort Lauderdale* rocked gently under his feet. For a ship this size—nearly seven hundred feet long and with a hundred-foot beam—this weather was more an inconvenience than a danger. The weather forecast called for two more days of rain and wind, with a high-pressure system moving in just about the time they were set to get underway.

He shifted his vantage point so he could better see the city of Batumi—or try to, at least. The metropolis was a scattering of watery lights shining through a veil of heavy rain and fog.

Still, rain or no rain, he was looking forward to getting to see the city when he had liberty tomorrow. He'd have a beer or two, walk the streets of

Batumi, and take a few selfies along the way. Reports from the crew that had already been on liberty said the Georgian city lived up to its nickname as the Las Vegas of the Black Sea.

Hardy sighed. Duty was calling his name. Might as well get this over with, he thought. He tugged his ship's ballcap into place, flipped up the hood of his raingear, and stepped outside.

It was like walking into a warm shower. He trudged through the water sluicing across the deck to the bow of the ship, inspected the lines that secured them to the pier for damage, and peered over the gunwale. The lines were securely tied to the white-painted bollards on the jetty and he could see nothing unusual in the rain-pocked waters.

He turned back and looked up. The bridge windows looked like a line of tiny black squares in the flat front of the forecastle. This was Hardy's fourth sea tour and the largest ship he'd ever served on.

Although he'd only been on board three months, he knew that he wanted to command an amphib like this one someday. The Aegis destroyers were faster, had more firepower, and were more fun to drive, but the mission of ships like the *Lauderdale* was to put Marines and materiel on the beach. They took the fight to the enemy. They lived in the middle of the action. To Hardy's mind, that mission was more interesting than firing anti-ship cruise missiles at a target a hundred miles away.

The 1MC speaker suddenly blared to life, breaking him out of his reverie. "XO, lay to Radio. XO, to Radio, sir."

Hardy jogged back toward the open doorway, already frowning. You didn't use the shipwide intercom to call the Executive Officer unless it was an emergency.

He caught the edge of the doorjamb and swung toward the nearest ladder, scrambling up the steep steps. The duty radioman held the door of the comms center open with his work boot.

"Secure call from NATO HQ, Mr. Hardy," he said. "They asked for the captain, but I said he was on shore, so he wanted to talk to you."

"Who?" Hardy asked, still trying to catch his breath.

"SACEUR, sir."

"No, I mean who was on the phone?"

The radioman stared at him and for the first time Hardy noticed the young man was sweating. "It's him, sir. Well, it's his aide, but he wants to speak to the captain—or you, now, I guess."

Hardy held up his palm. "Stop, Petty Officer Robbins. You're telling me that Admiral Limner, Supreme Allied Commander of Europe, is on the phone. For me?"

Robbins nodded.

Hardy picked up the receiver and punched the button to connect.

"Commander Hardy speaking."

"You're the XO of *Fort Lauderdale*, Commander Hardy?"

"I am, sir."

"Standby for the Admiral."

There was a click and the familiar warble of secure digital communications, then a new voice came on the line. Hardy had never met Admiral Limner, but he'd seen him speak a dozen times and he pictured the man's face in his mind's eye.

"Hardy, this is John Limner, how are you this fine Navy day?"

"I'm...I'm good, sir."

"I understand Andy is on shore and you're in charge."

"Yes, sir, Captain Dyson is on an archaeological tour outside the city. I expect him back later this evening, sir."

"Well, that's unfortunate."

"Sir?"

"Listen carefully, Hardy. In the next ninety minutes, six trucks will show up pierside. You are to load their cargo immediately into a secure area of your hangar deck. Once loaded, you will bypass force protection standing orders and get underway. Once at sea, you will receive further orders. Do you understand these instructions so far?"

Hardy's head reeled, but he said, "Yes, sir."

"Good. I know what you're thinking, Hardy. I can't go to sea without the captain and I need my crew, right?"

"Yes, sir."

"Do you know what the word *discreet* means, Hardy?"

"It means to do something without making a fuss about it."

"Well said. That's what I want you to do here. I want you to do everything I just told you, but I want you to do it discreetly. In the next hour, you call the captain and recall all the crew that you can find, but if they're not on board by the time you have the cargo secured, you leave them on the beach. Understand?"

"Yes, sir."

"Do not fail me here, Hardy. If I read an article in the paper tomorrow that the US Navy scrambled a ship from a Black Sea port on a secret mission, then you have failed your country."

"I understand, sir. I will be discreet."

"I have full confidence in you, Hardy. One last thing: You do not hold your departure for anyone, and that includes the captain. If he can't get back in time, then you leave without him."

"I understand, sir."

"Any further questions?"

Hardy racked his brain and came up empty. "No, sir."

"Then let's not waste your precious time. You've got work to do, Hardy."

The Admiral hung up.

Petty Officer Robbins watched him from the rear of the small room. "What's up, XO?"

"Robbins, get on the 1MC. Muster an all-hands meeting on the hangar deck in ten minutes. Everyone, no exceptions, whether they're part of the duty section or not."

"Marines, too, sir?"

"Marines are people, too, Robbins. Get moving."

Hardy looked at his watch. 1505. The captain wasn't due back until 2200 hours. He took out his mobile and dialed the captain's number.

"Dyson," the captain said.

"XO, sir. We have an emerging situation, sir. I need you to come back ASAP."

At the use of the code word *emerging*, the captain's voice sharpened with concern. The word meant emergency sortie.

"I'm on my way, Brett."

"Sir, time is of the essence."

"I understand. I'll be back by evening meal."

Dinnertime on board was 1800. If the cargo arrived as planned, the

Lauderdale would be long gone. Hardy tried to think of a way to tell the captain what was going on without just saying it out loud.

"We're having dinner early tonight, Captain. I may need to save you a plate."

There was a long pause on the other end. "I'll be there as fast as I can, XO."

"Thank you, sir."

Hardy hung up and jogged through the ship, ducking through hatches and riding the rails down the steep ladders. He arrived on the hangar deck to find a mass of about 150 ship's crew and about forty Marines. When he came out of the doorway, one of the senior chiefs called out, "Attention on deck!"

There was a buzz in the air and Hardy knew that the rumor mill was already churning. Good, he could use that energy to his advantage.

A row of Marine Humvees stood in front of the assembled men and women, so Hardy climbed on the hood of the nearest one.

"At ease." His voice echoed in the high overhead of the hangar deck. "I'll be brief because we have a lot to do and not a lot of time to do it. In the next hour, we will be receiving six trucks with cargo. Once we have the cargo on board, the ship will get underway. Immediately."

A ripple swept through the assembly. Hardy held up his hands. "I know what you're thinking. Two-thirds of the crew is on liberty, including the captain. We can't get underway without them. Well, I'm here to tell you that we can, and we will. You're all trained to get the job done—if we work together."

Hardy paused, scanning the sea of upturned faces. He felt like he needed to say something inspirational, but he was drawing a blank. He clapped his hands together.

"That's it, people. Make preparations to get underway immediately. We've got a ton of work to do and not a lot of time to do it."

Hardy flagged the Deck Division Officer and the Marine Combat Cargo Officer to consult about loading their cargo and securing shore facilities. By the time he left the hangar, the cargo team was already maneuvering the loading ramp to the pier.

Hardy's head was filled with the thousand details he needed to address before a ship of this size left the pier. He took the open deck walkway to the bridge. It was still raining hard. The Admiral wanted discreet, he reminded himself. This miserable weather is my friend tonight.

When he arrived on the bridge, he looked for the designated Officer of the Deck for Sea and Anchor detail.

"What's our status, Mr. Hampstead?" Hardy said as he stripped off his rain slicker.

"Diesels are online, XO. Engine room reports ready to answer all bells. Quarterdeck watch is secured, sir. Senior Chief Masterson reports that we'll have the brow off the ship in ten minutes."

"He was able to get a crane operator in this weather?" Hardy asked.

"Ask me no questions, I'll tell you no lies, sir. The Senior Chief knows a guy in every port."

"Very well, Mr. Hampstead. Keep me posted on underway preps. I want to know the minute we have that cargo aboard."

"Aye, sir."

Hardy stepped toward the bridge wing and stood inside, just out of the pouring rain. He pulled out his mobile phone and dialed the captain's number.

"Dyson," came the answer.

"Captain, XO. What's your status, sir?"

The network glitched, making Hardy miss the next few words. "Say again, sir."

"The rain washed out the road up ahead. I'm at least three hours out, Brett."

Hardy cleared his throat. "Captain, we have orders."

The line was silent for so long that Hardy wondered if he'd lost the connection.

"Sir? Are you there?"

"I'm here. Are you saying what I think you're saying, XO?"

"Yes, sir."

He heard the captain swearing in the background. This was a commanding officer's worst nightmare. His ship ordered to get underway in an emergency and he can't be there. Dyson had spent over twenty years getting to this point in his career. The situation was out of his control, but that didn't matter. The captain was responsible for everything that happened on his ship. Everything.

Dyson came back on the line. "Good luck, Brett. I mean it."

"Thank you, sir."

Hardy ended the call and turned to find Hampstead waiting.

"XO, the cargo is on board. The trucks are back ashore and the loading ramp is secured. Per your orders, there's a Marine guard posted. The ship is ready to get underway, sir."

"Very well, Mr. Hampstead. Set the Sea and Anchor detail." As the 1MC announcement rang throughout the ship, he stole a look at his watch. The time was 1628. It was hard to believe what he and his crew had accomplished in less than two hours. He felt a swell of pride. The bridge filled with watchstanders and the air buzzed with excitement.

"Sea and Anchor detail is set, XO," Hampstead reported.

"Very well." Hardy could feel the tension in the air. Outside, the rain lashed the steel skin of the ship. None of them knew what was going to happen. Hell, he didn't even know. He raised his voice. "Attention on the bridge. This is Commander Hardy. I have the conn."

"XO has the conn," came the replies from the watchstanders.

"Single up all lines, Mr. Hampstead," he ordered.

37

Moscow, Russia

The timepiece on Nikolay's desk read five minutes past midnight. The lights were turned low in the private office of his residence a few blocks from the Kremlin, giving the room a deceptively cozy look. The map of the Russian Federation, hand-painted on the wall of the office, was half-hidden in mysterious shadow.

Seated behind his desk, Nikolay yawned.

"I apologize for the late hour, Mr. President," said Gennady Abukamov, standing at ease before Nikolay's desk. "I thought it best to bring this to you immediately."

Nikolay nodded. The hour was late, but unfortunately Nikolay had not been sleeping. He'd been in bed, but his eyes had yet to close this night. Most nights were like that now and lack of sleep left him foggy in his thoughts.

But he had no intention of sharing his insomniac woes with the head of the Rosvgardia. He focused on the screen of the tablet.

A stock photo of a US Navy ship, blocky gray hull etched against a cloudless blue sky on a moderate sea. A snow-white bow wave frosted the slate-gray sea. He recognized it immediately as a *San Antonio*-class amphibious transport dock, used to carry US Marines and their equipment from ship to the shore. The aft third of the ship had a well deck that could be flooded down to allow amphibious landing craft to deploy out of the stern of the ship.

This ship, the USS *Fort Lauderdale*, LPD-28, had been on a port call in Batumi, Georgia, on the Black Sea. Nikolay hated the fact that the Americans felt they had a right to operate their warships inside the Black Sea, but after the devastating naval losses during the war in Ukraine, he had no say in the matter. International law said that large portions of the Black Sea were international waters and open to all nations, including the American warships.

"You're saying this ship got underway last night?" he asked Gennady.

"Yes, sir, at approximately seventeen hundred hours local, Mr. President."

Nikolay stewed. That meant for almost eight hours no one in his military chain of command or his security services brought this matter to his attention.

His thoughts took a dark turn. Unless they had been blocked from doing so by the Rosvgardia. Maybe Abukamov was making sure that he was indispensable to the President.

Games within games, he thought, then moved on. He would deal with that later. Right now, he needed to make sense of what this sudden ship movement meant.

"And you're saying their commanding officer was left behind?" he asked, not hiding his skepticism.

"Yes, sir. Also, over four hundred crew members as well as two hundred and fifty Marines."

"And no other ships? Just this one amphib put to sea suddenly?"

Abukamov nodded.

Nikolay leaned back in his chair, pressing his neck against the coolness of the leather head rest. None of this made sense. If this was some sort of drill, why would they leave their captain and hundreds of sailors and Marines behind? What kind of emergency would require a US Navy ship to get underway without their captain?

Nikolay had commanded ships in his naval career and knew the incredible pressures of command. As a captain, you were responsible for everything that happened on your ship, no matter how small. Every accident, every broken pump, every eighteen-year-old seaman who drank too much on liberty and got into a fight. You owned it all, good, bad, or somewhere in the middle. Command of a naval ship was an emotional pressure cooker. No captain in his right mind would allow his ship to get underway without him.

And yet it had happened, which meant that the Executive Officer had orders from above. Urgent orders.

He consulted the tablet again. "What is their heading?"

"Northwest, Mr. President. They established that heading as soon as they left port and have maintained it."

As a matter of habit, Nikolay still scanned the weather reports every morning and the mention of the Black Sea tickled his memory. He switched screens on the tablet and called up the weather report.

"There's a tropical depression in the Black Sea, Gennady," he noted.

Abukamov looked at him with a blank stare.

"You didn't think to mention that fact?" Nikolay asked.

"No, sir."

"Why would a ship leave port without her captain during a storm, Gennady?"

"I don't know, sir."

Nikolay pinched his lip in concentration. He could think of only three possibilities. The *Fort Lauderdale* had suffered some sort of accident and left port to cover it up. The Americans had a weather forecast that indicated imminent danger if she remained in port during the storm. Or they were sailing toward a rendezvous with another ship.

Nikolay opened up a new screen on the tablet and called up the Automatic Identification System used to track ships around the world. Any ship above a certain tonnage that operated in international waters was required to operate an AIS beacon.

The screen updated slowly. Ships showed as colored arrows, indicating their speed and direction. He immediately noted the speed of the American amphibious ship.

"They're making nearly twenty knots, Gennady," he said.

"Yes, sir." He could tell by the tentative tone in the Rodvgardia Chief's voice that the fact meant nothing to him.

Nikolay huffed in frustration. Maintaining that kind of speed in a heavy sea would be a punishing ride for the amphib transport as well as a tremendous fuel burn. Navy ships did everything possible to conserve fuel. That kind of maneuver meant the acting captain had urgent orders, but for what?

He studied the updating screen. Most of the sea traffic had changed their tracks to navigate around the storm except for three ships. Two were oil tankers headed south to the Bosporus and Turkey.

The third was more interesting to Nikolay. It too was operating at a relatively high speed for the heavy weather. He touched the icon to give him more information. The only additional data was the AIS ID number, which told him it was privately owned.

That only piqued Nikolay's interest more. He opened another tab and logged into a Russian naval database. In front of him, Abukamov cleared his throat to remind him of his continued presence.

"Wait," Nikolay growled without looking up, "I'm doing your job for you, Gennady. The next time you rush to bring me a report, get all the facts first."

He typed in the AIS number and waited. The screen cleared and an image of *Svarog*, Yuri Balinovich's yacht, filled the screen.

Nikolay spun the screen so that Abukamov could see it. He went pale. "I had no idea, Mr. President."

"Obviously," Nikolay snapped, acid in his tone. "This is not a coincidence, Gennady. Where is Balinovich coming from? What is his— Never mind. I'll do it myself."

He turned the tablet about and used the AIS app to retrace the track of the yacht. He stared at the screen.

"Where is Bogdan Rabilov right now, Gennady?" he asked.

The Rosvgardia Chief shifted his feet. "His last known location was Athens, Mr. President. We lost him there."

"When?"

"Day before yesterday, sir."

Nikolay rubbed his neck. The muscles in his shoulders felt like they'd been tightened with a torque wrench. "What if I told you that the day before yesterday, Yuri Balinovich sailed from Mykonos, Greece, on his yacht. That was his last port of call. Do you think it's possible that Rabilov managed to get from Athens to Mykonos and join Balinovich?"

Abukamov swallowed. "I'll find out, sir."

"I'll save you the trouble," Nikolay hissed. "It is possible."

He smashed his fist down on the tablet. "And I'm willing to bet Yuri and Bogdan are sailing home. In a storm. At a speed that would be very uncomfortable for the passengers of a luxury yacht. And it appears that they are being intercepted by an American ship." He posted his fists on the desk and stood. "What I want to know, Gennady, is *why*? What do the Americans know that I don't?"

"I'll find out, sir."

Nikolay sat down again. He took a measured breath. He could smell Abukamov's sweat. Good, Nikolay thought, at least somebody still feared him.

"Put the Black Sea fleet on alert. Get me surveillance assets on that yacht. Drones, satellites, whatever you can find—and do it yesterday, Gennady."

"Yes, sir."

Nikolay looked up. "Get out of my sight."

Abukamov started to beat a hasty retreat from the office when Nikolay had another thought.

"Wait! Don't do anything. I'll handle this myself." Abukamov started to speak, but Nikolay put up a hand. "I was angry, Gennady. My apologies."

Abukamov stared at Nikolay in confusion.

Nikolay gave him a tight smile. "Go get some sleep. You've done well tonight. Thank you."

As the office door closed, Nikolay picked up his phone and dialed a number from memory.

Nikolay felt a sudden buzz of emotion—part fear, part excitement. Something was happening. Rabilov was about to make his move. Knowing Bogdan, it would be big and splashy—and risky. And the Americans knew something, too.

He wanted a drink, but that was a bad idea. He needed a clear head. He needed to be smart. He needed to outthink his opponent if he wanted to win. This was his moment.

What would Federov do? he wondered.

Create chaos. There is opportunity in chaos.

But how? He could not trust his FSB Chief and Abukamov was clearly out of his depth. He needed to work outside his circle of advisors. Work with people he trusted. Friends.

It took fifteen minutes to get Admiral Kutenov on the secure line from Sevastopol. Nikolay had known Vasily Kutenov since grade school. They had come up through the ranks together and his old friend was nearing retirement. For his unwavering loyalty, Nikolay had rewarded him with command of the Black Sea Fleet, a posh assignment. It was time to call on that loyalty.

"Good morning, Mr. President," the Admiral said, his voice still rough with sleep. "It's one in the morning, which means you are either drunk-dialing me to reminisce about our wasted youth, or there is an emergency that I don't know about yet."

Nikolay felt a soft stab of loss for the life he'd once led and friends like this man. "Good morning, Vasily. Our youth was indeed wasted, but I did not call to reminisce. I need to know which submarines you have at sea right now."

Nikolay could hear Kutenov shuffling papers. After a few seconds, he rattled off hull numbers. Nikolay stopped him.

"The *Krasnodar*," Nikolay interjected. "Is Morosov still in command?"

"One of our finest submarine captains, Mr. President."

"I agree. Maxim will do well for what I have in mind."

38

Black Sea, 210 kilometers southwest of Sochii, Russia

After the pilot's first attempt to land the MV-22 Osprey on the deck of the USS *Fort Lauderdale*, Don considered renewing his trust in organized religion. He tried to think of a prayer that might be suitable for the moments before he died in a fiery plane crash and came up blank.

His head ached and his neck muscles were on fire. With the oversized ballistic helmet, which he'd worn at the suggestion of the crew chief, he probably looked like a bobblehead—he certainly felt like one. Normally, no one would be wearing protective headgear as a passenger, but on this flight even the crew chief had donned the bulky helmet.

Like at least half the men on the flight, Don had long since surrendered the contents of his stomach into an airsick bag and the cabin smelled like a porta-potty after twelve hours at a Grateful Dead concert.

Desperate for anything to take his mind off his roiling stomach, Don twisted to look out the window at their destination. The deck of the amphib landing ship was a square patch of light the size of a matchbook in an otherwise dark and seething ocean.

And it didn't sit still, either. Even from a few thousand feet up, the little square of light shifted and moved. When they got closer, it looked to Don like they were trying to land on a roller coaster. The big ship sloped down into the trough of a wave, then angled up the other side.

It wasn't like the tilt-rotor plane was stable, either. It pitched and bucked in the wind just as much as the ship.

After the second attempt, Don turned away from the window, where he found the dark eyes of Akhmet Orazov studying him. The two men had never met. The one attempted meeting in Turkey at the height of the Central Asian resistance movement had never happened because Akhmet refused to leave the combat zone.

Don supposed he should have some sort of resentment about that snub, but he felt nothing. It was impossible to be annoyed with a man who was willing to risk his life just because Don told him Harrison was in trouble. Orazov hadn't even hesitated at the request.

And now, in the garish red interior lights of the MV-22 cabin, where they were being bounced around like a pair of corks in a washing machine, Don searched that face for any signs of regret. He found none.

The team of eleven men Orazov had brought with him were a motley crew. Don heard at least five different languages and dialects in the brief time they'd spent in Trabzon Airport in northern Turkey.

These were not young men. The youngest, Don guessed, was mid to late thirties, but most were at least a decade older. Like Orazov, they were hard men, with wind-burned faces and wiry physiques and more than a few scars on their arms and faces.

As different as they seemed in dress and language, there was one common trait: their unwavering respect for Orazov. They called him Ussat, but when Don asked Orazov about the name, he'd ignored the question.

Don heard the pitch of the rotors increase again and shifted his gaze to the window behind Orazov's head. The rotors on each wing slowly tilted skyward and the aircraft descended. It bucked and heaved, throwing Don's bulk against the three-point harness.

Don was not a pilot, but he sensed they were descending faster on this run. The pilot understood that scrubbing the mission was not an option.

He risked another glance out the window and the square of light was coming into focus at an alarming rate of speed. Instinctively, Don tensed his body and gripped the straps on his chest.

He could see the painted markings on the deck now, and a man waving two lights. The engines screamed, the wind screamed back. The aircraft continued lower without hesitation. It hovered for a moment before slamming onto the deck with enough force that Don's jaws clicked together.

The crew chief was out of his seat as soon as they made contact. The ramp at the rear of the craft started lowering and he shouted for them to move. Warm wind and rain blasted into the cabin, washing out the fetid atmosphere. Don released the buckles of his harness and struggled to get to his feet.

He felt a strong hand on his left arm. Orazov pulled him upright and slapped him on the back. Don walked down the wet ramp into lashing sheets of wind and rain. His shoes landed on the rough surface of the ship deck. Don had never been so glad to get off an airplane in his life.

The crew chief seized Don's right hand and slapped it onto the right shoulder of the man in front of him. He felt Orazov's hand on his own shoulder. The line of men shuffled forward, giving the still-spinning rotors of the Osprey a wide berth. When Don cast a glance over his shoulder, he saw the crew chief raising the ramp.

The line of men entered the lee of the ship, blocking some of the wind. Behind them, the engines of the Osprey surged again and the aircraft took off. They shuffled into a red-lit aircraft hangar and stopped. The hangar door closed behind them. White lights came on and Don closed his eyes against the sudden illumination.

When he opened them again, there was a US Navy commander standing in front of him. The man had sandy-blond hair and a wan smile. He looked like he needed a drink and a nap.

"Mr. Riley?" he asked.

Don nodded.

"I'm Brett Hardy, sir. XO of the *Lauderdale*, er, acting captain, I guess."

Don's hand was cold and slimy, but he took Hardy's hand anyway. "You have our gear, Captain?"

"This way, sir." Hardy led them down a ramp into the main deck of the amphib. It was a disorienting feeling being inside the ship as it was being buffeted by the waves outside. The deck felt unstable and shivered every time a big wave hit, which seemed like every few seconds. Don felt his inner ear trying to find a balance in this shifting environment and he hoped he wouldn't be sick again.

The crates were lined up in a row next to a large table secured to the deck. A flat-screen monitor was lashed to the table, cables snaking away toward the bulkhead.

Hardy pointed at the crates. "If you want help unboxing, I can supply all the manpower and tools you need."

Don looked at Orazov, who nodded, and within minutes a swarm of Marines and Sailors descended on the shipping crates.

Orazov and Don stayed at the table. Hardy touched the screen and the video image sprang to life. "This is the overwatch feed you requested, sir. We're here"—he pointed to a ghostly shape on the infrared display—"and your target is here. Twenty-five kilometers northwest."

Don studied the screen. As large as he knew it to be, Balinovich's yacht looked like a toy on the ocean.

"Wherever they're going, they're trying to get there in a hurry," Hardy continued. They're making about fifteen knots. In seas like this, with a ship that small, that's a rough ride, sir."

The *Fort Lauderdale* absorbed another massive wave and Hardy nodded as if the weather had made his point for him. Behind them, one of the crate sides dropped to the deck with a bang.

"What the hell is that thing?" one of the Marines asked on a loud voice.

"It's a jet bike," Orazov answered matter-of-factly. "It uses turbines instead of wheels. Very maneuverable, very fast."

Hardy's eyebrows went up. "You're going out there? On that thing?"

The acting captain led Orazov and Don to a ramp at the far side of the space. "The well deck is down there. You don't need to go up to the flight deck, you can exit out the stern of the ship."

Orazov nodded his thanks and returned to his team. The men were donning ballistic wetsuits and checking their weapons.

It took another thirty minutes before all of Orazov's men were geared up and the jet bikes uncrated and tested for readiness. The team crowded around the table with the monitor, wetsuits unzipped to the waist, faces tense.

They were alone in the hangar. Don had dismissed the ship's crew, including the XO. Orazov's briefing was delivered in Russian, their common language, using a three-dimensional model of the yacht as a guide. Don's Russian was rusty, but he was able to follow.

The plan was not complicated. Six jet bikes for twelve men. One driver, one shooter on each bike. The high-speed approach to the target was at wave height to avoid radar, following a loose V formation on Orazov's lead bike.

After taking the bridge, two bikes would land on the forecastle, two on the stern, two airborne for overhead cover and backup.

Once they had control of the ship, execute a room-to-room clearance operation and search. He looked at Don for guidance.

"Expected resistance," Don said, "is three HVTs, security force of six, and crew of ten. Deadly force is authorized for any resistance." He looked at Orazov. "Commander's discretion is authorized for the crew."

"Tell us about the high-value targets," Orazov replied.

Don passed out three photos. "Bogdan Rabilov, Yuri Balinovich, and Roland Buhler are the HVTs." He passed out a fourth picture. "This briefcase must be retrieved. It will be with one of the HVTs at all times, most likely Buhler, so look for it. It has a two-factor biometric lock, so I will need two additional objects for verification."

Orazov studied the photo. "I see a fingerprint reader. What else do you need?"

Don dug into his duffel bag and pulled out a black cylinder that looked like a long lens for a camera. He weighed the object in his hand, scanned the circle of faces.

"The briefcase also requires a retina scan."

39

Black Sea, 180 kilometers southwest of Sochii, Russia

At forty-two years old, Denis Petrov had been living and working on boats of all sizes for his entire life. From the fishing trawler his family owned in Vladivostok to the Russian Navy destroyers he'd served on for twelve years, he'd done every imaginable job on the water from gutting fish to helmsman of a two-hundred-meter-long warship navigating the Straits of Hormuz.

For the last ten years, he'd worked for Yuri Balinovich as captain of his private yacht, the *Svarog*. The boss only visited a few times a year and never stayed more than a week or two. Denis had captained the *Svarog* to the Baltic in summer, the Spanish Costa del Sol in winter, and Cyprus twice. He took the *Svarog* wherever Mr. Balinovich wanted to go, no questions asked.

It was easy duty. When he had passengers aboard, his biggest concern was making sure that he delivered a smooth ride and that none of the guests fell overboard when they got too drunk or high, which was most of the time.

The men were powerful, the women stunning, and clothing was optional. He and his crew did their best to remain out of sight, collect their paychecks, and forget everything they saw. What happened on the *Svarog* stayed on the *Svarog*.

The last two days had not been easy duty. Normally, the job of the captain of a luxury yacht was to avoid bad weather. He gripped the armrest of his chair as he steered into another wave. Tonight, he was ordered to drive straight into a storm and maintain top speed the whole time.

In Mykonos, they'd laid in stores for a dozen guests on an easy overnight to the neighboring Greek island of Naxos. The cabins were prepared, the champagne chilled, and the dinner service set on the main deck. Then the boss changed his mind. In addition to Roland Buhler, who was never far from his boss's side, Balinovich was accompanied by only Bogdan Rabilov. He'd left all the other guests and their escorts on shore. Rabilov was a regular guest on the *Svarog*. The man's appetites for vodka and young women were well-known to the crew.

There was a third man on board, although not as a guest. The other man had come aboard drugged, inside of a fresh fish delivery container. Ivan, Mr. Balinovich's security man, put him in a bunk room down by the engines and ordered the crew to stay away. In his ten years with the boss, this had only happened once before and that guy never made it back to port.

Denis didn't know who the man was and he didn't want to know. What happened on the *Svarog* stayed on the *Svarog*.

"I'm still getting contact returns, Captain. Bearing one-two-three, range two thousand meters," called out Anton. He was a slight man who normally worked the galley but was on the bridge tonight because he was one of the few crew members who wasn't seasick. Even Denis, who'd never been seasick in his life, felt a headache building and his stomach churned.

"Hang on," Denis called out. A huge wave broke over the bow and for a second the clean white hull disappeared under green water. The windshield wipers sluiced water off the windows, barely keeping up with the weather.

He'd put Denis on the radar and taken the helm himself. Besides getting smashed to bits by the waves, his biggest fear tonight was getting run over by an oil tanker or some other large cargo ship. As big as the

Svarog was, he wasn't confident a merchant sailor would notice her in seas this rough.

He glanced at the radar screen. It was like looking inside a washing machine. The waves and heavy rain made trash of the radar returns. The radar made another sweep and he saw three blips show up. They were small, the size of a dinghy, which was preposterous. No boat that small could survive out here.

"It's just false returns from the waves," he told Anton. "I'm only worried about something big." Another wave rose up and he gripped the helm harder.

He looked longingly at the throttle. Common sense told him to reduce speed and ride out the storm, but the boss was adamant. He wanted to be in Sochii as soon as possible. Even when Denis advised him about possible damage to the ship, he was ordered to keep the speed on.

Denis heard a whining sound over the roar of the wind. He looked over to Anton. He'd heard it, too. He was looking up, at the ceiling of the bridge. The screaming noise seemed to be above them.

A flicker of movement ahead of them caught his eye. Denis leaned toward the glass, squinting through the thrashing wipers. Nothing.

THUMP, THUMP, THUMP.

The sound came from directly above his head like something had dropped on the roof. As he looked up, the doors on either side of the bridge opened. Black forms, slick with rain, rushed in.

Denis found himself on the deck, a wet hand pressing his face into the damp carpet. Without his hand on the helm, the ship heeled over, broadside to the waves. The deck tilted.

"You'll capsize us!" he yelled.

The hand seized his collar, hauled him to his feet, and placed him in front of the helm. Denis spun the wheel, turning the bow into the weather again. The ship took a wave across the beam and water rushed in the open bridge door.

"Shut the door!" Denis yelled.

Working the throttle and the helm together, he fought to get the *Svarog* stabilized. By the time he was done, he was shaking. Then he realized the muzzle of a gun was pressed into the back of his neck.

"Are you the captain?" The man spoke Russian with an accent. He stripped off the balaclava hood of his wetsuit and Denis was surprised to see the man had gray hair and beard.

Denis nodded.

"You have a prisoner on board?"

Denis nodded again.

"Where is he?"

Before Denis could respond, the phone next to the helmsman station buzzed, the red light winking in the darkness of the bridge.

"What is that?" the man asked.

"It's the boss," Denis said. "He probably wants to know what happened."

The man considered his answer. He nodded at Anton, who clutched the handgrips on either side of the radar like his life depended on it. "Can he steer?"

Denis nodded.

One of the men moved Anton from the radar station to the helm. Denis reduced the throttle and instructed Anton how to steer into the weather. The cook had an expression of sheer terror.

Denis squeezed his arm. He said the first thing that came into his brain. "It'll be okay. Just do what they say."

The phone buzzed again.

"What do you want me to do?" Denis asked.

The gray-haired man said, "Answer it. Tell Mr. Balinovich that you need to see him right away."

Denis picked up the phone.

40

M/V *Svarog*, Black Sea, 180 kilometers southwest of Sochii, Russia

The room reeked of pine-scented vomit and spilled vodka.

Roland, the originator of the vomit, was passed out on a white leather couch, his body curled around a plastic bucket. After he threw up the first time, Yuri called the cleaning staff. They scooped up the mess, scrubbed the carpet with something that smelled like pine needles, and left a bucket for each of the men.

As usual, Bogdan was drinking, but he was a happy drunk on this stormy night. He removed the cap from the bottle of vodka—he'd abandoned using a glass due to the weather—and took a slug.

"I'm invincible," he announced. "God is protecting me. Those thugs tried to car bomb me and the hand of God reached down and sheltered me from harm."

Yuri eyed his own white plastic bucket as he felt the ship heave into another wave. If the smell didn't make him want to throw up, then Bogdan's sanctimonious bullshit might just do the job.

Dariya's murder was a mistake. That's what the CIA spy finally told them, and Yuri believed the man. Even Ivan had been impressed with how long his subject lasted under the cocktail of drugs he'd administered. They had his confession recorded, just in case something happened to him before they put him in front of the television cameras in Sochii tomorrow afternoon.

On the opposite couch, Bogdan belched and then laughed at his own bodily functions like a child. His untucked shirt rode up, revealing a bubble of white belly bisected by his belt. He stared into space, a vacant smile on his lips. He was like a caricature of a once great politician, all of his vices and physical attributes amplified to cartoonish levels.

A wave of grief and disgust swept over Yuri.

How could this pig of a man have fathered Dariya? Beautiful, smart, vivacious, charismatic Dariya. Dead Dariya, sacrificed for the ego of this buffoon.

He wanted to scream and cry, but it would do no good. Dariya was dead. Her father was an idiot, flawed and broken, but he was Yuri's idiot and that would make it all right. Eventually.

Even in grief his mind churned forward. Bogdan was a liability now, but he needed the old man a little longer. He would use Rabilov to consolidate the inevitable gains the New Dawn party would make in this election, then sideline the aging politician. The trick would be to find someone charismatic enough to replace him as party leader.

The room tilted up again as the ship tackled another wave, then angled downward.

His thoughts turned to Anoushka. It pained him to leave her in Greece. When they reached Sochii, he would call her and apologize. Beg her to give him another chance. Somehow, he would make it right with her and rebuild their relationship. Whatever it takes, he vowed. I want her back in my life.

The ship changed course suddenly and the room heeled over. Bogdan, caught unawares, slid off the sofa, landing heavily on the floor. The uncapped vodka bottle slipped from his grip and spilled. Bogdan started to giggle, his bare belly jiggling in time with his laughter.

Roland's bucket of puke spilled and the smell immediately consumed the cabin.

Yuri gagged, cursed, reached for the phone. He pressed the button for the bridge.

No answer.

The ship started to turn back to the northeast, and the room stabilized. He hung up the receiver and helped Bogdan get to his hands and knees. The big man crawled across the floor to his sofa. He sprawled on his back, arms spread, breathing like a locomotive. He reached for the ceiling.

"The room keeps moving, Yuri."

"You're drunk."

"*Da*," he shouted back.

Yuri felt the thrum of the diesel engines lessen under his feet. A glance at the indicator panel on the wall told him they'd slowed to ten knots. He gritted his teeth in annoyance. The captain had strict orders to maintain speed. Now that he had the confession from the American spy, he wanted to be in Russian territory as soon as possible.

Yuri reached for the phone again, punched the button for the bridge.

No answer.

He was just about to hang up when the line connected.

"Captain speaking."

"Denis, why are we slowing down? Why did we veer off course?"

"We have a problem, sir. I need to see you right away."

"What sort of problem?"

"I-I can't explain it over the phone, sir."

"Fine," Yuri said. "I'm in the lounge."

Yuri slammed the phone down.

"Ivan," he yelled.

His security lead opened the door of the lounge. His pale skin had a greenish tinge, but he was still on his feet.

"The captain is coming down," Yuri said.

"Yes, sir." The door snapped shut again.

Bogdan got to his feet and tottered over to the bar in search of a fresh bottle. Yuri fumed, glancing at the speed indicator every few seconds. He knew he was overreacting, but he couldn't help himself.

Over the creak of the hull and distant whine of the wind, Yuri heard movement in the hallway. He sat up, his anger already bubbling over.

There was a knock at the door.

"Come in!" he called.

The door stayed shut. Yuri gritted his teeth in frustration.

"Ivan! Send them in."

Bogdan turned from the bar, a freshly uncapped bottle of vodka in his bear paw. "I'll get it." He lumbered to the door and swung it open.

There was a sharp snapping sound and Bogdan's body fell backward like a toppling tree. Yuri had time to register the bloody bullet hole in his friend's forehead, then four men swarmed into the room.

They wore skintight black suits, gleaming with moisture. Two of the men fell on the sleeping Roland, two on Yuri.

Roland screamed himself awake as they hauled his body off the sofa and onto the floor.

Yuri felt a cold, wet glove grip his jaw and he looked up into a man's face. Gray hair, gray beard, and dark brown eyes as dead as stones.

"Where is my friend?" he asked in Russian.

Yuri started to shake his head, but the heel of the hand dug into his throat and his windpipe closed off. The man put his face centimeters from Yuri's.

"Where is Harrison Kohl?"

The pressure on his throat eased and Yuri gasped in a lungful of air.

"Aft. In engineering."

The man with the gray beard nodded, then he cranked Yuri's head to the side so that he could see Roland. His breath caressed Yuri's ear.

"Watch, Yuri Balinovich. This is what I'm going to do to you."

He called out to the men restraining Roland in a language that Yuri did not understand.

One man sat on Roland's chest, pinning his knees on the banker's arms. The other drew a knife. He seized Roland's thumb and sliced it off, then he did the same with the other side. Screams split the air. The room slanted into another wave and Yuri felt his stomach heave with fear and disgust.

Then it got worse.

The man on Roland's chest pulled a black cylinder from the small pack on his back. To Yuri, it looked like a collapsed spyglass, like the antique one he kept on the observation deck. The man fitted the cylinder over Roland's right eye and slapped his open palm down on the top of the device.

The device sank into his eye socket. Roland's body convulsed and the screaming devolved into a terrified wail. Blood from the severed stumps of his thumbs pumped, painting the white carpet with crimson streaks.

The man jerked the cylinder out of Roland's face. There was an empty socket where his right eye had been. Roland moaned. His remaining eye rolled back in his head.

The man slipped the cylinder back into his pack, then he calmly pulled a handgun from the holster on his thigh and put two bullets into Roland's brain.

Yuri gagged. The whole evolution had taken fifteen seconds.

The hand pressing down on his face released and Yuri looked up.

"I have money," he begged. "I can pay you."

"No, you don't." The gray-haired man held up Yuri's briefcase. "I have your money now."

He stepped back and the other three men swarmed onto Yuri.

41

M/V *Svarog*, Black Sea, 180 kilometers southwest of Sochii, Russia

The world was motion. Up, down, side to side. Corkscrewing. Constant swaying.

And pain.

Every scrape against his bonds, every time his bare skin touched the metal chair, his nerves screamed.

Whatever drug they gave him, it would not let him sleep. His mind raced, his skin crawled, his guts clenched with unceasing agony. He felt as if he might shatter into little pieces.

But at least it was dark now.

They had come back three times. On each visit, they turned on the light and set up their video camera. The red recording light glared at Harrison as they asked him questions and he told them lies.

"I am an American citizen," he said. "I want to talk to the American embassy."

They laughed at him and gave him more drugs. He felt his nerves stretched like piano wires all over his body. His skin quivered at the slightest touch. When they slapped him, it felt like they'd ripped the skin off his face. It was all he could do to remember his name, much less hold on to his cover story.

They played a game where every time he gave an answer they didn't like, Ivan pricked him with a pin. It was a tiny pin, but it felt as if they were using a power drill on his arm. Like Pavlov's dog, he was conditioned. The mere sight of the pin made his skin pucker with fear.

Still, Harrison resisted.

Then they brought in the lamp. They taped his eyelids open and Ivan put him in a headlock. They shone the light in his face. It looked like an ordinary desk lamp, but it burned like the sun. It burned his face, scorched his eyeballs so badly that even now, in the darkness, iridescent purple blobs filled his vision.

The light had been the final straw, the thing that broke him. After that, he told them everything.

They had Semion's name, they had Victor's name, they had Don Riley's name. He answered any question they asked. He begged for mercy. He apologized for Dariya's death.

Murder, Balinovich corrected him.

Harrison remembered weeping then.

Finally, they removed the tape from his eyelids and turned off the light. He was alone again, in the dark.

It seemed like a lifetime ago, but he dimly remembered his survival training in the Army. If you are taken prisoner, an instructor told the class, it is your duty to hold out for as long as possible or until help arrives, whichever is longer. In the CIA, he'd received training as a case officer for peacetime government detention. Ask for the embassy, they said. Say nothing, stick to your cover story, and hold out for as long as possible. There were rules and conventions that most countries would observe.

There were no rules here, Harrison knew. No conventions. He was at sea, aboard the yacht of a Russian oligarch. No one was coming to save him.

Limits. The Army instructor had talked about limits.

Everyone has a limit, he told them. With enough time and enough pressure, everyone breaks. There is no shame in it.

But in the dark, Harrison wallowed in his shame.

The room heaved and rolled. The bonds raked his raw wrists and ankles, sending waves of fresh pain up his limbs.

How long had he lasted? he wondered. He had no idea.

His tongue rasped like a dry stick against the roof of his mouth. He couldn't remember the last time he'd had water or food.

What would they do with him now that they had his confession? A bullet in the brain, dump his body at sea. Soon, he figured, but his sense of time was slippery. Between the drugs and the darkness and the lack of sleep, all his thoughts seemed to run together in a muddy scrum.

Past became future, present the past.

He had a conversation with Tim Trujillo. But it wasn't the Tim he remembered, it was Tim's corpse, the way he'd found him on a hillside in Uzbekistan. His hands were still bound with zip ties behind what remained of his body.

The skeletal remains floated on the limits of his vision, Tim's voice on the edge of his hearing. He was telling a story about the night he met Jenny. Harrison remembered that night—he'd listened to Tim tell the story of how he met his wife a thousand times—and he'd laughed every time. He laughed now and his own voice sounded like a shriek in his ears.

The door of the room opened. They were coming back. Whether it was more questions or a bullet in his brain, it was going to be pain. His whole body shook with fear.

"No," he moaned.

The light from the hallway banished Tim's ghost from the room. The light scorched Harrison's damaged retinas and he slammed his eyelids shut. A hand touched his bare shoulder and he screamed in pain.

A voice in his ear. Akhmet's voice. Another hallucination. Harrison tried to twist away from the hand, but it was no use.

Then the bonds on his hands and feet released and he slid out of the chair. The linoleum floor was a new form of torture to his drugged senses, but at least he was free. He squirmed away, but hands held him back.

He felt his body being gathered and lifted and he heard Akhmet again.

"Harrison."

He knew it was a hallucination, but it sounded so real. He tried to open his eyes, but the light was like a knife in his skull.

They were moving. The taste of diesel grew stronger, the light brighter. The cold air washing over him made his skin prickle with a thousand tiny pinpricks. They rocked and swayed, bumped into a wall as the ship moved, climbed a steep staircase.

Then there was rain. And wind. It made his skin burn but he didn't care. He turned his face upward and opened his mouth.

"Sedate him," Akhmet's voice said.

There was a stab in his arm. He screamed again.

Then, nothing.

42

Russian submarine *Krasnodar*, B-265

The red-lit control room of the *Kilo*-class submarine shuddered as another wave smashed into the sail. Captain Second Rank Maxim Morosov gripped the periscope handles more tightly and kept his eyes pressed to the eyepiece.

"Having difficulty maintaining depth control in this weather, Captain," said Lieutenant Sidirov, belted into the chair behind his helmsman and planesman. The dry comment elicited a muffled chuckle in the crowded room.

"Do your best, Diving Officer," Morosov responded.

Submarines are meant to be *under*water, he thought, but kept the comment to himself.

They were twelve hundred meters behind the port quarter of a huge yacht that was being tossed on the stormy seas like a toy. The infrared image was a white outline on the dark water. The lighted windows, slightly warmer than the skin of the ship, showed up as bright squares along the hull.

He twisted the handgrip to shift to high-magnification and the image jumped closer. But between the motion of the submarine and his target, it was a challenge to keep the yacht in the smaller field of view. He shifted back to low-mag.

Morosov sighed. They would have to get closer.

"Diving Officer, all ahead full. Make turns for twenty knots."

Another punishing wave rocked the hull. Had he not been hanging on to the periscope, it would have knocked Morosov to the deck.

Twenty knots on the surface when the weather was calm was unusual. Twenty knots on the surface in a storm was insane. Still, the Diving Officer knew better than to contradict his captain.

"Twenty knots, aye, sir."

They gained on the yacht. Morosov made the mistake of pulling back a few centimeters from the eyepiece. Another wave arrived and he cracked his head on the periscope barrel. His vision filled with stars for a second. That was going to leave a mark.

He thought about manning the second periscope, but discarded the idea. In this weather and speed, damage to the raised scope was a real possibility.

For Morosov, putting his command in a situation where he was likely to sustain damage was anathema to everything he'd been taught. If he lost a periscope or bent one of his control surfaces, it could mean months of waiting for repairs. The point of being the captain of a submarine was to be *at sea*. There were no commendations to be earned pierside.

But Admiral Sokolov had been crystal clear in his instructions. Maintain visual contact with the target at all times. Contact him directly if there were any developments. When Morosov questioned the Admiral what he meant by developments, his answer was best summed up as "you'll know it when you see it."

There was no man in the world that Morosov respected more than Nikolay Sokolov. As a senior lieutenant commander, he'd served as the Admiral's aide in Vladivostok and witnessed the man deal with all manner of crises. Admiral Sokolov always managed to rise above the scrum of politics—not easy in the Russian Navy. When the Admiral went to Moscow and took over as President, Morosov went to church and lit a candle in his honor. Nikolay Sokolov was the kind of man who would lead Russia to a new, brighter future.

That future was not as bright these days, but Morosov still believed in the man. When the call had come from the Kremlin, and he heard Admiral Sokolov's voice on the phone, Morosov had to blink back tears of pride.

Of all the submarines in the Black Sea, the President had called on him for this important task. Whatever it took, Morosov would do the bidding of his President—even if he damaged his submarine in the process.

A wave slammed into the sail, rattling Morosov's teeth and making him lose his footing. He stepped back and stretched his neck, then leaned in for another look.

He pressed his forehead firmly against the periscope barrel and searched for his target. He toggled the laser rangefinder and got back a reading of six hundred meters.

Close enough. "Reduce speed to fifteen knots, Diving Officer."

"Fifteen knots, aye, captain," Sidirov repeated.

The sleek hull of the yacht was a whitish-gray color, sharp against the dark sea. He shifted to high-mag, focusing on a window to see if he could spot any people on board.

A bright spot flitted across his vision.

What the hell? He shifted back to low-magnification and the entire hull sprang into view. In the air above the yacht, he counted six bright flares like mosquitos buzzing about a carcass. He tried to use high-mag to focus on one of the bright lights but it moved out of his field of view too quickly.

You'll know it when you see it. This certainly counted as a development in his mind.

Morosov shifted back to low-magnification and toggled a thumb switch to begin recording. "Quartermaster, mark time," he called without taking his eyes from the periscope.

"0437 local, Captain."

Two of the bright lights hovered over the bridge of the ship and two did the same above the stern. He shifted to high-mag and saw dark figures slide off what looked like a flying snowmobile. They were dressed in hooded wetsuits, so only their uncovered eyes registered as heat signatures on the display.

The four converged on the bridge, two on each side.

Morosov's mind raced. An assault team was on the yacht.

"Radio, this is the captain," he called loudly enough that the microphone in the overhead would pick up his voice.

"Radio, sir."

"Get me a secure line to the Kremlin. Tell them I need to speak to the President."

"Aye-aye, sir."

"Diving Officer, raise the comms mast," Morosov ordered.

"Raise the comms mast, aye, sir."

Eight painful minutes passed as the radioman tried to get the connection established. Every time a wave washed over the communications mast, they lost their satellite connection.

Morosov grew impatient. "Diving Officer, surface the ship."

Lieutenant Sidirov's response held no hesitation. "Surface the ship, aye, sir."

The blower started to force air into the ballast tanks, increasing the buoyancy of the submarine. They would be visible on radar now, but that was a risk Morosov was willing to take. He needed to know what the President wanted him to do.

He watched the flares of light buzz around the yacht. Two had landed on the stern, but the other four stayed aloft with single riders.

"Quartermaster, mark time," he called.

"0449, Captain."

Morosov cursed. Twelve minutes had elapsed.

"Where is my radio connection?" he roared in frustration.

"Coming through now, Captain."

Someone pushed a phone receiver into his hand and he pressed it to his ear. A voice said, "Standby for the President."

He saw four figures emerge onto the stern and mount the flying craft. No, he realized. Five figures. One of the men held a naked body in his arms. The man being carried showed up as bright white on the IR display.

A boat detached from the side of the yacht. A lifeboat. He saw people crowded into it, wearing life preservers, which made them look like white disembodied heads in the belly of the boat.

Two of the flying vehicles descended to the bridge level and hovered. Men climbed aboard and the aircraft rose swiftly into the sky. The six vehicles formed a loose formation and accelerated east. The captain followed them with the scope until the flock of flaring lights disappeared.

"Morosov? Are you there?"

He'd forgotten he was still holding the phone to his ear. "Yes, Admiral, I'm here." He tried to form the words to explain what he'd just seen. "There was an assault on the yacht. I don't know who they were, sir. They just—"

His field of view saturated to a blinding white. An explosion rocked the submarine.

"Sound general quarters!" Morosov shouted, dropping the phone.

The control room erupted with activity. The general quarters alarm rang through the ship, the sound of running feet and new watchstanders crowded into control, buzzing with excitement.

"Silence in control," Morosov roared.

He pressed his face to the periscope, searching for their target.

The yacht was a burning hulk. Fires showed as bright white in the display. A wave washed over the flames, darkness consuming white.

Morosov blinked. The ship was gone.

43

Sochii, Russia

Watching on CCTV, Nikolay surveyed the ballroom of the Rodina Grand Hotel. The room was packed, every seat occupied and reporters lining the walls two deep. There were cameras everywhere and the space hummed with the energy of men and women hungry for their next story.

And Nikolay Sokolov was about to make their dreams come true.

He'd considered upgrading to a larger room or even a different venue, but there was a sense of cosmic justice in using the same space that Yuri Balinovich had rented to hold his own press conference.

Yuri had planned to use this place to bury Nikolay's political career. Now Nikolay would use that same room to bury the oligarch—literally and figuratively.

Nikolay watched his press secretary walk to the podium and wait for the room to quiet down. For the first time in months, he felt excitement building in his core. It made him want to grin like an idiot, but that would not do. Not yet.

He checked his appearance in the mirror. The dark blue blazer and red tie were perfect. Snowy-white cuffs and golden cufflinks. He smoothed the tie and frowned at his reflection to hold back the smile. When he heard the press secretary say: "Ladies and gentlemen, please rise for the President of the Russian Federation," he spun on his heel and headed for the door.

He entered from the rear of the ballroom. The buzz in the room turned to tense silence. He took his time walking to the front, camera lenses on all sides, faces wondering why the President was in Sochii.

He rested his hands on either side of the podium and scanned the crowd, his face solemn. The room was still—a rare condition for a room full of reporters. When he spoke, his voice was a carefully modulated baritone, equal parts empathy and strength. A leader doing his duty to his people.

"It is with a heavy heart that I have come here today to announce the passing of two Russian patriots. Yuri Balinovich and Bogdan Rabilov perished in a storm at sea last night."

The gasp in the room was like the rushing of wind followed by a burble of hushed conversation. Nikolay held up his palms.

"You can rest assured that there will be a full investigation, but first, I would like to introduce the commanding officer of the Russian Navy submarine *Krasnodar*, Captain Second Rank Maxim Morosov."

Morosov entered from the door to the adjoining ballroom. He wore his service dress uniform, freshly pressed. He was a handsome man, with a rugged jaw and piercing blue eyes, and he walked with a measured step. Morosov exuded professionalism and confidence.

Nikolay yielded the podium and the submarine captain took command of the room. "At approximately 0300 local, my submarine received a distress call from the *Svarog*, the ship owned by Mr. Balinovich. As the closest military vessel, we immediately located the ship and attempted to make contact. Unfortunately, by the time we arrived, a fire had broken out on board. We saw a lifeboat put to sea and then the ship exploded. There were no survivors of the explosion and the ship sank immediately. My submarine surfaced and recovered the survivors in the lifeboat."

Morosov twisted to look at Nikolay. "With your permission, Mr. President. I will ask the captain of the *Svarog* to say a few words."

Nikolay nodded gravely and watched as Captain Denis Petrov entered the room, escorted by Gennady Abukamov. The head of the Rosvgardia wore a black mourning band on the right sleeve of his gray suit. A little old-fashioned, Nikolay thought, but a nice touch.

Petrov had a cut above his right eye and he walked like he was sore. He did not meet the President's eye. Nikolay had been reluctant to put Petrov in front of the cameras, but Morosov had assured him that the yacht captain would stick to the script.

"My name is Denis Petrov," he began in a shaky voice. He said a few words about his background, then paused and cleared his throat. "Last night, at about 0230 local, the *Svarog*, Mr. Balinovich's vessel, began to experience an electrical problem which led to a fire on board. Because of the severity of the storm we were not able to cut power without capsizing the ship. We lost control of the fire and the passenger compartments filled with smoke. At 0330, I gave the order to abandon ship."

He paused again, licked his lips. He stared at the podium.

Don't look at Morosov, Nikolay thought. Don't look at me. Just say the words, Petrov.

"The last contact I had with Mr. Balinovich," Petrov said in a hoarse voice, "was when he ordered me to get the crew to safety." He broke down in tears.

Nicely done, Nikolay thought, as Morosov led the weeping Petrov away. Nikolay took the podium again.

"I am announcing that for the next two days, all flags in the Russian Federation will be flown at half-mast in honor of the passing of these two great patriots. Our thoughts and prayers are with their families in this terrible tragedy."

The energy in the room was so intense, he could almost see it like a shimmering fog above the scrum of reporters.

"I will take a few questions," he said.

A hundred hands shot into the air, everyone on their feet. Nikolay pointed to the journalist halfway down the center.

"Mikhail," he said, "please ask your question."

"Mr. President," the reporter said, "the election for the Duma is in five days. Do you have any intention of delaying the election?"

Nikolay rubbed his jaw as if he was considering a thoughtful answer to this planted question. "Mikhail, these were two great Russian patriots and their bodies are not even cold. Don't you believe it is too soon to talk of politics?"

"But, Mr. President, the New Dawn party—"

"The New Dawn party is alive and well, Mikhail! Neither of these men were on the ballot, so the election can go forward as planned."

Nikolay paused here and surveyed the huddle of people who had surged closer to the podium.

"The Russian people are strong. We know how to deal with tragedy. We know how to deal with loss. But I see a bright future for this country, a future that is everything the New Dawn party stands for: economic freedom, military strength, strong borders. It is also what I stand for. I believe, in Russia, our best days are ahead of us."

Nikolay took the time to make sure they got a good photo of this moment. He delivered his best you-can-trust-me smile. "If Yuri Balinovich and Bogdan Rabilov were standing here today, they would agree with me."

It was a breathtaking lie, but he could see it landing in the room exactly the way he'd intended. He saw journalists pause, then nod slowly.

Bogdan and Yuri were gone. Their voices silenced. Nikolay's message would fill that void. Over the coming days, his people would nurture his message in the press, on television and on social media until the lie became the truth.

Nikolay allowed a sad smile.

History is written by the victors. And I am the last man standing.

44

USS *Fort Lauderdale*, Black Sea, 150 kilometers south of Sevastopol

I'm blind. That was Harrison's first thought.

His eyes were open, but it was black.

He slid his hands away from his body. Clean sheets. More fumbling revealed an IV in his right arm. He raised his hands to his face—

Someone grabbed his fingers.

"He's awake," a woman's voice called.

"Where am I?" Harrison asked.

"We'll get to that, sweetie," said the voice. "My name is Dana. What's your name?"

"Harrison. Harrison Kohl."

"Nice to meet you, Harrison. Do you want some water?"

"Yes, please." A straw touched his lips. He latched on and sucked.

"Extreme thirst is a side effect of the drugs," said the voice. She pulled the straw away. "That's enough for now."

"I can't see anything, Dana."

"You have bandages on your eyes. The doctor will be here soon to explain everything. Right now, there's someone who wants to say hello."

A hand covered his. "Harrison." Don's voice.

"Don?" Harrison's eyes felt hot and wet. Was that a good sign? "Where am I?"

"*Fort Lauderdale.*"

"What? How did I..."

Don chuckled. "Sorry, couldn't resist. The USS *Fort Lauderdale*, it's a Navy amphib. You're in their sick bay and we're in the middle of the Black Sea."

"The Black Sea? I was...on Balinovich's yacht." It all came rushing back now. "Don, I told them everything. I tried to—" His eyes felt hot again.

Don's hand tightened on his. "It's okay. There's a lot for you to catch up on, Harrison. What's the last thing you remember?"

Harrison sighed. "They drugged me...I was hallucinating. I dreamed Akhmet was there. He cut me loose."

"Was I very handsome?" Akhmet's voice sounded in his opposite ear. He felt someone take his other hand.

"Akhmet," Harrison gasped. "I wasn't dreaming?"

"You were very drugged"—the hand tightened on his—"but I was real."

Don let go of his hand. "The doctor is here, Harrison. We're going to let her take over."

"How do you feel, Mr. Kohl?" The doctor was a woman with a brisk tone. "I'm Dr. Hammond."

"I feel like I've been hit by a truck and I think I'm blind."

"No wonder," she replied. "The amount of drugs they put in your system, it's a wonder you didn't have a heart attack."

"What about my eyes?"

He heard a smile invade her voice. "No, you have photokeratitis, more commonly known as snow blindness. You'll recover, but it will take a few days. I can remove your bandages if you like."

Harrison sat still as she peeled off the adhesive eye patches. The light in the room was dimmed, and his vision glassy from his watering eyes. He blinked. Dr. Hammond was a trim woman in her early thirties dressed in a Navy underway uniform of tan camouflage. She wore the rank of lieutenant commander.

"Take your time, Mr. Kohl," Hammond urged. "I am happy to report there will be no lasting *physical* damage, but you need time to heal. As for the psychological trauma, I strongly recommend you consult a professional."

"Thank you, Doctor," Don said.

When Hammond left, Don shut the door behind her. "There's some things we need to talk about."

Harrison used the controls to raise himself in bed. His vision still had purplish blotches, but he could see well enough.

"Look, Don, I don't know how long I lasted, but in the end I told them—"

Don held up his hand. "It's probably best if you watch this first." He took out a tablet and turned the brightness down so that the figures on the screen were dim shapes. "This is a press conference in Sochii this afternoon."

Harrison squinted at the screen. Nikolay Sokolov stood behind a podium.

"It is with a heavy heart that I have come here today to announce the passing of two great Russian patriots. Yuri Balinovich and Bogdan Rabilov perished in a storm at sea last night."

Harrison gasped along with all the reporters in the room.

"Just watch," Don urged him.

Harrison watched all the way through, then went back and watched again. Finally, he looked up. The questions piled up in his brain like a traffic jam.

"How did you find me?" Harrison asked.

Don shrugged. "We didn't. You just disappeared in Mykonos. There was no way we could be sure that you were on the yacht."

"And you came for me."

Don looked away. "A US team was out of the question. I improvised."

Harrison's damaged eyes found Orazov. "You came for me, Ussat."

"You would have done the same for me, my friend."

"Balinovich and Rabilov?" Harrison asked. "They're dead?"

Don shrugged. "The operation was not under US control. Therefore, the outcome was not ours to decide. Akhmet made the call."

"But Balinovich's assets," Harrison said. "The briefcase."

"We have the briefcase and the means to access it," Don said with a wry smile. "Considering you are still recovering from an eye injury, I'll spare you the details. Rest assured that Anoushka Balinovich will have control of her late father's estate."

More questions bubbled up. "She's safe? And Genevieve, too?"

"The team is all safe, Harrison. Yuri and Bogdan left them all behind in Greece. The only ones they took were you and Iliana." Don's face clouded. "She's still missing."

"No," Harrison said. "Iliana was the one who betrayed me. She was working for Balinovich."

"What?" Don said. "No, that's not possible. She gave us the intel about the coup."

The pieces started to click into place in Harrison's brain. "Yes. She did." He waited.

"No," Don said, but Harrison could tell by the look in his eye that his brain was already operating on the problem.

The anger Harrison felt gave him strength. "Iliana provided all the intel we used to set up the operation in Greece. She insisted—*insisted*, Don— that I deliver the knockout gas to her personally. Only hours before the operation went down." He paused. "Don, she made that demand in Paris, before we even had the operation fully planned."

"No," Don repeated.

"Yes," Harrison shot back. "Think about it, Don. Somehow, Bogdan Rabilov managed to get from Russia to Greece just in time to catch the boat that was leaving with me on it. How did he know?"

"Don," Orazov said. "The woman was a double agent."

Don Riley hung his head. Seconds ticked by. Slowly, he looked up, lips curled into a rueful smile. He pointed at the blank tablet.

"That press conference you saw. There's only one man alive who could have engineered that outcome." He walked to the door. "And I'm going to find him."

45

Montreux, Switzerland

Don stared out the window of the Mercedes sedan as dusk closed in on Lac Leman. The weather at Geneva Airport when he'd landed an hour ago had been gray and cold, drizzling rain. The weather only worsened on the hour-long drive to Montreux.

When the Deputy Director of Operations for the Central Intelligence Agency visited an ally, it was customary to give the host country notice of his presence. Even more so if he had agents operating inside the borders of the host country.

Don had extended neither of those courtesies to the Swiss. If either he or his operation were discovered, there would be angry phone calls to the Director. Carroll Brooks would express genuine shock. After all, he'd not told his boss either—and she hadn't asked.

Don's grandmother would have said that he was on thin ice with Carroll—and she would have been correct. He'd launched a kill operation in the Black Sea using foreign fighters off a US Navy ship. That operation had international disaster written all over it.

The only reason why Don Riley still had a job was because the operation was successful. But that didn't mean he was out of the woods with his boss. He had put the Director and the Commander in Chief in a terrible position.

What Don hadn't shared with either Director Brooks or President Cashman was that he had been played as well. What he didn't know was the extent to which he'd been duped.

But he was about to find out.

The car entered the outskirts of Montreux and the electric vehicle climbed from the shoreline drive into the houses stacked up the side of the mountain overlooking the lake. The driver went past their destination and ran a thirty-minute surveillance detection route in the winding streets of the city. Finally, he drew to the curb on Rue des Anciens Moulins.

Don walked up the cracked steps of the two-story stone building and rang the doorbell. On a clear day, the front step would have afforded a glorious view of the lake below and the Alps in the distance, but tonight the scenery was cloaked in darkness and fog.

Genevieve opened the door without turning on the outside light. "We're upstairs, sir."

Don climbed the narrow stairs to the second-floor operations center. The open space was normally a combination kitchen, family room, dining room, but most of the furniture had been pushed aside in favor of folding tables that held a battery of computer screens. Michael Goodwin used a rolling office chair to sweep back and forth across his computer domain. Don scanned the video feeds of a house as well as an EM spectrum analysis display.

"If Federov so much as farts, we'll have it recorded," Harrison said from behind Don.

Don turned to greet his friend. In the weeks since his rescue, Harrison seemed to have recovered, but Don was watching him. He knew from personal experience that trauma returned at the most inconvenient times. By being here, Harrison was missing therapy sessions, but Don hoped that the operation might give him some personal closure.

"Tell me what you've got, Harrison," he said.

"Federov's inside the house kitty-corner behind us." The drapes were drawn on all the windows, so Harrison used an aerial image to show Don the layout. "18 Rue du Pont. Three-story house, two exits. Front opens on the street, rear into a garden. We've had both under surveillance for the last seventy-two hours."

He moved his finger to the side of the house. "No side entrances, but we have eyes on all first-floor windows."

"Security?" Don asked.

Harrison shrugged. "Two guys. They look capable enough, but they're at least in their late sixties. They both live in the house. They act as doormen and run errands."

"Visitors?"

"Twenty-four-hour nursing staff, one on duty all the time. A doctor visits every morning at 0800 like clockwork and leaves about thirty minutes later. We've followed all the medical staff. They're all local and they are actual nurses and doctors."

Don glanced at Michael's electronic domain. "What about phone calls?"

Harrison shook his head. "They call local merchants. Groceries and the like, but no international calls."

"What about a satellite receiver?" Don asked.

Michael shook his head. "I've got an EM net over this place, Don. If they plug a light into a different socket, I'm seeing it. They're not communicating with the outside. I'm positive of that."

"One last thing, Don." Harrison's voice had an edge that made Don look up.

"She's in there," he said. "Iliana is with him."

"You're sure?" Don said.

Harrison took a photo off the table and handed it to Don. It had been taken at a distance through a partially opened curtain, but there was no mistaking Iliana Semanova.

Harrison watched him. "What's our move, boss? I can have a team here in twelve hours."

Don shook his head. Running an unauthorized surveillance operation on Swiss soil was one thing, but an extraction was something else altogether. He would need to get the Swiss FIS onboard, not to mention his own chain of command. Neither of those options were likely to happen. There were courtesies and procedures for these things among the democracies of the world. And Don had ignored all of them.

No, Don knew, what he really needed was answers, and there was only one way he was going to get them.

He buttoned his coat. "I'm going for a walk," he said to Harrison. "I want you to turn off all surveillance."

"Don, what about—"

"I'll be fine, Harrison. This is something I have to do."

Harrison nodded. He turned to Michael. "You heard the boss. Secure all monitoring until further notice."

"Aye-aye, sir." Michael rolled his chair in front of a keyboard and started hammering away. Monitors went blank.

Don walked down the steps and back out onto the street. It was cold and raw outside. Fat snowflakes drifted down and melted on the wet sidewalk. Streetlights glowed like golden bubbles suspended above the ground.

He turned up the collar of his overcoat, walked to the corner and turned onto Rue du Pont. The front light was on at number 18. Don climbed the steps and rang the doorbell. He heard it echo deep inside the house. There was a camera lens next to the door and Don made sure his face was visible.

It took almost a full minute for the door to open. The man who greeted Don had a patchy gray crew cut and wore casual clothes and work boots. He was fit, but the flaccid skin of his neck told Don that his age was closer to seventy than sixty.

He entered and waited as the man closed and bolted the door behind him. Don unbuttoned his jacket and held out his arms to be searched, but the man shook his head. He pointed at the staircase. "You can go up, sir."

The second floor of the house had been converted into a hospital room. A large hospital bed occupied the center of the room with a bank of monitors close by. An open cabinet showed shelves packed with bottles of medicine, IV bags, and other sundries.

Iliana Semanova stood next to the bed, her hand on Vladimir Federov's withered shoulder. The former FSB Chief's eyes were open and bright as they tracked Don's progress into the room.

"You found me," he said in a croaking voice. "I knew you would." Behind the breathiness, there was a hint of a laugh. "It is good to see you, Donald."

Don took off his coat, dropped it on a chair. "Maybe I'm here for her." He pointed at Iliana.

Her chin lifted defiantly, she maintained eye contact with Don.

"Leave us, dear," Federov said.

Iliana seemed reluctant, but she complied. Don crossed to the side of the bed and took Iliana's chair.

"Why did you do it?" Don said finally.

"Donald, don't waste time pretending to be stupid. Look at me. I don't have time to spare."

"You wanted Sokolov firmly in power before..." His voice trailed off.

"You can say it: before I die. Exactly." Federov fumbled for the bed controls and raised the head of the bed a few centimeters. "The damned ultranationalists were gaining ground again and nothing I did stopped them. Bogdan Rabilov was a cancer on the future of Russia. He needed to be dealt with..." His voice rasped as he tried to catch his breath.

"And you needed someone to do the dirty work," Don finished for him.

Federov nodded.

"Why us?" Don asked.

Federov shook his head. "Wrong question. Not *us*, Donald. *You*."

Don tamped down a flash of anger. "Why me, then?"

The sound that emanated from the skeletal figure might have been a chuckle or a choking gasp for breath.

"You're reliable, Donald. You always get the job done. And you always do the right thing, no matter how much you want to avoid it."

"It was all a setup then? How far back did it go?" he asked in a heated voice. "Did you stage the assassination attempt?"

Federov's bright eyes locked with Don's. He nodded.

Don's mind reeled. He opened his mouth to speak, then closed it again. He had no idea how to respond.

"Vladimir," he said finally. "People died. Innocent people."

Federov closed his eyes, nodded. "Everything has a cost."

Don sat back in the seat, suddenly deflated. His brain fired. Details that had been suspect now made sense.

"You tipped off Balinovich in Newcastle about the bribe to Bogdan."

Federov nodded. "It was a nice try, but it wouldn't have worked."

"And the coup that Iliana warned us about? Was that made up, too?"

Something like a smile stretched across Federov's chapped lips. "Maybe. You never know about these things. It is Russia, after all."

"The car bomb that killed Dariya Rabilova?"

Federov's shoulders sagged a fraction. "An unfortunate accident. Collateral damage. These things happen."

Don leaned forward. He didn't want to ask the question, but he had to know. "And kidnapping my agent? Did you tell Iliana to do that?"

"Yes." His voice was wispy but unapologetic. "I knew you would come after him, Donald. You're reliable."

"So that's all there is to it?" Don couldn't sit anymore. Anger drove him to his feet, made him pace. "The ends justify the means. Whatever the sacrifice, as long as we get what we want, it's all okay?"

"It's what we do, Donald." His thin chest heaved as he tried to catch his breath. "Nikolay Sokolov is secure for the foreseeable future. He will make Russia a viable, stable partner, and the world will be better for it. That's good for your country—and mine."

Don leaned over the bed, his face close to Federov's. He could smell the decay in the dying man's breath. He wanted to smash his fist into that twisted face.

"And when is the price too high, Vladimir? How many dead is too many?"

Federov's chest rose and fell. "Those answers are for historians, Donald. We have only choices. We rely on the people making those choices. People like you."

"And Iliana? What about her?"

"I made the choice for her. She did what you say, at my direction. We took a calculated risk that Rabilov would not kill your agent. We believed he would use him as a political prop to win the election. He probably would have won without your agent, but he's always been a greedy prick."

"So, if I arrest her, you're okay with that?" Don challenged.

Federov tried another shrug. "She knew the risks then and she's prepared for whatever happens, but you should think about that move. Iliana's client list is not just Russians, you know. Some of the most powerful men in the world are her best customers. Do you want that kind of publicity?"

Don sat down again. He put his head in his hands. He wanted to be sick. Federov had used him from the start. They'd achieved stability in Russia. That was good for everyone, but at what cost?

He felt a touch on his shoulder. Federov's hand felt as fragile as a bird's wing.

"You're a good man, Donald. A good man in a dirty world. Only you could have pulled this off. That's why I chose you."

The hand patted his shoulder lightly. "And now, if you don't mind, I'd like to die in peace. It's time."

Don got to his feet. He stared at the shell of the man who had once been the most feared person in the Russian Federation. He hated him, he admired him, but most of all, he pitied him.

"Goodbye, Vladimir."

Federov attempted another exhausted smile. "Goodbye, Donald. This time for good. I promise."

"I'll hold you to that."

Iliana met him on the steps but said nothing as Don passed by. He did not look at her. He pulled on his coat and let himself out the front door.

It was snowing harder now and fat white flakes clung to his shoulders and melted on the bare skin of his face. Washing away the smell of death and decay. Washing him clean again.

We are the sum of our choices, he thought. For every mission, we bear the cost.

He reached into his pocket and pulled out his mobile phone. He thumbed down to Harrison's number and dialed.

"Pull the plug. We're going home."

He hung up before Harrison could respond.

Don paused at the corner. He looked right. The falling snow formed a shifting veil that obscured the safe house from view.

Then he walked down the hill, alone.

46

Preobrazhenskoye Cemetery, Moscow, Russia

The ten centimeters of freshly fallen snow had not been plowed off the lane in this part of the cemetery when Nikolay arrived in his armored limousine. He spied the lone figure in black standing next to the open grave.

Nikolay reached across and patted the woman's hand. "This won't take long, my dear."

She started to pull on her lambskin gloves. "I'll come with you."

"No." Nikolay squeezed her hand. "It's all right. He wanted a small service. Private."

"I'll wait here, then." She took a well-thumbed book from her purse and opened it. She flicked her fingers. "Go, then. Leave me in peace."

Nikolay pulled on his gloves and opened the heavy car door. He filled his lungs with crisp, clean air. All around him, snow frosted the gravestones, softened harsh lines, and hid the dirt.

Vladimir Federov controlled everything, even in death. By rights, he should have been buried in the Novodevichy Cemetery alongside famous authors and poets and politicians. Transfiguration Cemetery was home to the Old Believers, an Eastern Orthodox religious sect. There were some notable residents here, but Federov had chosen a plot in a part of the cemetery where normal citizens were laid to rest.

Nikolay picked his way among the close-packed rows of modest headstones. There were no showy statues or ornately carved markers here, just simple granite with the facts of the deceased's life: names and dates, and not much more.

The open grave was a scar of black dirt in the pillowy white of the newly fallen snow. There was no red carpet for him to walk from his car to the gravesite, no chairs on which to sit. Another of Federov's demands had been that the cemetery personnel have no idea of who they were burying. To them, he was just a plot number in the cemetery plan.

Iliana Semanova wore black leather boots against the ankle-high snow. Her black wool overcoat hugged her slim figure and the fishnet veil of a black cloche hat shielded her eyes. She looked up when Nikolay approached.

"Good morning, Mr. President."

"Iliana, please call me Nikolay," he said. "Today, I am not the President. I'm just a friend who has come to pay his respects to a great man."

They embraced briefly and her lips brushed his cheek.

They stood together looking down into the open grave where the plain wooden casket lay.

"He was never one for ceremony, was he?" Iliana's voice broke at the end.

"Do you know that he even specified the exact model of the casket?" Nikolay said with a soft chuckle.

"He used to tell me it was all about the details." She mimicked Federov's high-pitched voice. "'Iliana,' he would say, 'I am the painter. You are the paint. Every detail, even the most insignificant, has meaning.'"

Nikolay drew in a deep breath of frigid air and blew it out in a long stream of vapor. Federov had found Iliana as a runaway teen on the streets of Moscow. When he looked at the elegant woman standing next to him, he could hardly believe the story.

And his story? Nikolay first met Federov as a teen, before Nikolay even entered the Navy. As Nikolay's military career progressed and his own influence grew, so did Federov's presence in his life. By the time he was an

Admiral, he and Federov communicated regularly and met every time he visited his uncle in Moscow.

With Federov by his side, Nikolay rose to power by staging a coup against his uncle.

They were the same, Nikolay realized. Like Iliana, he had been shaped and molded by this man. They were both products of Vladimir Federov.

The *putt-putt* of a small engine broke the silence and an ATV appeared around the bend of the lane. A bearded Russian Orthodox priest, dressed in a cassock and wearing a winter coat, gloves, and wool hat, rode the ATV. He stopped in front of Nikolay's limo, dismounted, and trudged to the graveside, eyes down.

"I'm here for the service," he announced. He looked up and Nikolay saw the light of recognition in his eyes. His mouth fell open. "Mr. President, I didn't—"

Nikolay cut him off. "This is a private service, Father. You didn't know because that was how it was arranged. I would like to preserve the anonymity."

The priest was nodding his head in vigorous agreement before Nikolay even finished speaking. "Of course, of course. Shall I get started, sir?"

"We're waiting for one more," Nikolay replied.

"We are?" Iliana asked.

Nikolay spied a car turning into the unplowed lane. It drew to a stop behind his limo. "Here he is."

The rear door opened and Don Riley got out. The Deputy Director of Operations for the Central Intelligence Agency looked down at the snow in dismay. He was wearing dress shoes.

Americans, Nikolay thought.

Riley had grown more stout since Nikolay had last seen him and his uncovered head showed more gray than red. He buttoned his overcoat, thrust his hands into his jacket pockets, and tramped through the snow to the graveside.

"Sorry I'm late, Mr. President," Riley said. "Traffic from the airport."

"It was good of you to come all this way, Don." Nikolay pulled off his glove and held out his hand. Riley's bare hand was chilled.

"I'll be on the ground less than two hours, I promise," Riley replied. "I appreciate you making the arrangements."

Nikolay turned to Iliana, still speaking in English. "Allow me to introduce Iliana Semanova. She was a close confidante of Vladimir."

Riley shook her hand. "It's a pleasure to make your acquaintance, Ms. Semanova. I'm sorry for your loss."

"*Spasibo*," Iliana replied and turned away.

The priest watched the introductions with dismay.

"Mr. President," he said. "I don't know English. The prayers will all be in Russian."

Nikolay eyed Don. "That will be fine, Father. Please proceed."

It struck him as odd that Federov even had a priest at his funeral. He'd never known the man to be at all religious.

Iliana leaned close. "Why is the CIA here?"

"Because Vladimir asked for him." Nikolay shot a look at the priest, who was opening a book and preparing to read. "Why is there a priest here?"

Iliana chuckled. "I think Vladimir is covering his bases."

Nikolay laughed and the priest paused. "Continue, Father. My apologies."

The priest raised his hand. "Let us pray," he began.

The service lasted ten minutes. There was no sermon, just a series of prayers. Nikolay was not even sure if the priest knew Federov's name. When he'd finished, Nikolay nodded to his security man standing next to the car to tip the priest and make sure he kept his mouth shut.

The trio stood graveside, each alone in their own thoughts.

Riley broke the silence. "How old was he?"

Nikolay frowned. He didn't know. He'd celebrated his own birthday with Federov many times, but he'd never celebrated Federov's birthday.

"I don't know," Nikolay replied. "Iliana?"

"I don't know either."

"Where's the headstone?" Don asked. "It'll be there."

There was a low mound of snow at the head of the open grave. Nikolay leaned down and cleared it.

The headstone was a simple angled piece of granite, half a meter wide and thirty centimeters tall. It bore a single word in bold Cyrillic letters.

Патриот.

PATRIOT.

Iliana began to laugh. She grabbed Nikolay's arm and rested her head against his shoulder. Nikolay put his arm around her, gasping because he was laughing so hard. Riley bent at the waist, his hands on his knees to catch his own breath. The air around them clouded with exhaled breath like they were a pack of smokers.

"What a bastard," Riley said.

"Agreed." Nikolay wiped his eyes.

Even in death, his mentor was determined to remain a mystery.

"A fitting end to a great man," Iliana added. "And now, gentlemen, I must go."

She shook Riley's hand again, bussed Nikolay's cheek, and walked off without another word.

Nikolay felt the continuing effects of their shared laughter. He threw an arm around Riley's shoulder. "Come, Don. There's someone I'd like you to meet."

He led Riley to his limo and opened the door. "My dear, come meet someone."

The woman got out of the limo. Her cashmere overcoat was unbuttoned, revealing fitted dark slacks tucked into boots and a silk blouse under a V-neck sweater. Her head was covered with a sable fur *ushanka* like a rustic crown for a Russian princess.

"My dear, allow me to introduce Donald Riley. Don, this is Anoushka Balinovich."

"Mr. Riley." She spoke in English, holding out a slim, manicured hand. "It's a pleasure to make your acquaintance."

"The pleasure is mine, ma'am." Don's brow wrinkled. "Balinovich? Any relation to..."

"Yuri was my father," Anoushka replied.

Nikolay put his arm around her and she moved closer to him. "I'm dating an heiress, Don. At least I know that she's not in this relationship for the money." He laughed and Anoushka kissed his cheek.

"I'm very happy for you, Mr. President," Don said, "and thank you again for allowing me to be here today."

Nikolay embraced him European-style with a kiss on both cheeks. "That was how Vladimir wanted it, and it was my distinct pleasure to fulfill his last wish." He patted Riley on the shoulder, smiling. "Now get out of my country, you filthy spy."

Riley raised his hands in mock surrender. "Consider me gone, Mr. President." He winked. "But not forgotten, I hope."

Nikolay watched Riley get into his car. He slid into his own limo. Anoushka took his hand. "Was it a nice service?"

Nikolay nodded. "It was the service he wanted."

Anoushka was quiet as the limo driver navigated the big vehicle along the narrow unplowed lane. Nikolay sighed and relaxed into the seat cushions.

They were headed to Anoushka's dacha outside of Moscow for the weekend, a very special weekend. He felt in his jacket pocket for the square box. He was going to propose to Anoushka tonight after dinner.

"Darling?" she said, still looking out the window.

"Mmm?"

"What did you mean when you called Mr. Riley a spy?"

Nikolay opened one eye. "Promise you won't tell anyone?"

She leaned over and kissed him.

"Don Riley works for the CIA."

Anoushka's eyes flew open. "No! You're teasing me."

"I'm not. You can trust me."

Anoushka kissed him again. "Of course I can. And you can trust me."

Nikolay closed his eyes.

Weapons Free
The Third Option Series #1

The Chinese Navy has unleashed a game-changing weapon that will tip the balance of power in the Pacific.

Harrison Kohl, newly appointed Director of the CIA's Special Activities Center, faces an impossible assignment: acquire the plans for China's new long-range, superfast Torpedo.

As Commander Janet Everett, commanding officer of the USS *Illinois*, tracks the Chinese Navy from under the waves of the South China Sea, Kohl's team makes a risky move to recruit an asset from the Chinese development team. They find only more bad news: the new weapon is far more advanced than they realized. The Chinese are preparing to test-fire the torpedo, proving its power to the world.

Amidst this devastating intelligence, Harrison sees an opportunity to execute one of the boldest covert actions in the history of the CIA. But an operation of this scale requires a massive diversion. The US Navy and Everett will have to challenge the powerful Chinese Navy in the contested waters of the South China Sea—without letting their power play spiral into World War Three.

Get your copy today at
severnriverbooks.com

30% Off your next paperback.

SCAN ME

Thank you for reading. For exclusive offers on your next paperback:

- **Visit SevernRiverBooks.com** and enter code **PRINTBOOKS30** at checkout.
- Or scan the QR code.

Offer valid for future paperback purchases only. The discount applies solely to the book price (excluding shipping, taxes, and fees) and is limited to one use per customer. Offer available to US customers only. Additional terms and conditions apply.

SEVERN RIVER
PUBLISHING

ACKNOWLEDGMENTS

Although our names are on the covers of all seven books in the *Command and Control* series, the truth is that much of the credit belongs to others.

The Severn River Publishing team has been there since Word One. Their professional execution of editing, covers, narration, formatting, marketing, and the thousand and one other details that transform a story into a book stands out in our experience in this industry. Our sincere thanks to Amber, Mo, Andrew, and most especially, Cate.

About 1 in 100 readers take the time to leave a written review on Amazon or other review platforms. We are humbled by the fact that some of our readers have bought, read, and reviewed every book in the series (and we hope this one as well!). With a few exceptions, we've never met these men and women and know them only by the pseudonyms they leave on their reviews. Nevertheless, these are our people. While this list will undoubtedly be incomplete, cheers and thanks to Mike Beason, David C Taylor, Sprari, InTTruder, Walter Scott, IndianaHappyTraveler, Thomas L. Savarino, EJ Schumacher, Cody Mason, Claude Buettner, Ron Robson, JRL, Ken 575, Simon Mayeski, Kent Zimmerman, and dragonsmama. (If we missed you, our apologies.)

This novel was made more special by a cameo from one of David's favorite authors, Kate Quinn. Kate generously allowed her persona to be fictionally employed in the recruitment of an American asset to go after the Russian President. (We *may* see Anoushka Balinovich in a future Bruns-Olson novel...) The two works mentioned in the book, *The Diamond Eye* and *The Briar Club*, are two of Kate's excellent novels. If you haven't read them, then get thee to a bookstore!

Line of Succession marks our eleventh novel as a co-writing team in as many years. None of them would have been possible without the love and support of our spouses, Melissa and Christine.

ABOUT THE AUTHORS

David Bruns

David Bruns earned a Bachelor of Science in Honors English from the United States Naval Academy. (That's not a typo. He's probably the only English major you'll ever meet who took multiple semesters of calculus, physics, chemistry, electrical engineering, naval architecture, and weapons systems just so he could read some Shakespeare. It was totally worth it.) Following six years as a US Navy submarine officer, David spent twenty years in the high-tech private sector. A graduate of the prestigious Clarion West Writers Workshop, he is the author of over twenty novels and dozens of short stories. Today, he co-writes contemporary national security thrillers with retired naval intelligence officer, J.R. Olson.

J.R. Olson

J.R. Olson graduated from Annapolis in May of 1990 with a BS in History. He served as a naval intelligence officer, retiring in March of 2011 at the rank of commander. His assignments during his 21-year career included duty aboard aircraft carriers and large deck amphibious ships, participation in numerous operations around the world, to include Iraq, Somalia, Bosnia, and Afghanistan, and service in the U.S. Navy in strategic-level Human Intelligence (HUMINT) collection operations as a CIA-trained case officer. J.R. earned an MA in National Security and Strategic Studies at the U.S. Naval War College in 2004, and in August of 2018 he completed a Master of Public Affairs degree at the Humphrey School at the University of Minnesota. Today, J.R. often serves as a visiting lecturer, teaching national security courses in Carleton College's Department of Political Science.

You can find David Bruns and J.R. Olson at
severnriverbooks.com